"So what makes this balcony so special?"

Dalton turned to Virginia and smiled. "A fond experience with a girl." His expression became dreamy as he continued. "She had a long, blond ponytail tied back with a blue ribbon. I watched that ponytail all through the movie. After the movie ended, I jumped up and ran after her. I think I was trying to reach for her shoulder, but my hand automatically gravitated toward her hair, and I wound up with a fistful of ponytail instead. She jerked around at my touch. And naturally after that I didn't stand a chance."

"Naturally."

"In a last-ditch effort, I reached for her again, but my hand went back to her hair. This time I came away with a trophy, though."

"A trophy?"

"I yanked the blue ribbon out of her hair."

"Do you recall if the blue ribbon had a small, white rose pattern embroidered through it?"

Dalton's eyes widened. "That was *you?*"

Dear Reader,

Welcome to Silhouette **Special Edition** . . . welcome to romance.

Last year, I requested your opinions on the books that we publish. Thank you for the many thoughtful comments. For the next few months, I'd like to share quotes with you from those letters. This seems very appropriate while we are in the midst of the THAT SPECIAL WOMAN! promotion. Each one of our readers is a **special** woman, as heroic as the heroines in our books.

Our THAT SPECIAL WOMAN! title for October is *On Her Own* by Pat Warren. This is a heroine to cheer for as she returns to her hometown and the man she never forgot.

Also in store for you in October is *Marriage Wanted,* the third book in Debbie Macomber's heartwarming trilogy, FROM THIS DAY FORWARD. And don't miss *Here Comes the Groom* by Trisha Alexander, a spin-off from her *Mother of the Groom.*

Rounding out the month are books from Marie Ferrarella, Elizabeth Bevarly and Elyn Day, who makes her Silhouette Debut as Special Edition's PREMIERE author.

I hope you enjoy this book, and all of the stories to come!

Sincerely,

Tara Gavin
Senior Editor

QUOTE OF THE MONTH:

"I'm the mother of six, grandmother of ten and a registered nurse. I work in a hospice facility and deal with death and dying forty hours a week. Romance novels, light and airy, are my release from the stress."

L. O'Donnell
Maine

ELIZABETH BEVARLY

RETURN ENGAGEMENT

Silhouette®

SPECIAL EDITION®

Published by Silhouette Books New York
America's Publisher of Contemporary Romance

For Terri Medeiros,
a wonderful writer
and a fabulous friend.

SILHOUETTE BOOKS
300 East 42nd St., New York, N.Y. 10017

RETURN ENGAGEMENT

Copyright © 1993 by Elizabeth Bevarly

ISBN: 0-373-09844-8

First Silhouette Books printing October 1993

All the characters in this book have no existence outside the
imagination of the author and have no relation whatsoever to
anyone bearing the same name or names. They are not even
distantly inspired by any individual known or unknown to the
author, and all incidents are pure invention.

®: Trademark used under license and registered in the United States
Patent and Trademark Office and in other countries.

Printed in the U.S.A.

Books by Elizabeth Bevarly

Silhouette Special Edition

Destinations South #557
Close Range #590
Donovan's Chance #639
Moriah's Mutiny #676
Up Close #737
Hired Hand #803
Return Engagement #844

Silhouette Desire

An Unsuitable Man for the Job #724
Jake's Christmas #753

ELIZABETH BEVARLY

is an honors graduate of the University of Louisville and achieved her dream of writing full-time before she even turned thirty! At heart, she is also an avid voyager who once helped navigate a friend's thirty-five-foot sailboat across the Bermuda Triangle. "I really love to travel," says this self-avowed beach bum. "To me, it's the best education a person can give herself." Her dream is to one day have her own sailboat, a beautifully renovated older model forty-two-footer, and to enjoy the freedom and tranquillity seafaring can bring. Elizabeth likes to think she has a lot in common with the characters she creates, people who know that love and life go hand in hand.

WISCONSIN

Lake Michigan

MICHIGAN

Ann Arbor

Chicago

Fort Wayne

ILLINOIS

Comfort

INDIANA

OHIO

Champaign

Dayton

Indianapolis

Cincinnati

Bloomington

Louisville

KENTUCKY

All underlined places are fictitious.

Chapter One

As he stood before the looming brick building silhouetted like some abstract monster before the noonday sun, it occurred to Dalton Cameron that the place was perfect. In many ways, this dilapidated old building was just what he had been looking for, although until that moment, he didn't even realize he'd been muddling along on a quest.

The decaying, sixty-year-old movie house was less glorious now than it must have been in its heyday. The crumbling wood paneling studding the front of the building was something Uncle Eddie must have added during the tacky seventies, because Dalton recalled the front of the theater being a beautiful art deco mosaic of tile. He shielded his eyes as his gaze traveled up to the broken, grungy neon sign, its faded letters spelling PAL C instead of PALACE, the way he knew it should. The cashier's window bore an ominous crack from top to bottom, a scar sustained, he'd been told, when an unruly *Rocky Horror Picture Show* crowd had gotten out of hand one Saturday midnight years ago. One showcase window still housed a faded, weather-rumpled poster advertising a film Dalton recalled seeing in his late teens, a banner stretched across it proclaiming in nearly unreadable lettering, Return Enagement. He smiled at the irony, jingling the keys in his hand with a proprietary shake.

The Palace Theater had legally been his for the last five years, but he hadn't even looked at it until now. He hadn't had time. In fact, Dalton had spent those five years trying his best to unload the old relic, never quite understanding why his uncle Eddie had bequeathed it to him in the first place. He hadn't seen or spoken to his mother's brother for more than ten years, since shortly after Dalton's mother died. And since signing the papers that had made it his, the Palace Theater had simply been something else to clutter his mind, something else to worry about.

Yet as his responsibilities at the hospital had lately become more hectic, more stressful, Dalton had gradually begun to feel an urgent need for an excuse to leave Indianapolis behind for a little while. The Palace Theater had suddenly seemed like a perfect escape, the perfect reason to get away. Maybe if he renovated the place, got it up and running again, he'd have a better chance of selling it, perhaps to one of the locals.

So he'd requested a leave of absence from the chief of staff, a period of six months that might allow him to put his life in order again. Despite the fact that losing his best pediatric surgeon would put the hospital in a bind, Dr. Addison Parker hadn't hesitated in agreeing to Dalton's request. Since the deaths of Dalton's wife and young son two years ago, Addison had known his head of pediatrics hadn't been able to keep his mind on his work as well as he should. A temporary leave of absence was in no way an unreasonable request.

And when Dalton had picked up the Palace keys from the local Realtor a half hour ago, any concern for River Crest Hospital had been completely erased from his thoughts. There was something more urgent to worry him now. He had his own peace of mind to think about.

This was the first time he'd seen the theater in more than twenty years. Twenty-two to be exact, he remembered now, because he had been fourteen years old when he and his mother had come to spend a summer with Uncle Eddie. It had never occurred to Dalton to seek solace here, to seek escape in this little town from the troubles that had been plaguing him for the past two years. And yet even the name of his uncle's hometown was perfect. Comfort. Comfort, Indiana. And now—for a while—it would be Dalton Cameron's hometown, too.

The keys in his hand were warm from the way he had been stroking and palming them since the Realtor had pushed them across her desk toward him thirty minutes ago. She told him she had arranged to have the electricity turned on, and had even volunteered to accompany Dalton, to show him the theater he now owned. But he had softly declined her offer, unwilling to share this moment with anyone else. As he inserted one key into the dead bolt above the handle on the entrance door and turned it, the tumblers groaned and creaked before reluctantly sliding aside to allow him entry. Inside the lobby, it was dark and close, the air pungent with the loamy aroma of mouse droppings and mold. Cobwebs decorated every corner, and a thin film of dust lined every surface.

Dalton smiled. He'd been hoping the place would challenge him, hoping it would be something to occupy his thoughts and keep the memories and bad dreams at bay. And it was beginning to look as if a challenge was precisely what he'd be finding here. He raked his fingers through his light brown hair, lingering at the ends that were beginning to curl. He hadn't had it cut since requesting time off, and his hair hadn't shown any curl since his undergraduate days at Indiana University.

Maybe he wouldn't cut it for a while longer, Dalton thought absently, rubbing the rough stubble that darkened his hard jaw. And maybe he'd let his beard grow, too, just to see how it would come out. He didn't have to worry about other people's rules. For now, he could make his own.

He pushed both entrance doors open wide, then crossed the tiny lobby in a small arc to the exit doors paralleling them and opened those as well. The light pouring through the two gaping holes in the room reflected off the dancing motes of dust as if they were snowflakes, enabling Dalton to find the manager's office, where he let himself inside with another key. There he found a slender metal door in the wall above a battered desk, and he flipped it open to reveal two long rows of switches. Fully unaware of which switch would do what, Dalton shrugged optimistically and began to flip them all one by one.

Click. The lobby came softly aglow with yellow, recessed lighting. *Click.* A single, naked fluorescent bulb sputtered to life immediately above him. *Click.* The glass showcases of the concession stand were illuminated to display a myriad of fingerprints still smudged across them. A single, flattened box of Raisinets was stuffed into the corner of one. *Click, click, click.* With every flick of his fingers, Dalton revealed more of the theater for his inspection. By the time he'd thrown the last switch, his heart was pounding with excitement and anticipation.

He left the office and turned to his left, staring through an entryway that led to the viewing auditorium. The huge white screen on the other side of the cavernous room was spattered in more than one place where some disgruntled viewers had apparently displayed their disgust with the movie by hurling their soft drinks at the actors above them. The faded purple curtains on each side hung in near tatters. Further investigation revealed that the floors were covered with sticky remnants of sodas spilled long ago, and the seats were more bare thread and stains than their original burgundy velvet.

Upstairs in the projection room, Dalton found even more decay. The equipment was ancient, quite possibly original, and a quick scanning of the projector had not offered him a clue as to how he might go about running it. Still, he ran a strong hand over the cool metal casing as if the piece of machinery were the most sensuous woman he'd ever met. Because for Dalton Cameron, the Palace Theater was a sensuous woman of sorts. One who could offer him more than anyone else ever had in his life—sanctuary, solace, perhaps at some point, even a little serenity.

But first, he had some work to do. Quite a lot of work, he thought with only a half-felt frown as he lifted his hand away from the projector to find his fingertips stained with black dust. The Palace Theater would once again return to her original glory, he promised himself. And by the end of four months, she would open again. He already had the bookings planned, a double feature of *Casablanca* to be followed by *A Night at the Opera*—to Dalton, two of the greatest movies ever made.

"Four months," he promised himself aloud, his voice low and rusty sounding as it bounced off the concrete walls of the projection room. He promised himself that was when his life would begin again.

"Oh, Ginnie, you should have *seen* him. God, he was absolutely *gorgeous!*"

Virginia Gennaro gazed at her lunch companion mildly, shifting around the spinach leaves on her plate until they were sufficiently covered with hot bacon dressing. "Mmm," she mumbled with an indulgent smile before tasting the first bite of food she'd had time for today. For most people January was probably a pretty slow month, a comedown after the holiday season. But for Virginia, the beginning of the new school quarter caused January to fly by. And naturally, it hadn't helped at all that she'd over-slept this morning, and had never quite caught up. Her second graders had run circles around her all day.

Now she was enjoying her regularly scheduled late Friday afternoon lunch at Rosie's Diner with Natalie Hogan, a ritual the two of them had practiced since high school. They had both called Comfort, Indiana, home since the day they were born—which, coincidentally, just happened to be the exact same day thirty-four years ago—and had been best friends since the first grade. For that reason, Virginia knew quite well how easily Natalie tended to be swept off her feet by nearly any man who made eye contact with her, and she was certain that her friend's enthusiasm now was nothing to be concerned about.

"He was!" Natalie insisted. "He was the handsomest man I've ever had for a client."

"I'm sure," Virginia agreed with a vigorous nod, fingering back a strawberry blond wave of hair that fell forward over one eye. "So was the guy to whom you sold Henderson's Hardware store. And the guy who listed Montgomery Lake with you. And the guy who bought old Mrs. McCabe's house. Oh, and that doesn't even begin to include the men who were your clients at the jewelry store, before you went into real estate."

Natalie made a face at her. "Well, Eddie's nephew and new owner of the Palace Theater really is the single most incredible looking man I've ever seen. Green eyes, Ginnie," she whispered with a melodramatic sigh, squirming with delight. After a thoughtful moment, she added, "You know, I don't think I've ever met a man with green eyes."

Virginia shook her head. "You're hopeless where men are concerned, you know that?"

Natalie's shoulders drooped in resignation. "I know." Then she brightened somewhat as she asked her usual Friday question. "How's your brother, by the way?"

Virginia smiled. "Evan is fine, as usual. Why do you ask?"

Natalie smiled back. "Just curious. As usual."

"He's in New York for a couple of days, on business. But he should be back in plenty of time for the county Realtors' banquet next month."

Natalie affected an air of nonchalance. "Why should I care when Evan gets back?"

Virginia sipped her tea leisurely before replying. "I just figured you would be asking him to accompany you again this year, as you usually do."

"And no doubt he'll turn me down again this year. As he usually does."

Virginia shook her head mildly and patted her friend's hand in sympathy. "Poor Nat," she cooed. "Evan is just too dumb to realize what he's missing."

Natalie sighed melodramatically. "I think at this point, his avoidance of me is nothing more than tradition. I guess I can't blame the guy. I've been drooling over him ever since I was twelve years old and he was sixteen. He just never drooled back. Then again, I guess I can't blame him for that, either. I looked like a stork with a bad dye job when I was twelve. All legs, no bod, and a shock of hair that did nothing but stand straight up. Anyway, it doesn't matter," she asserted conclusively, confidently tossing a long lock of professionally permed dark hair over her shoulder. "There are lots of other eligible men in Comfort for me to harass. At least six or seven, anyway."

Virginia couldn't help but laugh at her friend. The two of them were notorious around Comfort for the escapades in which they'd indulged all their lives. "Look out," people would always say when they saw Nat and Ginnie walking down the street, "trouble always comes in twos." Yet they were complete opposites in every way. Where Natalie had dark hair and brown eyes, and skin that seemed tan all year, Virginia claimed strawberry-blond hair and porcelain skin, and eyes the color of a summer sky. And where Natalie would try anything once and overexaggerated everything, Virginia was at least quiet and cautious enough to prevent their creating too much turmoil around town. Despite that, the two had latched on to each other immediately and never let go. And unlike most best friends, they'd never envied or begrudged each other the tiniest thing, and they'd never had a fight. Even over a boy. That's because their taste in that department was generally at opposite ends of the spectrum as well.

"Hey, if you like Eddie's nephew, Nat," Virginia said, returning to the conversation at hand, "I hope the two of you will be very happy together."

"Oh, but I wasn't thinking about him for me," Natalie said quickly. "As soon as he came through the door of my office, I thought, 'Oh, gosh, he'd be perfect for Gin—'"

"Stop right there," Virginia cut her off with a decisive wave of her hand. She dropped her fork to her plate with an ominous clatter, and stared Natalie right in the eye. "You know better than that. I have no desire to get involved with any man, something you and my mother seem to consistently forget. And you two, above all people, should understand why."

"I know, but—"

"No buts," Virginia reminded her. "And no matchmaking. Do you promise?"

Natalie twisted her lips into an exasperated line, but nodded once reluctantly. "All right." She was about to sink her teeth into her club sandwich when she added, "But he really is a nice man, Ginnie. I know you'd like him."

"Natalie..."

"Okay, okay, I won't say another word about it."

Until later, Virginia finished her friend's remark. Because she was certain that was exactly what Natalie was thinking. Ever since Virginia had come back to Comfort four years ago, Natalie had been parading one man after another in front of her, assuring her that each was the "handsomest" or "nicest" or "gentlest" or "decentest" or some other contrived superlative of manhood. And each time, Virginia had politely reminded her friend that she'd already been down the matrimonial path once and had absolutely no intention of following it again.

She had married her high school and college sweetheart, Dean "The Dream" Dawson, and lived a life that had bordered on idyllic for almost seven years. Unfortunately that fantasy had ultimately turned into a nightmare, and it had cost Virginia a lot more than her dreams. She wasn't likely to share her life with a man again anytime soon. Or ever, if she had her way, something that Natalie refused to see. Virginia's ex-husband had become a stranger to her in the end, a very dangerous stranger. Who was to say the same thing wouldn't happen with another man?

"That theater's a wreck, though," Natalie went on with her mouth full of sandwich, evidently unwilling to completely drop the subject of the new man in town. "I can't remember the last time anyone set foot in there. I hope Eddie's gorgeous nephew doesn't come barreling back into my office this afternoon demanding to know why it wasn't better cared for."

"It's nice, though, that someone's going to reopen the Palace," Virginia said. "I can't believe it's been closed for so long. It's like having lost a place of pilgrimage or something. How long has it been anyway?"

"Five years," Natalie replied thoughtfully. "Since old Eddie Schneider passed away. Originally his nephew didn't want the theater, wanted me to unload it on anyone who made a halfway decent offer. That offer never came, so I guess now he's taken it upon himself to fix the place up a bit."

"Five years," Virginia repeated dreamily. "That's right. I remember when I came back to Comfort, the first place I went, before even going to Mom's, was back to the Palace. Remember how much time we used to spend there as teenagers?"

Natalie smiled with genuine delight. "Every Friday and Saturday night. And just about every other night of the week once we got hired on."

Virginia smiled, too, only hers was melancholy. "I cried the day I returned home and saw the Palace was closed. Just sat down in front of the theater and bawled like a baby. It was almost symbolic, you know? After everything that had happened with Dean..." She elaborated no further, because both she and Natalie knew better than anyone what everything with Dean had involved. Instead, she just continued softly, "All I'd wanted after that was a little escape. And that meant going to the Palace. But it was closed. Gone. Eddie was dead...." She sighed with genu-

ine sadness. "After that, I felt like I didn't have any escape."

Virginia dropped her gaze back to her salad lest her eyes
reveal all the turmoil her memories evoked. Coming home
to find that her youthful haven from troubles had been shut
down and locked up had caused Virginia perhaps even more
pain than her marriage had provoked. When she'd seen the
Palace closed, that was when she'd begun to feel hopeless.
It had taken her more than five years to work through all
that had happened—five years to battle the anger and resentment and terror, and come to terms with all that had
passed. And now that was precisely where it all lay—in the
past. She would not let what Dean had done to her color the
life she enjoyed today.

"I wonder if Eddie's nephew will show recently released
movies or go back to the revival house format that Eddie
followed," Natalie wondered aloud.

"Oh, I hope he shows the old stuff," Virginia said enthusiastically. "And some of the foreign stuff. That would
be wonderful."

Natalie laughed. "Except that we'd probably start
spending all our time in a darkened theater again and never
see the light of day."

Virginia laughed, too. "Maybe we could get hired on as
concession girls again."

Natalie pretended to consider it. "Maybe if we did, Dr.
Cameron would let us in free, the way Eddie used to do."

"Eddie's nephew is a doctor?" Virginia asked.

Natalie's eyes fairly twinkled. "Why are you interested?
You have no desire to get involved, remember?"

Virginia looked down and brushed at a nonexistent speck
of dust on her white blouse, smoothing a wrinkle out of her
full, flowered skirt. "No, just the idle curiosity anyone in
Comfort would have about a newcomer, that's all."

"Uh-huh," Natalie teased.

Virginia looked up and went back to her salad. "Oh,
never mind. Forget I asked."

Natalie's smile was dazzling as she eagerly offered what she knew of the client she'd had for years but whom she'd only recently met. "He moved here from Indianapolis, and he's signed a six-month rental lease on one of those old houses on Dumont Street. He's thirty-six years old, *single*, devastatingly attractive, about six feet in height, maybe one-eighty in weight."

At this point, Natalie had stopped looking at Virginia, and her eyes were straying toward something over Virginia's shoulder, as if she were envisioning again the handsomest man she'd ever had for a client. "He has the most beautiful wavy brown hair, almost golden," she continued dreamily, "killer green eyes, and he's—"

"I know, I know," Virginia interrupted before Natalie could say it, "he's perfect for me."

"No," Natalie countered with a shake of her head. "No, he's—"

"But you just said he was perfect for me." Virginia was confused, both by Natalie's denial and by the fact that she was more than a little perturbed by her friend's flip-flopping over such a thing. She called herself crazy for caring, and assured herself she did *not* sound petulant.

"No, I don't mean not that," Natalie muttered absently, still looking over Virginia's shoulder, now intensely focused on something she saw there. "I mean, I wasn't going to say that."

Virginia leaned to the left a little so that she could put herself in Natalie's line of vision and bring her friend's wandering attention back to the conversation. "Then what were you going to say?"

Instead of looking Virginia in the eye, Natalie leaned further to her right to look past her lunch companion again. "I was going to say he's coming through the door right now. He's coming right at us."

Before she could stop herself, Virginia turned around, cursing the reflexive action that so clearly indicated her curiosity. But even when she realized she was staring, she couldn't make herself turn back around. Eddie's nephew,

Dr.—what had Natalie said his name was?—was indeed one
of the handsomest men Virginia had ever seen. And he did
indeed claim all the qualities Natalie had so lovingly described, and then some.

For example, her friend hadn't mentioned how well built
and solid the man was. He must be very athletic, Virginia
thought vaguely. Doctors' work wasn't particularly physical, was it? And Natalie hadn't pointed out how...
scruffy...the good doctor was. Although on him, it seemed
somehow appropriate, as if he were the kind of man who
would normally shun social courtesies and conventions in
favor of his own relaxed comfort. Nor had Natalie brought
up the fact that his face was so angular and strong-looking,
and lined with furrows around his jaws and eyes that spoke
of more experience than most people saw in their life-
times. It occurred to Virginia that he somehow looked older
than thirty-six. He also looked kind of angry.

"He seems pretty mad about something," she voiced her
thought out loud as she turned to meet her friend's gaze
once again.

"What did I tell you?" Natalie whispered hoarsely.
"He's ticked off about the state of the theater. He's going
to call me to the mat. Dammit, I *knew* it. I knew something like this would happen. I'll bet he's really steamed."

But if Dr. Whoever was gunning for Natalie, Virginia
decided he wasn't searching for her very hard. He walked
right past their table without so much as a glance in their
direction, headed apparently for the lunch counter in the
back of the diner where so many solitary figures hunched
over their blue plate specials. Never one to appreciate her
good luck when things were running in her favor, Natalie
stopped him with a loudly offered, "Oh, Dr. Cameron!"

He stopped and turned around abruptly, clearly startled
to hear his name called out in a place where he was unknown. When he saw it was Natalie, he seemed to relax a
little, but his surprise was quickly replaced by an unmistakable annoyance.

"Ms. Hogan," he greeted her stiffly as he approached their table with what Virginia thought looked suspiciously like wariness. "Nice to see you again so soon."

Funny, Virginia thought, he sure didn't sound as if he thought such an encounter were nice.

Natalie bit her lip thoughtfully before saying, "I thought you might be looking for me."

"Why would I be looking for you?" he asked her bluntly, almost rudely.

Because Natalie had already dug her own grave by attracting the doctor's attention, Virginia now waited silently and expectantly to see if her friend would follow up by hurling herself into it face first. Never one to disappoint, Natalie did just that.

"I just thought maybe...you know...the Palace wasn't exactly what you were expecting." Her voice had shifted from its usual devil-may-care timbre to the no-nonsense model of efficiency Virginia knew Natalie adopted in the workplace. Except that this time, Natalie sounded like a no-nonsense, efficient six-year-old. Dr. Devastating, she decided, could make any female feel like a giddy little kid again.

Dr. Cameron shook his head thoughtfully as he responded, "No, Ms. Hogan, it's perfect."

"Really?" Natalie squeaked.

Virginia watched the byplay between the two with a superior smile. Natalie was so easy, she thought smugly. No one would ever catch Virginia falling under a man's spell that way. Just as the thought formed in her head, however, Dr. Cameron turned his attention from Natalie to her. The moment their gazes met, she knew she was in trouble. His eyes really were green, she thought. Really green. Like a vast, sweeping plain of summer grass. Immediately her heart began to pound out an alarm, one that shouted *Warning* with every thump of life.

"Perfect," Dalton repeated, although suddenly the theater was the farthest thing from his mind.

The woman who sat across from who he was fast beginning to consider the somewhat bothersome Ms. Natalie Hogan, Realtor, with more idle curiosity than was comfortable, was rather...intriguing. She reminded him of Veronica Lake, with those high cheekbones and that cool sweep of strawberry-blond hair, parted on one side to fall in a dangerous wave over spectacularly blue eyes. Dalton had always loved Veronica Lake. And like his favorite actress, this woman's bone structure was delicate, her body willowy and probably a little on the short side—even though she was seated, he could tell that she'd probably barely reach his chin. Yet despite a seemingly fragile frame, she exuded a raw strength and conviction that Dalton could see was impenetrable. Simply put, he could tell she would never tolerate being walked over.

"Dr. Cameron," Natalie Hogan began again when she evidently realized where his attention had strayed. "This is my friend, Virginia Gennaro. She teaches art over at the elementary school. Did I, uh, did I ask if you had any children?"

Dalton glanced over at her again, hoping his expression reflected his exasperation. "No, Ms. Hogan, you did not. You did, however, ask me my age, my birthplace, my favorite food and my favorite color. You also asked me whether or not I was married, and when I replied that I was not, you finally moved on to another subject. But, no, just for the record, I don't have any children." Not anymore, he thought before he could stop himself.

To force the numbing reminder out of his head, Dalton looked at Virginia again. Veronica, Virginia, even their names were similar. He took an almost involuntary step forward and extended his hand toward her, and she took it graciously with a surprisingly robust grip.

"It's nice to meet you, Dr. Cameron."

"Dalton," he told her, calling himself an idiot for encouraging any kind of familiarity.

"Virginia," she replied in kind.

Dalton held her hand for a moment longer than was necessary, then dropped it hastily when he realized what he was doing. It was just that her hand was so soft and warm. And it had been years since he'd allowed himself to get so close to things like softness and warmth. Of course he'd be drawn to a woman like her, he told himself. So what? There was nothing so wrong about that, was there? Just a natural attraction. All he had to do was make certain it didn't go any farther than that. All he'd have to do was stay out of her way. And despite the fact that Comfort, Indiana, was a pretty dinky town, such an evasion shouldn't be too difficult. He'd have no need to bother himself with the workings of the local elementary school, because he no longer had a son. And where else was he likely to meet up with the attractive Virginia Gennaro?

"Natalie tells me you're planning on reopening the Palace," she said then, and suddenly Dalton realized he might very well be seeing more of Virginia once the theater was up and running again.

Natalie Hogan had told him this afternoon about how the old movie house had been one of the most social institutions in Comfort up until the time it closed. It made sense that people would be looking forward to its reopening. And that Virginia Gennaro would be one of those people.

"Yes," he told her. "In about four months, I hope to complete the work necessary to get her rolling again. I'm aiming for an opening sometime in May. By then the weather should be nice and warm, and people will be anxious to get out and do something to chase away the winter doldrums."

"And what better way than a movie?" Virginia asked with a smile.

He nodded. "I can't imagine a better one."

"Will you be showing new films?"

Dalton shook his head decisively. "No way. I'm working on a format of old classics and foreign films that might not receive play in this part of the country. It will be a rather eclectic schedule."

"Just promise me you'll show *Casablanca* and *A Night at the Opera*, that's all I ask," Virginia requested with a smile. "They're two of my favorite movies."

Dalton was stunned. Before he realized what he was doing, he told her, "I've already planned on opening the theater with a double feature of those two movies. That's amazing. It's as if you read my mind."

Virginia's smile broadened, a smile that was at once wary and delighted. "I'll bet you're a Truffaut fan, too."

Dalton couldn't help but chuckle nervously. "*Small Change* is another of my favorite films."

Virginia looked at Natalie, and Dalton could tell the two of them were sharing some private joke. "Looks like we're going to have our Friday and Saturday nights pretty well tied up starting in May," she said to her friend.

Natalie laughed. "Good thing we both have such crummy social lives."

Dalton didn't like the way this conversation was going one bit. He had way too much in common with Virginia Gennaro, and now Natalie Hogan was looking at him as if he was a choice loin cut in the butcher's window. He had to get out of there. Fast.

"I seem to be keeping you ladies from your lunch," he said abruptly, taking a few steps backward as he spoke. "If you'll excuse me, I'll just catch a quick bite at the counter and get out of your hair."

Before they could decline, Dalton hurried away, hoping he hadn't looked like the idiot he felt, fleeing in terror from two beautiful women. He really was a disgrace to his gender. But Virginia Gennaro had begun to creep under his skin, into some part of him deep down inside that he had cemented over and sealed tight. It was a place he had sworn no one would ever enter again. Yet she had reached out a warm hand and touched it without fear of rejection.

And that was what had scared Dalton the most. That his defenses against Virginia had been absolutely nil.

Chapter Two

The sun had already settled below the horizon by the time Dalton decided to send out for a pizza. Unconsciously, he rubbed his knee as he rose from the kneeling position he'd folded himself into while painting the concrete floor of the projection room. The thing he hated most about the winter months was not that the biting cold and dampness brought constant achiness to his knees, a throbbing pain that would probably stay with him the rest of his life, along with the memories that haunted him. No, the thing he hated most was that darkness came so early and stayed so damned long.

Dalton despised the darkness. Since the accident two years ago, there hadn't been a single night when he'd slept soundly. Two years without good sleep could put anyone in a bad mood, he told himself as he limped awkwardly down the stairs to the manager's office. But tonight's bad mood went beyond fatigue. It was the result of an unwanted preoccupation. A preoccupation with thoughts about Virginia Gennaro.

Three weeks had passed since Dalton's arrival in Comfort. He'd moved into the furnished house he was renting just inside the outskirts of town, an old, brick monstrosity that predated the First World War, and one that needed about as much fixing up as the Palace did. Between making the two places habitable enough to even begin all the work that needed to be done, Dalton had been busy day and night, another reason he hadn't been getting much sleep. But he liked the hard work, liked the movement and strain on his muscles. Every fiber in his body ached from overuse, but Dalton didn't grumble or complain. At least he was feeling *something,* he reminded himself. And physical pain beat emotional pain any day of the week.

He pulled the Comfort phone book from its place on the shelf above his desk in the manager's office, marveling again at the slenderness of the volume compared to Indianapolis's heavy tome. The population of this town was only something like seven thousand, he had to remind himself. Nowhere near the metropolitan and commercial center that Indianapolis was. Here, the business district consisted of fewer than a dozen city blocks, and the closest thing to a shopping mall was a flat length of outdoor shopping center that claimed a discount chain store and combination book/gift shop run by two elderly sisters as its anchors. Still, the slower pace and quiet atmosphere appealed to Dalton. It was a complete and welcomed change from the hurried, stressful string of activity that his life in Indianapolis had become.

Dalton rubbed the back of his neck until he flipped to the yellow page topped by the heading Pizza. God, he was beat. He couldn't ever remember being this tired, even during his residency, when he'd been forced to remain awake literally for days. A quick snooze on an unoccupied gurney would be the only rest allowed him back then, but even that sounded like a dreamless delight compared to the patchy instances of semiconsciousness he'd been experiencing lately.

Pushing the memory away, Dalton rose without even checking his dinner choices and began pacing around the tiny office to work the stiffness out of his lower limbs. Inevitably, once his mind was cleared, memories of Virginia Gennaro swam into his brain with all the clarity and color of a seventy-millimeter film print. He'd seen her once since their initial meeting at the diner three weeks ago, in the supermarket near his home. She'd been standing in the produce section, gently fingering tomatoes, and Dalton had just stood there, transfixed by the way she handled the vegetables. She'd looked up to find him staring at her, and had smiled, then she'd blushed a little, as if she'd been caught in some mildly illicit act. Nonetheless, she had approached him to say hello.

She'd been wearing a long, amber wool coat with a cream-colored lacy scarf thrown around her shoulders. The coat had been open to reveal an old-fashioned, flowered dress, and her hair had been swept back, loosely bound with a black velvet bow. And she had smelled wonderful, he remembered now, inhaling deeply as if trying to recreate the scent in his mind. She'd smelled like an English garden full of white flowers. Dalton had thought that if Virginia Gennaro were a movie, her image would be softly blurred, her features mellowed by sepia hues and a glazed lens.

They had chatted for only a moment, the small talk of people who'd met only recently and knew each other not at all. Yes, he was settling in nicely, thanks, and the house on Dumont Street was more than ample for his modest needs. Yes, the theater work was moving along right on schedule, but he was going to have to hire some professionals, because he had absolutely no knowledge of plumbing, and the thought of working with electrical wiring made him a little edgy. Virginia had given him the names of a plumber and electrician—both men she had known in high school—and then had suggested a number of local attractions Dalton might be interested in hearing about. She had also mentioned that he lived near some very nice restaurants if he didn't like cooking at home, she herself favoring one called the Purple Iris Café.

Dalton glanced at his watch. Pizza really didn't sound all that appetizing right now, he thought. And his diet this week had been lousy. Maybe what he needed was a decent, well-cooked meal, something with a few vegetables on the side. This Purple Iris Café that Virginia had mentioned might be just the ticket. Not wanting to waste any more time than necessary, Dalton quickly cleaned up his painting supplies and changed from his painter's clothes back into the brown corduroys and baggy beige sweater he'd worn into the theater that morning. In no time at all, he was decent enough looking to go out in public, and his appetite was bordering on ravenous.

The Purple Iris Café, he thought again. Sounded like a nice place to have dinner. And if Virginia Gennaro just happened to show up there, too, well, then maybe for the first time in years, Dalton wouldn't have to eat alone.

Virginia was there, as he'd somehow known she would be. She sat alone at a table for two in the corner of the Purple Iris Café, cradling a glass of white wine in one hand and a copy of Bruno Bettelheim's *The Uses of Enchantment* in the other. She wore a pale lavender sweater and faded blue jeans, her cream-colored wool scarf draped shawl-style over her shoulders. Dalton studied her for long moments, but she never felt his eyes upon her. Instead she continued to be utterly absorbed in what she was reading.

Virginia Gennaro was completely unlike any woman he had ever been attracted to or dated. He'd scarcely ever gone out with blondes. He'd never gone out with a redhead. Virginia Gennaro's hair was like a compelling mixture of both, a color he'd never quite seen on another woman. She taught art to elementary school-age children and read books by child psychologists. She wore very feminine clothes that fairly screamed at any casual observer she was a soft woman, yet she carried a look in her eyes to assure such an observer she would not tolerate being taken lightly. She seemed to Dalton sedate, refined, no-nonsense, and a borderline intellectual. And if such were the case, she had very little in common with the carefree, fun-loving adventurous sorts he'd dated before he married.

She also seemed to be nothing at all like his wife, Penny. And perhaps that was precisely why he was attracted to her, he thought, his analysis stemming from some faintly recalled undergraduate psychology classes. Or maybe, he finally admitted, the reason he was attracted to her was simply that she was a beautiful, articulate woman. A woman who touched some forgotten place deep inside him that hadn't been touched in years. A woman he should probably avoid at all costs.

As quickly as the warning sounded in his brain, Dalton ignored it. Before he even realized he had decided to join Virginia, his feet were moving leisurely in her direction. His low-heeled boots scuffed softly across the blue-and-white-tiled floor as he walked, and he noted idly the framed artwork of purple and blue flowers that adorned the white walls of the café. Inevitably, though, his gaze fell back on Virginia, and despite the fact that he paused to stand a mere two feet away from her table, she still didn't look up from her reading.

"Virginia?" he finally asked, his voice sounding too loud to himself, too anxious.

She started a little when she heard her name, but finally glanced up from her book. Dalton could tell she was surprised to see him standing there, but she was also clearly delighted by his appearance. Only when he felt himself relaxing did he realize he had been fearful that she might not be pleased to see him.

"I wasn't sure, but I thought that was you sitting back here all alone," he lied softly, hoping he sounded suave and self-confident, instead feeling like a high school senior who must hide his interest in a girl until he's certain she reciprocates it.

"Hi, Dalton," she greeted him warmly, closing her book with infinite care before setting it on the table beside her plate.

To say she was surprised to see him wouldn't exactly be the truth. Ever since Virginia had told him at the grocery store that the Iris was one of her favorite places to eat, she had been hoping she would run into Dalton Cameron there. In fact, she had eaten here so frequently over the past few weeks that even the waiters and waitresses were beginning to ask questions such as whether her stove was working all right, or if she no longer had time to shop for groceries.

Virginia would always laugh and reply vaguely, yes, something of the sort. But deep down, she had to admit that despite all her reminders that she would be better off maintaining a polite, but very real distance between herself and the very attractive Dr. Cameron, she couldn't help but be fascinated by him, couldn't help but want to know more.

When she had run into him at the grocery store, she almost hadn't recognized him right off. He'd been letting his hair and beard grow out, and as a result had passed from the somewhat scruffy stage of their first encounter to enter the fashion-model-with-a-trendy-but-rugged appearance phase. Now his hair was unfashionably, but pleasantly, long and curly, and his beard had become thick and lustrous, with a hint of red amid the pale brown softness. Now he looked like a successful, sophisticated businessman. Or an English professor. Virginia couldn't quite decide which.

"I hope I'm not interrupting your dinner," he said, indicating her glass of wine and empty plate.

"No," she was quick to respond. "I just ordered an appetizer. I haven't ordered dinner yet. Would you . . ." She hesitated. How would he construe her invitation to join her for dinner? Would he think she was coming on to him? Was he one of those men who assumed that an invitation from a woman—any invitation—also indicated she would welcome him in her bed? Or would he be reasonable and normal enough to understand that such an invitation simply meant she was willing to share her dinner table and conversation with him?

Ultimately Virginia decided Dalton was one of the latter, and said softly, "Would you like to join me? I'll share my green chili wontons with you when they arrive."

Dalton smiled, a glacier-melting, typhoon-inducing smile. She felt every cell in her body warming to a dangerous temperature. If she'd been a woman of less self-control, she would have actually squealed with utter delight.

"I'd love to," he said. His voice reminded Virginia of expensive cognac, gently warmed in the cradle of a gentleman's hand.

He shrugged out of his leather bomber jacket and hung it on a nearby hook, then pulled the opposite chair away from the table and sat. Suddenly, and not a little nervously, Virginia realized he was closer to her than he'd ever been before. If she'd wanted to, she could have reached a hand across the table and stroked the silky strands of his beard, or traced the deep lines that fanned out from his eyes. He smelled faintly of mineral spirits, an aroma that always reminded her of summertime, when her father would come home from a construction sight redolent of such scents. For a moment she closed her eyes and recalled how happy she'd been back then, and for just a moment, sitting here with Dalton made her feel exactly the same way.

And suddenly Virginia could think of absolutely nothing to say.

But as if she'd sent out her distress telepathically, her waiter returned with a plate full of fried wontons accompanied by a green sauce upon which she was forced to comment verbally.

"Watch out," she cautioned Dalton. "This stuff is *very* hot and spicy."

"A woman who likes the Marx Brothers *and* very spicy food," he replied with a smile. "Where have you been all my life?"

Virginia laughed, although she felt more uneasy than jubilant, and quickly turned her attention to the waiter to order dinner. Dalton offered the menu a perfunctory glance and made a quick decision, and the waiter left again, to return momentarily with a glass of red wine for him. For a moment, Virginia and Dalton simply sipped their wine in silence, hastily glancing away every time they made eye contact. Finally, when she couldn't tolerate the awkward tension any longer, Virginia reached for a wonton and groped for small talk.

"How's the theater coming along?" she asked before popping the spicy nugget into her mouth, chewing quickly so that she could swallow before it would be necessary to talk again.

Dalton seemed relieved by the harmless question. "Pretty well. There's just so much that needs fixing, it was hard to decide where to begin. But now things are moving along right on schedule. The plasterers are plastering, the plumbers are plumbing, and the electricians are..."

"Electrifying?" she asked.

He eyed her with a smile. "To say the least."

She smiled back as fond memories tumbled into her mind like a nearly forgotten film. "I can only imagine how much work needs to be done. That place was a wreck sixteen years ago when Natalie and I started working there. My God, has it really been that long ago?" she marveled aloud to herself. After an incredulous shake of her head, she added, "Since the theater has been neglected for five years, the decline must be overwhelming."

"You used to work at the Palace?" Dalton asked, clearly very interested in her reply.

Virginia nodded. "All through college. It was a wonderful place to work. I'm sure you already know about how your uncle was hired on there as an usher in the thirties when he was a teenager, and bought it in the fifties as a first-run movie house."

"Vaguely," he confessed. "To be honest, I don't know much at all about Uncle Eddie. My mother and I spent one summer here when I was a kid, but that's the only time I really met him. The Palace format was strictly first-run movies back then. When did he start showing old and foreign movies?"

"In the late seventies," she told him, "when he started losing business to the new multiplex at the shopping center. He figured the only way to challenge them was to show old classics people couldn't see on the big screen otherwise and charge a buck and a half instead of the three dollars new movies commanded. Every now and then he'd throw a foreign film into the schedule just to give the good citizens of Comfort something to talk about at the dinner table. *Grand Illusion, The Bicycle Thief,* that sort of thing. It was quite an ambitious thing to do in a small town like Comfort."

"I can imagine," Dalton said thoughtfully.

Virginia continued. "But your uncle Eddie was never a man to turn and run in the face of adversity. Some of the local churches tried to shut him down when he showed Fellini's *Satyricon,* but Eddie jumped up on a chair in front of the theater and went on for about forty-five minutes about freedom of expression and the American Way." She glanced at Dalton, who was watching her with just the hint of a smile. "If you'll recall, your uncle was only about five foot one. It was a very stirring sight."

"I'll bet."

"Anyway," Virginia continued after she dipped another wonton into the green chili sauce and tasted it, "by the eighties, the Palace became something of an institution, and word spread. It was the only place of its kind for miles around. Eddie even showed *Gone with the Wind* one night. Do you realize how few people have seen that movie on the big screen? It was incredible. People came from as far away as Indianapolis to see that. I remember one Saturday before Natalie and I worked there, we sat through five movies in a row—everything from *The Lady Vanishes* to *Godzilla Versus Megalon.* That was the beauty of Eddie's movie schedules. They claimed absolutely no rhyme or reason."

He gazed at her thoughtfully for a moment before responding. "So basically what you're telling me is that, despite my uncle's modest height, I have some mighty big shoes to fill."

She turned the plate between them until the last wonton was in front of him. He offered her a chiding expression, but took it anyway.

"I've had four and you've only had three," she pointed out before commenting on his remark. "People in Comfort have missed the Palace all these years. I'm afraid the community will be scrutinizing you very closely, Dr. Cameron."

Dalton halted his hand in its movement toward his mouth for only a heartbeat, but when he did, Virginia could see it tremble just the slightest bit.

"Just Dalton, okay?" he said softly, but his tone was in no way gentle. "I've taken a leave of absence from my position at the hospital where I've been working. I'm not practicing medicine right now." His next words were offered in a way that made her feel as if he were saying them against his will. "And whether or not I go back to it is . . ." His voice trailed off as he polished off the last of the green chili wontons. "Never mind," he concluded when he swallowed.

Virginia wanted to ask more, wanted to know what would make a man even consider leaving a position for which he'd spent more than a quarter of his life preparing, but she was too polite to pry. If he wanted to tell her, he would, she thought, and it was clearly a topic he had no intention of pursuing. Instead he began to ask her questions about her own job.

"So what grade do you teach?" he wanted to know.

"Second," she told him with a broad smile. "That's the age when they're still very curious and inquisitive, but independent and aggressive enough to put you on the spot if you don't answer their questions to their satisfaction."

Instead of smiling back, Dalton was frowning at her when she met his gaze again, as if she'd just uttered the foulest expletive in the English language. She had no idea why, but Virginia suddenly felt very small, and had the urge to sink into her chair until she was completely invisible. Thankfully their telepathic waiter arrived with their dinners then, and after his departure, she strove to reclaim their earlier light mood by returning to the theater as subject matter.

"So, um, are you planning to introduce a format similar to the one Eddie followed?" she asked cautiously.

He poked at the food on his plate as if he had no idea what he had ordered and couldn't quite identify what the waiter had placed before him. "Yes," he said quietly.

"Foreign films, too?"

A quick nod.

"Maybe if you have time someday, I can offer a few suggestions about scheduling. Which films were most popular with the locals, that sort of thing."

"Okay."

Virginia paused, hoping Dalton would offer some indication that he wanted to be a part of this conversation, but he remained silent with his head bowed toward his chest, thinking about something she suspected had nothing to do with what they had discussed so far. Despite that, she pressed on valiantly.

"The Rotary Club always loved it when Eddie ran the John Wayne Festivals. And my mom's cooking club was especially fond of the Ginger Rogers-Fred Astaire and Jeanette MacDonald-Nelson Eddy combinations."

"Mmm."

She bit her lip nervously. What had gone wrong with this conversation? she wondered. What had she said that had robbed him of his earlier vitality? Where had she gone wrong?

"Dalton?" she asked experimentally.

"Hmm?" he replied without looking up, still stirring his food into a bland mess.

"Did I . . . have I done something wrong?"

His head snapped up then, and his eyes were stormy when they met hers. "What do you mean?" he demanded gruffly.

Virginia swallowed with some difficulty, now very confused about what she could only describe as his anger. "Uh, just that we were having a nice conversation, then suddenly... suddenly you went a little quiet. Was it something I said?"

Dalton couldn't very well tell her that when she had described her second-graders, she had described his son, Dylan, perfectly. Dylan had just entered second grade the September before the accident, and he had been every bit as inquisitive and demanding of answers as Virginia's students apparently were. How many times had he heard his son utter the question, "But really, Daddy, why?" only to offer Dylan a quick rebuff and say he was far too busy to explain it right now?

He couldn't tell Virginia that because to do so would be to reveal a hell of a lot more of himself to her than he wanted her—or anyone in Comfort—to know about him. And it would open up wounds Dalton did not want to see bleeding again. So he simply shook his head and muttered, "No, it's nothing. I was just reminded of something, that's all." He forced himself to relax, and even managed a half-felt smile as he reached across the table to briefly squeeze her hand in reassurance. "I'm sorry. I didn't mean to get weird on you."

She smiled back at him a little tentatively. "You weren't weird," she assured him. "I just thought maybe I'd—"

He held up a hand to cut her off. "You're fine, Virginia," he told her. Almost too fine, he added to himself. To steer the conversation away from his past, Dalton went back to his earlier line of questioning. "But you were telling me about yourself. Are you from Comfort originally?"

Virginia nodded, chewing her food completely before swallowing. It was so awkward trying to get to know someone over a meal. Whoever had come up with the notion that dinner would be an appropriate occasion for a first date must have been out of his or her mind. Then she reminded herself insistently that what she and Dalton were enjoying was certainly *not* a date, first or otherwise. A chance encounter perhaps, she decided. Or maybe a fortuitous meeting. But not a date. Dates led to relationships. And relationships . . . well, they just led to trouble.

"Born and bred," she replied after a swallow of her wine. "I lived in Atlanta for nearly eight years, but I moved back here about four years ago. It's good to be home," she told him with a satisfied sigh.

"Your family is here?"

"My mother and older brother. My father died right after I graduated from college."

"I'm sorry," Dalton said softly.

Virginia smiled sadly. "Thanks. Me, too."

"This must have been a wonderful place to grow up," he went on quickly. "It's like living in a Norman Rockwell painting."

She chuckled. "You must have grown up in a big city."

"Indianapolis," he verified.

"I knew it. People from big cities always think it must have been nice to grow up in some little corner of the heartland." She placed her fork and knife appropriately across her plate in what her manners-minded mother had taught her meant "I'm finished with my meal now, thanks," then she leaned back in her chair. "It was actually pretty boring. There never seemed to be anything to do. Natalie and I were always in trouble for something because we kept coming up with these outrageous schemes to keep our brains from turning into pudding."

"You? In trouble?" he asked skeptically. "I don't believe it for a minute."

She shook her head at him mildly, brushing her hair back from her forehead to tuck a strand behind her ear. "You're going to have to trust me on this one, Dalton. I was a wild kid."

"You'll never convince me of that," he assured her as he tipped back his glass for the final sip of wine. "To you, being wild probably meant you listened to the Cowsills instead of the Osmonds and drank Cherry Coke instead of regular Coke."

Virginia gazed at him levelly and tried not to smile when she revealed, "I played electric guitar in an all-girl punk band called PMS. We even sold one of our songs, 'Uterus Envy,' to an L.A.-based band who was passing through and heard us play one night. We got shafted, though. In the excitement of the moment, we agreed to a sum of money much smaller than what we could have gotten had we been properly represented. Anyway, it didn't matter because finals were coming up, and we didn't have time to write any more songs for them."

Dalton had been about to place his wineglass on the table, but his hand had stilled in the action several inches short of completing it right after Virginia had voiced her first sentence. When his eyes met hers again, they were full of laughter and disbelief. "You did not," he denied. "You're making that up."

"Natalie played drums," she continued as if he hadn't spoken. "The first time we performed live, we got this spray-on hair coloring, thinking it would wash out the next day...." She chuckled from somewhere deep inside at the memory. "Boy, were our folks mad when it didn't. My purple hair kind of faded to a soft lavender by the end of summer. For months, Natalie's held this dark green hue you could only see when the sun was out. It was pretty interesting."

Dalton stared at her for a long time when she finished speaking, and finally decided she was telling him the God's honest truth. Maybe he'd been wrong about Virginia Gennaro, he thought with a silent shake of his head. Maybe she was more adventurous than any of the women he'd ever dated. But he sure couldn't picture her with lavender hair.

Despite the subfreezing temperatures outside, Dalton walked Virginia home from the Purple Iris Café, surprised—and more than a little pleased—to discover that her house was less than four blocks from his own. Lights shone warmly from nearly every window in front, and two cats were perched in the living-room window, their silhouettes made more prominent by the long drapes behind them.

"Thanks for walking me home," she told him. "It was nice of you to go out of your way, what with it being so cold and all."

When Dalton turned to say good-night, warm, silvery wisps of her breath spiraled upward to form a gentle halo around her face, her features made more luminous by a streetlight that stood sentry at the end of the Gennaro driveway. Her cheeks and the tip of her nose were pink from the brisk night air, and without realizing what he was doing, he reached for the scarf knotted loosely above the collar of her coat and pulled it snug. Virginia chuckled when he did so, covering his bare hands with her mittened ones to playfully brush them away.

He was shocked to realize that he suddenly wanted to kiss her. Not the passionate, drugging embrace of a man with the intent to seduce, but a soft, chaste brush of his lips against hers that would simply bring the two of them a little bit closer, create a little more intimacy than what he was already beginning to feel with her. It was an odd sensation, he thought, one he'd never experienced with a woman before, and one upon which he knew he most certainly should not act. However, he couldn't deny the intensity of his desire, couldn't deny that he wanted more than anything to see Virginia again. He tried to convince himself there was no point to such a meeting, that there would be no future in it, but the feeling remained strong. He would simply have to ignore it, he told himself. Pretend it did not exist.

"You're welcome," he finally replied in response to her thanks. "You realize of course we're practically neighbors."

She nodded. "Natalie told me you're renting a house over on Dumont Street. I used to play with a couple of girls who lived on that block when I was a child. This whole neighborhood was rampant with children back then. Now it's mostly older people. It's much quieter now than it used to be."

"This is the house you grew up in?" he asked, inclining his head toward the building behind them.

Again, she nodded, shrugging a little self-consciously when she confessed, "I, uh, I kind of live with my mother."

Dalton wasn't sure how to take her statement. Certainly there was nothing wrong with such a situation, and it was becoming more and more common for adult children to live with their parents with the economy being what it was these days. But Virginia seemed to be less than ecstatic about the arrangement. Perhaps she and her mother didn't get along.

"You'll have to introduce me to her sometime," he said finally. "I'd like to know what kind of woman could produce a lavender-haired electric guitarist."

She grinned, then reached up to push back a stray strand of his hair with her fingertips. As soon as she realized what she was doing, her eyes widened in surprise and worry, and she quickly dropped her hand. Dalton could tell she'd frightened herself by the forwardness of what she'd just done, but she quickly recovered.

"Mom's kind of a combination of June Cleaver and Emma Goldman," she told him in a shallow voice. "So you better be careful. Someday I'll take you up on your request and introduce the two of you, and then you'll be sorry."

He laughed. "I'll look forward to it."

Silence came again after that, and Virginia wished she knew what Dalton was thinking. A cold breeze kicked up, ruffling her hair and making her shiver. He must have noted the action because he rubbed his hands quickly up and down her upper arms, then turned her toward her house.

"Go," he instructed her playfully. "Get inside where it's warm."

She turned one final time and lifted a mitten in farewell. "Thanks again, Dalton," she said quietly. "Good night."

And with that she turned again and made her way silently into her house. When she was safely inside, she lifted her hand once more and closed the door behind her.

Dalton raised his hand, too, watching her actions with a number of conflicting emotions. He'd had fun with Virginia tonight, and had enjoyed her company tremendously. She was smart, funny, irreverent, and she shared with him a love of nearly every movie ever made, even *Plan 9 From Outer Space*. She knew who Ray Harryhausen was. She'd seen *Harold and Maude* twenty-six times. And she was beautiful, too, he reminded himself needlessly. Way too dangerous a woman for him to be around.

When the lights in the living room went dark, Dalton turned to leave. Film buffs were a dime a dozen, he knew, and every little kid in America had escaped to the movies now and then. And everyone had a favorite, the one roll of celluloid they were unequivocally certain was the best thing that had ever come out of Hollywood.

But, Dalton thought further, there were a few others who had ventured a little more boldly into the realm of film, beyond the usual buff stage. They were the ones who could quote obscure statistics and identify unknown actors about whom no one else would possibly ever care. They were the ones who could flip through a film compendium and tell you something about more than half of the movies on any given page. They were people who had found more than escape at the movie theaters of their youth. They'd found shared experiences and camaraderie of spirit. They'd found something they simply couldn't find anywhere else—understanding.

Dalton himself was one of those people. And so was Virginia Gennaro. And when two people like that discovered each other, they simply forged a bond without even trying, without even realizing what had been done. As much as he might wish that he could keep away from her, he already knew it would be pointless to even try. He liked her company, and she clearly liked his. They were two of a kind in a very small town. So why deny himself the pleasure of being around her? he asked himself logically. Why shouldn't the two of them spend time together talking and laughing and sharing? He'd done so little of that in the past two years.

And somehow, Dalton got the feeling the same was true for Virginia. She had her friend, Natalie, of course, and that was probably what had kept her sane in Comfort all these years. But he got the impression that there was some part of Virginia even Natalie didn't quite reach, a part she was unwilling to reveal to anyone. He recognized it so easily, because he carried a part like that within himself.

As he turned the corner of Virginia's street to make his way slowly toward his own, Dalton shoved his hands deep into his pockets and looked up at the sky. It was black—not the moon or a star in sight. The streetlight behind him was fast fading into a meaningless gleam of white, and the darkness was closing in around him. Normally he would feel a little edgy about such a thing. Normally he would hurry his steps in order to get home where he would be amid more familiar surroundings. Instead, he thought about Virginia Gennaro, and for some reason, the darkness didn't bother him quite as much as it usually did.

He'd made his first friend in Comfort, he realized with a broad, happy smile that was crooked and rusty from lack of use. He only hoped Virginia would understand when he wanted to keep their relationship at that. And once again, somehow he knew such an arrangement would be perfectly fine with her. In that respect, too, they were two of a kind. They would be two friends who knew better than to botch it up with hearts and flowers, two people who were strong enough and smart enough to know not to mess with something good.

But way, way back, in the very corners of Dalton's mind, he could hear somebody laughing. And with no small amount of fear, he realized he was laughing at himself.

Chapter Three

"Are you the guy who advertised for an artist?"

The woman's voice came to Dalton from several feet below. He stood at the top of an eight-foot ladder, the upper half of his body hidden thanks to an open panel in the lobby ceiling as he inspected the state of the material used to construct it. He sighed in frustration. As with nearly everything else in the Palace Theater, the lobby ceiling would have to be replaced. Not only was it a water-stained eyesore from below, but from this vantage point, it also looked like it might collapse at any minute.

"Yeah, that's me," he called down his reply, not moving from his lofty perch. "You interested?"

"You bet," the woman called back.

Dalton balanced his flashlight under his chin, steadying himself on the edge of the open ceiling panel with one hand as he raked the thumbnail of his other over a length of fiberboard. The material crumbled into dust as he did so. He started to grumble something about shoddy workmanship, then reminded himself that he was the one who had allowed the theater to sit neglected for five years.

Frowning, he recalled that he was interviewing a potential employee and asked further, "What are your qualifications?"

"Well, I'm an artist," he heard in response. He smiled in spite of himself. "And I'm very good," the woman added quickly.

"I'm not necessarily in the market for someone who can copy the Mona Lisa," he told her, switching off his flashlight and taking a step down the ladder. Two more steps down brought his head and shoulders out of the ceiling. As he replaced the panel, he turned his attention to the first applicant who had responded to the job he'd had advertised in the *Comfort Courier* for the past two weeks. "I'm looking for..." He stopped in midstep, staring down at the woman who stood chuckling at the foot of the ladder. "Virginia."

She smiled. "Well, if you're looking for me, here I am."

He couldn't help but smile back. He hadn't seen her for nearly a week, and was startled to realize just how much he had missed her. "No, that's not what I meant," he said.

"You're not looking for me?" Virginia tried to appear crushed, but being near Dalton again after six days of doing without him made her feel too good to pout.

"No, that's not what I meant, either," he told her as he completed his journey back down and came to a stop on the floor.

"Then I'm still in the running for the job?"

He didn't respond right away. Instead he only stood before her and marveled at the warm feelings meandering through his body at the sight of her. He shook his head as if to clear it, but remained silent.

"Why do you want to hire an artist anyway?" she asked conversationally, as if she were unaware of the goofy way he must be looking at her.

But Dalton could only continue to stare at her as if she were a miraculous vision who had appeared from thin air.

The late-afternoon sun shone through the lobby doors behind her, creating a hazy aura around her that only added
to the ethereal quality of her appearance. Her hair hung
over one shoulder in a loose braid bound at the end with red
ribbon, and she was wearing another one of those Depres-
sion-era flowered dresses beneath her long coat. Why did
Virginia Gennaro always make him feel as if he'd stepped
back into a quieter, gentler time? he wondered. Why, by her
simple presence, did she somehow make him feel almost at
peace?

"Dalton?" she asked softly, warily, making him realize
how long he'd been staring at her in dumbfounded silence.

"What?" he replied stupidly, unable to remember what
her original question had been.

She smiled a little nervously, as if she, too, were aware of
some strange, ill-defined something stirring up the air between them. "I asked why you had advertised for an artist
to begin with. A painter I can understand," she added,
nodding toward his own paint-spattered khaki trousers and
faded blue sweatshirt. "But an artist?"

Dalton hesitated only a moment before replying, a moment he needed to collect himself and be certain his voice
was steady. "I found some of my uncle's things upstairs in
a locked cabinet in the projection room. There was a box
full of old photographs of the Palace interior, taken shortly
after the theater originally opened back in the thirties. I
noticed a lot of art-deco detail painting around the doors,
along the walls near the ceiling, around the ticket booth and
behind the concession stand. Somewhere along the line,
someone painted over all that. I thought it might be nice to
recreate it again."

Virginia nodded, then turned to view her surroundings
with a critical eye. "You know, that's not a bad idea at all.
I could do a spray of palm trees behind the concession
stand, maybe stencil a fan-type motif along the walls near
the ceiling and around the ticket booth. Or maybe something less angular. What kind of lighting are you planning
on using?"

He didn't point out that he hadn't yet hired her, and knew such an idea probably wasn't such a good one to begin with, considering the major attraction he felt for her. Instead he replied to her question instantly, stating completely his intentions. "I'm staying with the recessed lighting, but I'm removing the yellow lights to go with blue instead. I've also ordered some wall sconces from a company in California that specializes in period reproductions, semicircular frosted globes affixed to three metal triangles."

She nodded again. "Then the fan motif would work very nicely."

"Yes, it would."

She smiled at him. "And the palm trees?"

Dalton nodded, too. "I like it."

"So do I get the job?"

He eyed her cautiously, knowing he should tell her no, but honestly looking forward to working with her. Besides, he reminded himself unnecessarily, no one else seemed interested in the work. "Don't you want to know how much it pays?"

She shrugged. "Actually I'm not all that concerned about wages."

"Then why are you applying for the job?"

She extended her arms restlessly out to her sides, then let them drop. Striding slowly past him, she paused to gaze through the open doors leading into the auditorium. "I just... I don't know. This old theater means a lot to me, Dalton. I spent some of my best times here as a teenager. Thanks to the wide range of movies Eddie showed, I learned about the world here, learned about human nature." She turned around again and made her way back across the lobby to where he still stood watching her. "It would make me feel good to be a part of bringing the Palace back to life again."

Dalton inhaled deeply, lifting a hand to rub it over his beard. The fuzzy growth on his face still felt strange to him, and his fingers lingered in their task. He couldn't help but notice that Virginia seemed fascinated by his gesture, watching the back and forth motion of his fingers as if mesmerized. Immediately he dropped his hand back to his side, pushing aside images that had become emblazoned at the forefront of his mind—images centering on what Virginia's hands would feel like caressing the silky strands herself.

"All right," he told her. "The job is yours. But it only pays minimum wage. I wasn't expecting anyone of your caliber to apply for the position. I figured I'd be lucky to land a student from the local college."

"Have you had other applicants?" she asked.

Dalton shook his head. "You're the first."

She grinned at him. "Don't worry. You won't be sorry."

That remains to be seen, he thought.

"So when do I start?"

He threw his arms out at a halfhearted angle. "Who knows? I probably should have the ceiling replaced in here first. Then I need to roll another coat of paint on the lobby before you can get started."

"I like the color you chose," Virginia said of the subtle mauve hue. "What color were you thinking of using for the detail work?"

He shrugged again. "You tell me."

Virginia tilted her head to one side as she considered the possibilities. "How about dark blue, outlined with black, then outlined again with silver?"

"Sounds nice."

"Or black outlined with dark blue and silver?" she added as an afterthought. "Or a soft turquoise, or teal even. Or gold outlining. Or maybe... what are you chuckling at?"

His chuckles became full-fledged laughter then, a sound that sent ripples of delight down her spine. She hadn't heard him laugh until this moment. And although she had considered him handsome before, confronted now by his cheerfulness, she was forced to realize just how breathtaking Dalton Cameron could be.

"Well, maybe I'll just try a few variations for you," she offered, hoping her voice reflected none of the heated turmoil she felt bubbling up inside her, "and you can decide which one you like best."

"Fine," he said as he brought his laughter under control.

An awkward moment of silence followed. Dalton looked at Virginia, Virginia looked at Dalton, and neither seemed to know quite what to say. Finally she stuffed her hands nervously into the pockets of her coat as if intent on leaving, then quickly withdrew them as if intent on staying.

"Would you, um, would you mind if I had a look at those photographs you found upstairs?" she asked. "They might give me some ideas."

"Sure," he replied quickly. "They're still up in the projection room. Come on up."

As she followed his progress up the stairs, Virginia was overcome with a bittersweet feeling of déjà vu. Had twelve years really passed since she had last been inside this theater? That was nearly a third of her life. She was appalled by the passage of so much time. So many things had transpired in that period. So many things had gone sour. Working at the Palace had probably been the only truly sweet period of her life. Her father had still been alive, she and Natalie had still been kids in college ... and Dean had still been just her boyfriend. He'd still been a dream. There had been no responsibilities, no worries or expectations beyond what the next day would bring. Had she really ever been so innocent? Virginia wondered. Had there really been a time in her life when nothing had been wrong?

"You're awfully quiet back there," Dalton said, bringing her out of her reverie.

"I was just remembering," she told him. "Remembering what it was like to work here."

"Is the place still the way you remember it?"

She nodded, considering her surroundings. "Pretty much. Back here behind the scenes, anyway. The lobby has changed since you painted it, of course. It's much brighter, more inviting now."

"Oh, watch that last step," Dalton cautioned as he topped the stairs. "It's a little—"

"A little loose," Virginia finished for him with a smile. "It was a little loose when I started working here sixteen years ago, too. And still a little loose when I left. Eddie wasn't one for keeping on top of repairs."

Dalton uttered an irreverent sound. "Tell me about it."

Despite the fact that she was reminded of the impairment, when she stepped up onto the metal stair, it tilted forward, and she lost her footing. She pitched toward Dalton, who caught her ably and steadied her. Yet even after she had comfortably regained her balance, he continued to hold her. With a slow, fluid motion, he pulled her up off the top step and onto the metal landing outside the projection room, an action he completed with infinite care. Virginia felt her body pressed intimately against his, her breasts pushing heavily against his abdomen, her thighs rubbing along the length of his. She had spread her hands open wide over his chest at some point during her rescue and could feel the irregular thumping of his heartbeat beneath her fingertips. When she stood before him on the landing, Dalton continued to grip her upper arms fiercely, his eyes boring into hers as if he were making the most supreme effort to keep himself under control.

"Thanks," she said in a shallow voice, releasing a ragged breath she hadn't been aware of holding. "I'm sorry. I can't believe I did that."

She was so close to him. Too close. Her nostrils were filled by the alluring aroma of something spicy and elusive and utterly masculine. Below his clothing, she could detect the solid strength of corded muscles and heated skin, and all she could do was speculate about how silky and smooth his naked flesh would be to her touch. She wished she were the kind of woman who could throw caution to the wind and act on impulse. Because right now all Virginia wanted to do was rise on tiptoe and kiss Dalton Cameron within an inch of his life. Fortunately for her, she wasn't an impulsive woman. Fortunately for her, she was terrified of that kind of behavior.

Another long moment passed in which neither she nor Dalton made a move to disengage themselves, so Virginia forced herself to take a step backward, and then another, and another. As she withdrew, his hands lingered on her arms so that she felt a searing heat from his touch that stretched from her shoulders to her fingertips. Only when a good three feet of space separated them on the landing did she trust herself to speak again. After a quick sigh, she shifted restlessly, nervous laughter threatening to bubble up at any moment. Groping for subject matter that might get their conversation started again, Virginia spoke the first thing that came to mind.

"I remember once," she said suddenly, "I came up here to bring Mickey a soda, and he made a pass at me—tried to kiss me, right here on this very spot. Boy, was Dean furious when he found out."

Dalton gazed at Virginia as if he couldn't quite remember her name. "Mickey?" he finally asked. "Dean? Who were they?"

"Mickey ran the projector," she explained, grateful to have some image to focus upon that would push memories of Dalton Cameron's glorious physique to the back of her brain. "He was about five years older than me, but he was always coming on to me or Natalie. It was all just in fun, but Dean didn't realize that."

"Dean?" Dalton repeated.

Oops, Virginia thought, her nervous mental meanderings ricocheting out of control inside her brain. Had she actually mentioned Dean? Twice? Talking about Mickey Mazzoni was one thing. He was a harmless, distant ghost from her past, and suitable enough subject matter for Dalton. But her ex-husband was the last person she wanted to bring up in conversation nowadays.

"Uh, yeah," she stalled. "Dean was my boyfriend at the time. He didn't like Mickey at all. The two of them got into a terrible fight over me after that."

Dalton nodded. "Teenage boys usually have too many hormones inspiring them. Fighting over a girl is one way to let off steam."

Of course, he remembered another, infinitely more enjoyable way to work off steam where a girl was concerned, but he didn't think this was a good time to be discussing sex with Virginia. Not while tangling naked with her was first and foremost in his mind. He still hadn't quite gotten over the warm, mushy feelings that had turned his stomach upside down while holding her in his arms. He still hadn't come to terms with the fact that he'd been *this close* to kissing her. Sex was something he hadn't allowed himself to think much about for a long time. Not until he'd met Virginia. Now suddenly he couldn't seem to think about anything else.

And from the look on her face, she appeared to be suffering from the same ideas as he, Dalton thought.

"The pictures are in here," he said suddenly, wishing the two of them were anywhere but alone in a dark movie theater where anything could happen.

Virginia followed him into the projection room, trying not to notice the way the muscles in his back rippled and danced beneath the tight sweatshirt as he moved smoothly across the room. Nor did she focus on the solid length of bare forearm exposed below the bunched-up sleeves. Nor the poetic grace of his hips and thighs as he walked . . .

For heaven's sake, Ginnie, stop it! she commanded herself. She would have sworn on her life that there was no such thing as sexual frustration. That any suggestion that people reacted anxiously as a result of too little copulation was nothing but some overblown propaganda instigated by Freudian eggheads on the payroll of the perfume and flower industry. However, now she was beginning to wonder. Maybe five years of avoiding physical contact with the opposite sex had in fact turned her into some kind of loony.

Because all Virginia could think about suddenly was getting to know Dalton Cameron intimately. And that was the last thing she could allow herself to do.

He opened a metal cabinet and retrieved an oblong box from the top shelf. He had to stretch as he did so, an action that caused his sweatshirt to shift, revealing a tantalizing band of flesh around his waist, she noted before she could stop herself. After placing the box on a desk strewn with power tools, unidentifiable pieces of hardware and bits of broken celluloid, Dalton gestured that she should help herself to a look, then took a giant step backward. Evidently he wanted to keep as big a space between them as she did, Virginia thought. Yet for some reason, this obvious evidence of his reluctance to be near her heartened her not at all.

"They should be right on top," he told her as she stepped forward and began to pick carefully through the contents in the box.

The photos were where he told her they would be, but Virginia stole a moment to dig deeper. Apparently Eddie had kept quite a collection of Palace memorabilia, because she found more recent photographs in addition to the old ones, as well as newspaper clippings, advertisements and copies of the schedules Eddie used to send out in the mail. She shook her head in wonder at the memories this box must contain, then picked up a handful of pictures from the top.

"Yes, this is almost exactly what I had in mind," she said, running her finger along the photo on top. "Originally there was a fan pattern painted around the doorways." She sifted through the other pictures until she came across one of the concession stand. "Oh, this is great," she mumbled to herself. "I love this. What do you think?"

She held out the photo for Dalton's inspection, and he took it from her warily, as if expecting it to burst into flame at any moment. Behind the concession stand was a painting not of palm trees, as Virginia had suggested, but an art deco rendition of the Palace Theater itself, complete with full moon and spotlights that threw two long, thin triangular beams into the sky.

"I like it," he told her. "I like it a lot. Can you do this?"

She nodded enthusiastically. "Sure. It would be fun."

"But I like the idea of the palm trees, too. Can you think of someplace else they might work?"

She thought for a moment, then answered triumphantly, "How about the alcove near the rest rooms? You could put a couple of real potted palms on either side of the entry to add a little flavor."

Dalton nodded, smiling, all concerns about his questionable intentions toward Virginia Gennaro placed temporarily on hold. "Yeah," he said thoughtfully. "That'll work. That sounds great."

Feeling oddly pleased that she had been instrumental in adding a personal touch to the Palace Theater, Virginia smiled back. "So when do you want me to start?"

He inhaled deeply and released his breath slowly, once again reminding himself that he should discourage any further contact with her, but once again helpless to make himself say the words that would put an end to their time together. "How about if I give you a call in a few weeks to let you know for sure?" he said instead.

Virginia's smile broadened. "Sounds good. I'll see you in a few weeks."

Actually she saw him again much sooner. The following Sunday evening found Virginia and her mother, Lana Gennaro, seated along with Natalie in the center of the balcony at the Miles Cranston Playhouse, waiting for the curtain to go up on the Comfort Repertory Theater's production of "Fiddler on the Roof." Virginia could think of a million other things she should be doing instead—grading five classes' worth of art projects, finishing the last three chapters of a book she'd been reading for what seemed like months now, bathing her two cats, organizing her closet... It wasn't that she didn't like repertory theater—she and her mother had been subscribing with Natalie and her mother for years, after all. But the productions always seemed to arrive on days when she had other things on her mind. Important, demanding things. Things like Dalton Cameron, for instance.

Terrific, Virginia thought. There she went again, thinking about something she couldn't have, something she shouldn't be wanting to begin with. Try as she might, she hadn't been able to prevent herself from dwelling on the way Dalton's hard, solid body had felt pressed so intimately against her own. Her mishap on the stairs at the theater last week was a scene she'd been helplessly replaying over and over again in her mind, and always with a disturbingly different outcome than the one she had actually experienced. Sometimes the mishap ended with Dalton kissing her, while other times it ended with Virginia kissing Dalton. Once or twice she'd even allowed the fantasy to progress a bit further—ending with their two bodies entwined in naked, robust passion—but now she tried to keep thoughts like those at bay. They were simply too troubling to consider.

"Oh, Jerry Cochran is playing Tevye tonight," her mother said from her position between the two younger women. Lana turned to Natalie, who was seated on her right. "Your mother's going to be so mad she missed this. She had the biggest crush on Jerry back in junior high school. Of course, he wouldn't give her the time of day."

Natalie nodded. "I know. She told me she wants to hear all about it if he messes up his lines or accidentally trips and hurls himself into the orchestra pit. She thinks it would be great if he flubs up. She said it would help her recover much more quickly."

Lana chuckled. "How's she feeling?"

"Better. She still has a temperature, but it's not as high. She's well enough to get out of bed at least. I just wish I could have found someone to use her ticket," Natalie added, gazing wistfully at the empty seat to her own right. "Too bad your brother was busy, Ginnie. What was it Evan had to do again?"

"I think he said he had to figure his taxes," Virginia said with a smile as she perused her program.

"Right," Natalie muttered dryly. "God knows that April fifteen deadline is just over two months away. Wouldn't want to wait until the last minute, would he?"

"The way Evan is with math," Virginia remarked, "it will probably take him two months to decipher his W-2s."

"You should have asked that nice Dr. Cameron," Lana told Natalie. "You know, Comfort's most prominent newcomer and most eligible bachelor?"

"Oh, no, I couldn't ask him, Mrs. G. He's Ginnie's." Natalie bent forward to grin devilishly at Virginia. "Isn't he, Ginnie?"

Lana turned to gaze at her daughter, her eyebrows arched in speculation. "Have you been holding out on me, sweetie?" she asked, feigning a lack of concern Virginia was sure she didn't feel. "Are you and Dr. Cameron... you know... seeing each other?"

Virginia shook her head resolutely. "No, Mom, I'm not holding out on you. Anything Natalie thinks is going on between me and Dalton—"

"Oh, so it's *Dalton*, is it?" her mother asked with a smile.

"They had dinner together a few weeks ago," Natalie added quickly. "At the Iris."

Lana's expression was full of mock censure when she turned back to look at her daughter. "You *have* been holding out on me."

"Mom, Dalton Cameron is just a nice man to whom Natalie introduced me when we ran into him at Rosie's last month. Since then, I've bumped into him a couple more times, including once at the Iris, but that's all there was to it. He got there just before I ordered, and since it seemed silly for both of us to sit at separate tables, we ate dinner together."

"And then what?" Lana asked.

"What do you mean?"

Her mother rolled her eyes hopelessly toward the ceiling. "What happened after the two of you finished dinner?"

"Nothing," Virginia insisted. "He walked me home—"

"He walked her home," Lana repeated in an aside to Natalie. "Did you hear that, Natalie? He walked her home."

"Ginnie's going to help him paint the theater, too," Natalie threw in for good measure.

Lana's expression was reproachful when she turned back to look at her daughter, but she remained silent.

Virginia bent forward in her seat to glare at her best friend. She should have known better than to confide in her. Natalie couldn't have kept a secret if she'd been offered a gazillion dollars to do so. When Virginia spoke again, her response was addressed to Lana. "I was going to tell you," she said quietly, feeling suddenly the way she had in high school when her mother had caught her necking with Dean on the living-room sofa. "It's just that Dalton doesn't need for me to start until a few weeks from now. I didn't see any reason to mention it until I began work."

"Uh-huh."

"He's just some guy," Virginia assured her mother.

"I hear he's a single guy," Lana replied.

"He also just walked into the theater," Natalie interjected suddenly. "Look, he's headed down the center aisle."

The other two women turned to find Natalie leaning over the balcony, waving her program at the tall, brown-haired, bearded man who was indeed threading his way down the center aisle below them, studying his ticket stub as he searched for his seat.

"Yoo-hoo!" Natalie called out before Virginia could stop her. "Dr. Cameron! Dalton! Up here! It's me, Natalie Hogan!"

Dalton pivoted around and looked up into the balcony, his expression somewhat perturbed as he lifted a hand in greeting to Natalie. He seemed to be about to glance down at his ticket stub again, intent on finding his seat, until his gaze traveled to Natalie's left and settled on Virginia.

For a moment, Virginia couldn't breathe, because when her eyes met his, she was assailed by memories of their innocent yet heated encounter of a few days before. Unfortunately those memories brought with them reminders of the explicit fantasies in which she had so frequently indulged as a result, which of course caused her face to flame in embarrassment. For some reason, she felt as if Dalton were looking right through her skin, enjoying the picture show of tangled bodies flickering to light inside her brain. But of course, that was ridiculous, she tried to remind herself. How could he possibly know what she was thinking? Unless, maybe he'd experienced a few racy mental film clips of his own lately.

She watched as he raised his hand again in greeting, this time for her. But whereas he had seemed a bit annoyed by Natalie's presence, his expression when he waved to Virginia was clearly pleased. She smiled back at him, lifting her own hand at half-mast in a weak gesture, all she was able to manage thanks to the irregular thumping of her heart. Dalton stood still for a moment, simply staring at her, and all she could do was stare back. When a woman came up behind him and tried to pass, he realized he was in the way and, with a final, wistful smile for Virginia, quickly returned to seeking his seat below them once again. Until Natalie's loudly uttered offer halted him in his search.

"Oh, Dr. Cameron, why don't you join us up here?"

"Natalie!" Virginia snapped.

"No, sweetie, don't stop her," Lana said with a smile, tucking an errant white curl behind her ear. "I'd like to meet your Dr. Dalton."

"It's just Dalton, Mom," Virginia corrected her. "And he isn't mine."

But he was coming her way, she noted as he pivoted around and proceeded back up the aisle to disappear below the balcony.

"Oh, boy," Natalie said. "This ought to be good. Here, scooch down, Mrs. G., so we can make an empty space next to Ginnie. Dalton will want to sit beside her."

"Oh, good idea, Natalie."

"Will you guys knock it off?" Virginia whispered.

But Natalie and Lana had already moved to their right, creating a gap between Virginia and her mother. She considered her option of rebelling to their gesture by staying put, but that would unfortunately leave Dalton seated beside her mother, should he in fact choose to join them. The thought of Lana leaning over to sing songs in the good doctor's ear about matchmakers and sunrises and sunsets helped make Virginia's decision immediately. She moved into the seat her mother had just vacated, hoping Dalton would simply stay long enough to say hello, then return to his own seat below. Surely he must be sitting with someone else anyway, she tried to reassure herself. Yet the thought that he might be attending tonight's production with another woman was anything but reassuring.

Just as she resettled herself, smoothing out her black dress and tugging anxiously at her lace collar, Dalton appeared at the end of their row. She opened her mouth to greet him, but was cut off by Natalie.

"Come on down," her friend encouraged him. "We have an empty seat here. Join us."

Virginia swiveled her head quickly to the right so she could throw Natalie what she hoped was a killing look. But her friend only grinned back at her like a matchmaking fool. Upon turning back to her left, Virginia found Dalton politely excusing himself to the other people seated in the row, because he was slowly but deftly making his way toward her. When he reached her, however, instead of seating himself in the empty space beside her, he simply gripped the chair with his right hand as his left settled on the seat in front of it, and he bent forward.

"Virginia," he greeted her warmly. "How have you been?"

"Hello, Dalton," she returned, feeling nervous and giddy and utterly delighted to be so close to him again. Yet she assured him, "I'm fine."

He looked wonderful. So far, she had seen him clad only in casual or work clothes. Now Dalton wore dark trousers matched with a dark olive blazer, a plum-colored dress shirt and silk necktie patterned in green, black and purple abstracts. Over one arm was draped a heavy, black wool topcoat, whose label indicated it was of expensive manufacture indeed. Having spent much of her married life surrounded by wealthy bankers and businessmen, thanks to Dean's line of work, Virginia knew quality men's clothing when she saw it. She had, after all, watched her husband don such expensive garments before heading off to the bank for seven years. Dalton's taste in fashion was definitely upscale and high-priced. For some reason, his clothes didn't fit her image of him as a man. However, they certainly enhanced his already striking looks.

"Ladies," he said further, inclining his head toward Lana and Natalie.

"Dalton, I don't think you've met my mother," Virginia said quietly. "Lana Gennaro, Dalton Cameron. Dalton, my mother."

"Mrs. Gennaro," he said with a smile, extending his hand.

Lana took it graciously, offering him a vigorous shake. "Nice to meet you, Dr. Cameron."

"Dalton, please."

Lana's smile became radiant. *Oh, no,* Virginia thought. *Not my mother, too!*

"Charmed, I'm sure," Lana told him. "And call me Lana."

"All right, Lana. And Ms. Hogan," Dalton said further, conjuring a smile for Natalie. "Nice to see you again."

"Natalie," she returned with an easy grin, shaking his hand as well. "Nice to see you again, too."

"Well," Virginia said hastily, "now that we've all made clear how nice it is to see each other again, I'm sure Dalton will have to return to his seat. You must be meeting someone, after all.''

He straightened. ''Actually I came alone.''

''Oh, really?'' Lana and Natalie chorused. Virginia hoped he didn't notice the way she jabbed her elbow delicately into her mother's side.

''The Chamber of Commerce sent me a welcome packet when I first moved here, and two tickets to tonight's production came with it. But I didn't know of anyone who would be interested, so I came alone.''

Dalton noted immediately the way Virginia's expression changed when he uttered his hastily crafted lie. She went from vibrant and excited to completely crushed. He knew what she was thinking. She was thinking he knew her, could have asked her. Which of course is what he had wanted to do upon realizing he had the two tickets. He'd even gotten as far as looking up her phone number in the Comfort directory, stroking his index finger back and forth over her name at the top of the white page until his hand had come away smudged with black ink. But he hadn't quite worked up the nerve to call her. Every time he'd reached for the phone, he'd talked himself out of dialing.

Why did he find her so damnably attractive? he wondered. What was it about her that drew him like a lemming to the sea? As he gazed at her now, he still found no answer to his questions. He saw only Virginia, a woman who had his heart tied up in knots. And perhaps for that reason alone, he had tried to avoid seeing her. He just didn't think he could survive falling in love again.

''Then you can sit with us,'' Lana said quickly, as if she, too, had noted an awkward silence Dalton hoped he had only imagined.

''That's all right, Dalton,'' Virginia rushed to his rescue. ''Your seat downstairs is probably better than ours up here. We always count on the cheap seats. Of course we'll understand if you sit on the main level.''

He should have jumped on her opening, should have hied himself forth to escape from the bevy of beautiful women who were eyeing him like a fish to fry. He didn't mind sitting alone, he told himself. In fact, he preferred sitting alone. Hell, he'd been alone for two years now. He didn't know any other way to be.

But instead of fleeing, Dalton settled himself comfortably in the seat next to Virginia. He didn't know why he reacted the way he did, but for some reason, the gesture just felt natural. And when the lights gradually began to grow dim, heralding the start of the play, he was inexplicably relieved. It saved him from having to ponder his actions further, gave him an excuse not to blather on to her like a love-struck idiot.

Unfortunately it also placed the two of them in darkness. And he realized suddenly that in darkness, anything could happen.

But surprisingly, nothing did. Nothing, that is, until Virginia crossed her legs, a motion that caused her foot to brush softly against his shin. She mumbled a quiet apology, but he scarcely heard it. Because when he'd felt the soft touch of her foot, he'd naturally glanced over, only to observe that her long dress had a button front. A button front that was undone enough at the bottom to allow her what he supposed would be a comfortable walking range. This was a good thing for her, he was sure, but a rather discomforting fact for Dalton. Because by unbuttoning her dress enough to allow her walking comfort, she had also provided him with an exquisite view of slender calf, knee and thigh, encased in creamy white silk and beckoning to him in a way no woman ever could vocally. Suddenly all Dalton wanted to do was run a long finger slowly up her leg from toe to wherever she would allow him. And as a result, he saw and heard very little of the first half of the play.

When the lights in the auditorium came on to announce intermission, he was surprised, but not enough to stop staring at Virginia's leg. Only when he felt her eyes upon him and saw her yank the skirt of her dress primly over her exposed flesh was he able to force himself to look away.

Yet, that, too, disconcerted him, because he found himself gazing into the stormy eyes of Virginia Gennaro.

"Seen enough?" she snapped.

For some reason, though, Dalton got the impression she wasn't mad at him for ogling her, but mad because she had rather liked it.

"Not really," he murmured back before he could stop himself.

Her eyes blazed like two blue flames, their heat evident in her flushed cheeks as well. He could only smile, glorying in the knowledge that he could set her atilt. It was only fair, he thought. Why should he be the only one who didn't know which way was up?

"Would you like to go down to the lobby for a glass of wine during intermission?" he asked, forcing himself to include the other two women in his invitation, despite the fact that he wanted nothing more than to be alone with Virginia. "I'm buying."

"Oh, well, since you put it that way," Lana replied enthusiastically, "I'll have Chardonnay."

Dalton smiled. He liked Virginia's mother. "Come on then," he told them.

The group filed out to the lobby, Virginia hanging ominously in the back, he noted. Only when Lana and Natalie became caught up in conversation with someone they recognized did Dalton turn to Virginia again.

"I'm sorry if I offended you," he said, knowing she would realize he was referring to his leering of some moments ago. When her blush confirmed it, he grinned mischievously. "But you've got great legs, Ginnie, how could I resist?"

Hearing him compliment her so intimately and address her by the nickname only those closest to her ever used made Virginia grow warm inside. "That's okay," she told him, her voice sounding shallow and uneasy. "I didn't mean to...I mean, I wasn't trying to..."

"I know," he was quick to reassure her. "But you can't fault a man for taking advantage where he finds it."

No, she supposed she couldn't. However, she could discourage right now any notion he might have about getting to know her better. She couldn't afford to offer him even the slightest indication that she was interested in him. Even though interested was precisely what she was. Still, her fascination with Dalton was pointless and would lead nowhere. She simply could not, would not, ever get involved with another man. She'd barely survived her first marriage, both figuratively and literally. How on earth was she supposed to be expected to trust someone again?

"Dalton, look," she said quietly, thankful that her mother and Natalie had disappeared. "I'm flattered, really I am, but I'm not interested in getting involved with anyone right now." When he started to speak, she held up her hand to stop him. "You seem like a very nice man, and I know guys hate it when women just want to be friends, but really...couldn't we just leave it at friendship? We're going to be working together, after all, and from what I understand, you're not planning on staying in Comfort anyway, so wouldn't it be easier if we just—" she shrugged, suddenly at a loss for words "—stayed friends?" she finished lamely.

Dalton nodded. "Yes, it would."

Virginia couldn't understand why his quick agreement made her feel so annoyed. "It would?" She wanted to slap a hand over her mouth for uttering what sounded like such a petulant whine.

"Yes," he repeated. "I'm no more interested in getting involved right now than you are. And you're right. I'll probably be leaving Comfort in July. I'm sorry if I led you to think otherwise, I—"

"No, you didn't," Virginia quickly interrupted. "You didn't mislead me at all. Honest."

Then why do I feel so betrayed? she wondered. *Why do I feel so cheated?*

Dalton smiled at her, cupping his hand over her shoulder in what she was sure he meant to be a comforting gesture. It was a light, warm, tender touch, something she hadn't felt from a man in a very long time. Unfortunately Virginia found that the feel of his hand on her shoulder was in no way comforting.

The lights flickered once, twice, three times overhead, signaling an end to the intermission. As she sipped hastily at what was left of her wine, she glanced around in an effort to catch sight of her mother and Natalie. Yet she couldn't find them anywhere.

"I wonder where they went," she said to no one in particular.

"They're probably already back inside."

She nodded. That made sense.

"Are you finished with your wine?" he asked her.

"Yes, thank you."

When his fingers closed around her empty glass, they also enclosed her own fingers, and seemed to linger a bit longer than was necessary. Virginia let herself enjoy the momentary touch, savoring the warmth and strength, the grace of his big hands. All she could do was recall again how long she had denied herself such an innocent masculine caress. And with that she was gripped by a loneliness unlike any she had ever known. Because only then did Virginia realize she might never experience such an intimate contact again.

Chapter Four

"I still can't believe Mom and Natalie dumped us. What an incredibly obvious ploy. How embarrassing."

Dalton laughed and lifted his glass of wine to his lips for an idle sip. He and Virginia had returned to their seats at the playhouse only to find the two chairs immediately to her right ominously vacant. Even when the theater lights dimmed in deference to act two, Lana and Natalie were nowhere to be found. And when the play had ended, the couple discovered that not only had Virginia's companions fled the scene, but they'd also beat their retreat in Lana's car, leaving Virginia stranded. Dalton, ever the gentleman, had naturally offered her a ride home, but only if she agreed to escort him to the Purple Iris Café for a nightcap on the way.

She couldn't figure out why he'd bothered. Her mother and Natalie couldn't have been more blatant in their attempt to contrive a situation that would force Virginia and Dalton to be alone together. She only hoped he was taking the matchmaking scheme with a smaller grain of salt than she was herself. Honestly sometimes her mother could be impossible.

"I'm sure there's a perfectly logical explanation for their disappearance," he said magnanimously. "Didn't you say Natalie's mother isn't feeling well? Maybe Natalie was worried and wanted to go home to check on her."

Virginia uttered a quiet sound of disbelief. "Mrs. Hogan is the heartiest, most robust woman I've ever met. It would take a lot more than the flu to keep her down. And Natalie knows it."

"Well, then maybe Natalie or your own mother is coming down with something and wanted to get home."

Her sound of disbelief this time was much more emphatic. "Oh, they're coming down with something, all right. Both of them suffer from a chronic condition called 'bachelor frenzy,' a malady they've experienced in fits and starts ever since I came back to Comfort."

"Bachelor frenzy?" he repeated warily.

She nodded. "In Natalie's case it's harmless enough, I guess. She's more preoccupied with snagging my brother for herself than in getting me hitched."

He laughed. "And your brother isn't interested, I take it?"

"I think Natalie will just always be twelve years old to Evan."

"I can see where that might inhibit a healthy romantic relationship."

Virginia nodded again. "But my mother is far worse than Natalie where trying to fix me up is concerned. Every time a single man moves to Comfort, my mother is at his front door with a casserole, an invitation to dinner and a sacrificial daughter to offer him."

"She hasn't been at *my* front door."

Her heart skipped a beat at his softly uttered remark. "You sound almost disappointed."

"Maybe I am a little."

When her eyes met his over the rim of her glass, he was smiling at her, a smile that could have meant anything. "Why would you be disappointed?" she asked softly.

His smile broadened as he revealed, "There's nothing I enjoy more than a good casserole."

Virginia grinned back. "And you're missing a treat, too," she assured him. "My mother's casseroles are wonderful."

Dalton almost confessed that her mother's daughter was pretty wonderful, too, but he checked himself. Flirting could be fun, but it was best not to let it go too far in this instance. For some reason, he was sure that if left to their own devices, he and Virginia could create more than a few sparks. Sparks would only generate flames, and from flames grew fires. And everyone knew that fires consumed whatever they burned.

He watched her shake her head in what he supposed was wonder at her mother's behavior before she apologized again. "I hope Mom wasn't obvious. Sometimes she can be kind of pushy. She's made more than a few people uncomfortable in her day."

Dalton laughed again. "I didn't notice her being pushy at all. And she certainly didn't throw you at me." However, he decided then, should Virginia feel like throwing herself at him anytime soon, he certainly wouldn't find such a situation uncomfortable. Before his thoughts could get tangled into subject matter he'd expressly forbidden himself to consider, he quickly continued. "The way you talk, your mother serves you up on a silver platter with an apple in your mouth."

She eyed him thoughtfully before replying, "That's probably what she has planned next."

"I'm sure she doesn't mean anything by it. A lot of mothers just naturally want to see their children happily married."

"But that's the point. She knows better than anyone that I have absolutely no desire to be married again."

The words were out of Virginia's mouth before she realized the gravity of their implication. For a moment, when Dalton didn't immediately respond, she thought he hadn't been paying enough attention to notice. Then she looked up from her glass to find him gazing at her with an expression that was far from disinterested.

"Married *again?*" he repeated.

His voice belied nothing of what he might be thinking or feeling, but she received the distinct impression that he didn't find her revelation particularly pleasing.

"I'm divorced," she told him, mentally begging him not to press the issue.

But evidently, he wasn't the kind of man to let such a disclosure go by unchallenged. "Since when?" he asked.

For some reason, Virginia thought he sounded almost . . . upset. But why would he be upset that she was divorced? she wondered. For one thing, her marital status was really none of his business. They didn't know each other especially well, despite having spent a significant amount of time together. And since each had already made a point of assuring the other that neither had plans to pursue a romantic relationship, her marriage to Dean should be of complete irrelevance to Dalton. Why should he care if she was once married? And why should she be obligated to discuss a topic that was dead and buried to her, a topic she definitely had no desire to explore ever again?

Nonetheless, she found herself replying, "For nearly five years now."

He nodded and sipped his wine again. He said nothing more, but she could sense he wanted to ask her about her experience. She sighed fitfully, scooping a lock of hair into her hand and pushing it over her shoulder.

"I'm sorry I didn't say anything sooner," she told him, wondering why on earth she should be apologizing for such a thing, "but it was a period of my life that wasn't particularly happy. I don't like to talk about it."

"Your marriage ended badly?" he asked quietly.

Virginia didn't know whether to laugh or cry in response to his question. Badly? Yes, her marriage to Dean had ended badly. Horribly. Viciously. Almost fatally.

"Yes," she simply replied softly.

"I'm sorry."

When Virginia looked up, it was to find Dalton studying her curiously, as if trying to figure out for himself exactly what had gone wrong between her and her husband. If he only knew, she thought. God, if he only knew.

"Well, it's getting late," he said suddenly, tipping back his glass to swallow what little was left of his wine. "And I really do need to be up early. I'm getting an estimate on a replacement for the ceiling in the theater lobby tomorrow morning."

Virginia was pleased to have their conversation steered back to the harmless and mutually agreeable subject matter of the Palace Theater. "I guess this renovation is going to be pretty expensive, isn't it?"

He lifted one shoulder in a careless shrug. "I pretty much expected it would be. And I have some money stashed away that I've been saving for no real reason. The Palace seems as likely a project as any. In the long run, I'm sure it will pay off."

Actually his statement about his finances wasn't entirely true. The savings to which he referred came from the settlement on his wife's life insurance policy. For some reason, for the past two years, Dalton hadn't felt it was his place to draw from the bank account where the money had lain untouched. For some reason, the money had never felt as if it belonged to him. But now somehow, using the funds to pump life into the Palace Theater, a place that might bring a little fun and happiness into the lives of others seemed appropriate. Penny would have liked it this way, he told himself. She'd been a movie nut, too.

"I'm surprised you were willing to take six months away from your medical practice to complete the work yourself," Virginia added. "Especially when most of it could have been contracted out. Your patients back in Indianapolis must miss you.''

For a long moment, Dalton said nothing in reply. He told himself she was only making idle conversation, that her comment was an innocent one made simply to keep the conversation going. Unfortunately he wasn't quite able to mask his irritation with her statement when he responded, ''If you want to ask me about my job, Virginia, then ask. Quit dropping hints like some curious, gold-digging, empty-headed debutante. Deception doesn't become you.''

She stared at him as if he'd just slapped her. And he supposed, in a way, he had. But it was too late for him to recall his thoughtlessly uttered remark, too late for him to apologize and have the matter forgotten. So he remained silent, waiting to see how she would parry.

''I...I'm sorry,'' she stammered. ''I didn't mean to insinuate, to imply anything. I was only—'' She halted abruptly and rose from her chair, reaching for her coat on the wall hook behind her as she did so. ''Never mind,'' she finally snapped. ''If you'll excuse me, Dalton, I should get home.''

''Virginia,'' he began as he, too, rose from his seat.

But she ignored him, throwing her scarf over her shoulders, shoving her arms into the sleeves of her coat. When she tried to push past him, he thrust out an arm to stop her, circling her wrist gently with strong fingers. Without acknowledging his gesture, she pulled her hand free and continued toward the door. Dalton snatched his own coat from the chair where he'd draped it, hastily donning it as he followed her out into the cold night.

''Don't you want a ride home?'' he asked as he caught up with her.

''I'll walk, thanks,'' she told him curtly.

''Virginia, that's ridiculous. The temperature must be less than twenty degrees out here.''

''I'm very warm-blooded. And if you'll recall, I only live a few blocks away.''

She quickened her footsteps, and Dalton nearly had to run alongside her to keep up.

"Then I'll walk with you," he offered.

"What, and leave your car behind?"

"I'll come back for it."

Virginia slowed her pace somewhat then, but continued at a brisk walk. Dalton matched her stride admirably, but neither furthered their conversation. Only after they'd rounded a street corner near her house did she suddenly stop and turn to face him.

"What did I say?" she demanded crossly. "What did I say? This is the second time you've turned on me for absolutely no reason, just for bringing up your medical practice. I wasn't dropping hints, Dalton, and I sure wasn't being deceptive. And as far as curious, gold-digging, empty-headed debutantes are concerned . . ."

She turned and began to walk briskly once again, feeling suddenly restless and anxious to get away from him. "Yes, I confess to being very curious about you," she added coolly, "because I find you a likable, friendly companion. So sue me. But my financial situation is just fine, thanks very much, and I'm a very well-educated woman. As for being a debutante, I, for one, can't remember a single cotillion ever being held in Comfort. There was certainly never a white dress for me."

"Virginia, I'm sorry," he said, seizing her arm to halt her speedy departure. When she turned to gaze at him again, he shook his head helplessly. "I didn't mean . . . Look, you touched a nerve, all right?" He ran a gloved hand anxiously through his hair, then shoved it back into his coat pocket. "In the same way that you don't like to talk about your marriage, I don't like to talk about my practice."

Her expression was puzzled. "Why not?"

Dalton inhaled deeply, the weary breath he exhaled appearing as a silver-tipped haze in the cold night air. Only when the fog cleared did he respond. "Did I ask you why you don't like to talk about your marriage?"

She dropped her gaze to the ground. "No."

He curled his index finger below her chin, cursing the gloves that prevented him from enjoying the softness of her skin, then tilted her head back so that she could meet his eyes once more. When he spoke again, his voice was calmer, gentler. "I'd appreciate it if you'd show me the same courtesy."

Looking into his eyes this way caused Virginia no small amount of distress. Even in the dim light of a distant street lamp, she could see that he was hurting. She wanted to reach out to him, touch him in the same tender manner he was touching her. Yet somehow, she knew he would rebuff such a gesture. Somehow, she knew closeness was the last thing he wanted to feel right now.

"I'm sorry," she said quietly. "I won't bring it up again."

Dalton nodded silently. "Thanks."

"You're welcome."

As if they had reached some unspoken agreement to do so, the two of them began walking again, this time at a much more leisurely pace, but still in virtual silence. When they arrived at her house, they saw one light burning in an upstairs window.

"Mom's room," she said. "She's probably reading, waiting up for me."

If she didn't feel so strangely melancholy, the irony of her situation might have struck her as funny. However, the hopeless anguish she'd seen reflected so deeply in Dalton's eyes only moments ago still haunted and chilled her, and all she wanted to do was curl up in her own bed and try to get warm. She inhaled deeply of the sharp, cold air surrounding her. It seemed to Virginia as if it had been winter forever. She hadn't felt warm, truly warm, for a very long time.

"Thanks for walking me home again," she told him, forcing herself to climb the front stairs.

For some reason, her expression of thanks felt so final, so conclusive, as if she were saying goodbye to him for good. The pleasant friendship the two of them had hit off so quickly a few weeks ago seemed to be dissolving before her very eyes. When had that happened? she wondered. What had they done to extinguish what had ignited as so warm a flame?

"I'll call you in a few weeks to let you know when the ceiling has been replaced," he told her. "Then you can get to work on your painting."

Virginia nodded. "My schedule is pretty flexible once school lets out. Classes end at two o'clock, but I usually hang around until four. I leave much earlier on Fridays. If it's all right with you, I'll do most of the work in the theater at night and on the weekends."

Dalton hadn't thought about the fact that Virginia would be working at night. Not that such a factor would create a problem for him, because he was usually working at the theater at night, too. He just hadn't expected to wind up there alone with a beautiful woman about whom he had taken to frequent obsessing. He and Virginia in a darkened movie theater all alone. The possibilities for such an arrangement were endless . . . and frightening.

"Nights are fine," he told her anyway. "I'm frequently at the theater until midnight myself."

She nodded again. "Okay. Just call me when you're ready for me."

Dalton wished she hadn't said that. If she wanted him to call her when he was ready for her, he'd be dialing his phone tonight. Right after he woke up from one of those dreams he'd been having lately. Dreams where Virginia played a very integral, very intimate part.

"I'll do that," he said softly, hoping his voice didn't reveal the turmoil he felt roiling around inside himself. *But don't be surprised if that call comes sooner than you think.* Lifting a hand in farewell, Dalton turned and made his way back to his car.

"Well, did you and Dalton have a nice time last night?" Lana's voice rang out crisp and clear from the Gennaro kitchen, reaching Virginia before her foot had even settled on the last step of the back stairway leading into the warm room below. She had not slept well last night. Despite her hopes to the contrary, her dreams had been very troubling indeed, filled with erotic images of Dalton Cameron, images that had only grown more vivid and explicit every time she had awaked and tried to sleep again. Now her mother's cheery question was the last thing she felt like answering this morning.

"Is there any coffee?" she asked instead, embracing the vain hope that her mother wouldn't press the issue of the previous evening's events.

"A fresh pot," Lana informed her with a smile. "I won't bother you until you get about halfway through your first cup and can speak coherently. Then I want to know all about you and the good doctor."

Virginia grumbled something unintelligible and poured herself a generous mug full of coffee, lacing it heavily with cream and sugar.

"What did you say?" Lana asked.

After slugging back a healthy portion of the strong brew, Virginia repeated, "You and Natalie should be ashamed of yourselves."

Lana's smile broadened. "I suppose we should be. But we're not."

"You embarrassed me in front of Dalton, Mom. You couldn't have been more obvious about trying to get the two of us together if you had handcuffed us." Virginia cinched the belt of her blue chenille bathrobe more tightly over her flannel pajamas and took a seat at the kitchen table across from her mother.

Lana waved a hand airily in her daughter's direction. "Sweetie, you worry too much. I'm sure Dalton took our machinations purely in the spirit in which Natalie and I intended them."

Virginia jumped on the remark with both feet. Pointing her finger at her mother, she assumed the voice of a prosecuting attorney and accused, "So you admit that you and

Natalie are deliberately trying to get me and Dalton together romantically.''

Lana gazed at her daughter blandly from over the rim of her own coffee cup. ''Well, don't act so surprised, sweetie. And don't point. It's impolite. Remember, whenever you point at someone else, you've got three more fingers pointing back at you.''

Virginia gazed at her mother through slitted eyes, but flattened her hand against the tabletop. ''What on earth is that supposed to mean?''

Lana shrugged and sipped her coffee.

''Mom, please stop trying to fix me up,'' Virginia pleaded softly. ''Dean and I have been divorced for almost five years. Don't you think I'd be involved with someone else by now if that was what I wanted?''

''I know, sweetie, but—''

''But nothing. I don't want to tie myself down with a man again. Any man.''

Lana set her cup down on the table and reached across to take Virginia's hand in her own. ''Dalton seems like a very nice man, Ginnie. He's . . . he's not like Dean at all.''

''Dean was nice, too,'' Virginia reminded her mother softly, trying to keep the inevitable edge out of her voice. ''He was the greatest guy who ever lived, remember? Dean the Dream, that's what Natalie and I used to call him. You did, too, after he and I got married.''

''Dalton *is* different from Dean,'' Lana insisted. ''I could tell right away. He's strong. He has good eyes. He's not the kind of man who would turn on you.''

''I know he won't. Because I won't let him get close enough to turn on me.''

''Virginia . . .''

''Mom, please. My marriage to Dean is the last thing I feel like talking about this morning.'' Or any morning for that matter, she added silently to herself.

Lana squeezed her daughter's hand sympathetically one final time before releasing it, but continued to study Virginia with a critical eye. "I think that may be your problem, you know."

The coffee had finally cleared the remaining cobwebs from Virginia's brain, and now she met her mother's gaze unflinchingly. "What's my problem?"

"You never have talked to me much about your marriage to Dean."

"Well, isn't it kind of obvious why I haven't?"

Lana shook her head. "Not to me it isn't."

Virginia stared at her mother incredulously.

"No, you're misunderstanding, Ginnie," Lana was quick to state. "The whole time you and Dean were married, you were living in Atlanta. I only saw the two of you twice a year, and everything always seemed fine on those occasions. I recall perfectly well that your marriage ended horribly." She dropped her gaze from Virginia's to stare into her cup. "But until I got the call from the hospital, I had no idea you and Dean were having problems of the magnitude you did. I thought everything was fine."

"I didn't want you to know how bad things had gotten," Virginia said quietly. "Or maybe I was lying to myself about how far gone our marriage was by then, I don't know anymore." Her voice grew softer as she allowed herself a brief memory of her time in Atlanta. "Although Dean and I did have our share of arguments after he lost his job, we didn't fight any more than a lot of couples, and under the circumstances, our arguments didn't seem so unusual. He'd become accustomed to living rich, and we just couldn't afford to anymore. But he was so sure he'd find another position right away. And when he didn't, when we started having trouble paying our bills, we started arguing more. But it was only after he started drinking that he became so... so difficult."

"Difficult?" Lana repeated bitterly, not even trying to disguise the contempt she felt for her former son-in-law. "Ginnie, he nearly beat you to death that night. He caused you to lose the baby you were carrying and made it impossible for you to ever have children again."

"Dean didn't know I was pregnant," she pointed out in a miserable voice, amazed to realize that she sounded almost as if she were trying to defend him. "I hadn't told him about the baby because he was so worried about our financial situation. A baby coming would have just made things worse. Maybe if I'd said something to him, maybe he wouldn't have..."

Virginia shook her head slowly, her eyes burning at the sharp pain in her heart that her mother's unnecessary reminder provoked. She didn't need Lana to repeat the things she already knew herself. She remembered perfectly well what her ex-husband had done to her. Her life would never be what she had once hoped it would because of his attack. But there was no reason now to rehash something with which she'd finally come to terms, something she'd buried firmly in the past and tried her best to forget. Dean had served thirteen months in a Georgia prison for what he'd done to her, and now he was getting on with his life in a place she didn't want to know about, a place that most importantly wasn't Comfort, Indiana. That was all Virginia cared about now—that Dean was gone from her life for good. Because despite the fact that he'd paid his debt to society, the debt he owed her could never be recouped.

Quietly, hopelessly, she insisted again, "Mother, I don't want to talk about it."

"But maybe if you did—"

"Mom, enough," she bit out. "I have done my share of talking about it. Maybe not with you as much as you'd like, but I talked to doctors and counselors and social workers after it happened. I even joined a support group for a while. I talked, Mom. God knows how much I talked. And finally, after years, I've learned to deal with it. Talking more would only reopen wounds that have finally stopped bleeding. Don't make me go over it anymore."

Lana hung her head and gazed blindly at her unfinished breakfast. "I'm sorry, Ginnie," she said quietly. "I shouldn't be so selfish. Maybe *I'm* the one who needs to talk about it. I should have noticed that *something* was wrong somewhere in your marriage. I should have interceded somehow, been able to protect you. Sometimes... sometimes I blame myself for what happened.''

Virginia rose and hurried around the table to hug Lana fiercely from behind. This was the first time she had heard her mother say such a thing. No one could have prevented what had happened. No one except for Dean. And he'd been too far gone to even consider the repercussions of his actions.

"How could you possibly blame yourself?" Virginia whispered, her voice breaking on the final syllable. She swallowed hard to steady herself before continuing. "How could you have noticed something was wrong when *I* didn't even realize how serious the situation had gotten, and what Dean was capable of doing?''

"I know, but when I remember how you looked when Evan and I got to the hospital... when I think about what that bastard did to you...''

"Shh,'' Virginia urged her mother. "Don't think about it, Mom. Just don't think about it.''

Lana propped her elbow on the kitchen table and rested her palm against her forehead. "I'm sorry,'' she repeated softly. "I shouldn't have brought it up.''

Virginia hugged her mother one final time, then seated herself in the chair beside her. "It's okay. I just don't talk about it, Mom, for the same reason I don't want you to think about it. What happened, happened. And nothing, *nothing,* can ever change that. But it's over now. It's taken me five years, but I've come to terms with what happened the best I can. Dean's gone, out of my life for good. There's no reason to dwell on something that's over and done with.'' This time it was Virginia who reached for her mother's hand. "Trust me on this one, Mom. It's best if we leave what happened with Dean well and truly in the past.''

"And you really don't have any desire to get married again?'' Lana asked. "You know, the right mate can make all the difference in the world. I don't know how I could have made it without your father.''

Virginia smiled reassuringly. "And Daddy died almost twelve years ago. But I haven't seen you going out with anyone. You seem to be getting along fine without a man."

Lana smiled back. "That's because I was lucky enough to find the right one the first time around. Once you've had the best, you don't settle for less."

Virginia laughed. "No, I guess not." She glanced at the clock over the stove. "I'm running late," she said. "Sorry to cut this conversation short, but something tells me it's come to an end anyway." As an afterthought, she added, "How come you don't focus as much energy on getting Evan to settle down as you do me? He's single, too, remember? And the right woman might turn his life around."

"I don't have to worry about Evan," Lana told her daughter. "Natalie's doing just fine wearing him down."

Virginia shook her head hopelessly. "Sometimes I wonder if Natalie and I were switched at birth. She's so much more like you than I am."

Lana waved an unconcerned hand at her daughter and sipped her coffee.

Virginia smiled, then bent to kiss her mother briefly on the cheek. "Just promise me you'll stop trying to fix me up with men, okay, Mom?"

Lana traced an ivy pattern in the tablecloth. "Even Dalton Cameron?" she asked innocently.

"Especially Dalton Cameron."

Lana looked up at that. "Why him especially?"

Virginia rose and went to pour herself another cup of coffee to drink while she was readying herself for school. "I'm not sure, really. There's something about him, though . . . Some kind of tragedy or something in his past. I can sense it somehow. He has very sad eyes."

"Maybe the two of you could help each other," Lana said.

Virginia shook her head. "Mom . . ."

Lana lifted her hands in mock surrender. "Okay. I won't say another word about it. For now."

Virginia sighed impatiently, but the clock overhead halted any protest she might utter. "I don't have time to argue. I'll see you this evening."

And with that she turned to make her exit. Her mother was wrong, she thought as she ascended the stairs to her bedroom. There was no way she and Dalton could help each other. Because Virginia had made her way past needing any help now, and she was positive he wouldn't accept any. Besides, she wouldn't be seeing him again for weeks. That gave her plenty of time to deal with the disconcerting emotions he had raised in her since his arrival in Comfort. Emotions she had no business experiencing, emotions that had only brought her trouble before.

Despite what she had told her mother only moments ago, she often thought back upon her marriage to Dean. And those recollections had precisely the effect she wanted them to have on her. Those recollections reaffirmed her conviction that she would never tie herself romantically to a man again. At one time, she had trusted Dean to love, honor and cherish her for the rest of her life, and he had betrayed her in every way. Who was to say that Dalton Cameron wasn't the same kind of man? She had met too many women during her recovery who had experienced something similar to, or even worse than, her own situation. A great number of women had suffered at the hands of men they trusted. And unfortunately, that cycle of violence showed no sign of ending anytime soon.

But her mother was right about one thing, too. Dalton was different from Dean. Virginia had detected that difference right away. But that didn't make him any easier to trust, or any easier to fall in love with. All too often, people twisted love into something different, something it was never meant to be. And all too often, someone wound up getting hurt. Virginia had experienced more than her share of the pain. And she simply could not—would not—allow herself to be wounded again.

Chapter Five

"Hello? Anybody home?"

Dalton almost didn't hear the shouted query, perched as he was atop a twelve-foot ladder behind the screen in the Palace Theater's viewing auditorium. "In here!" he called back.

After a moment's pause, he heard another question, originating this time from much closer. "In where?"

He smiled at the bewilderment he could clearly detect in Virginia's voice. Although it was already the middle of March, it didn't seem as if a month had passed since he'd seen her. Her voice sounded exactly as he remembered, exactly as it had sounded in his dreams. He was startled to discover he had missed her profoundly. "Behind the screen, Virginia," he told her in a more normal volume. "Go to your right and up the stairs—"

"Dalton, I know how to get behind the screen. I used to work here, remember?"

He hadn't forgotten. He was simply coming to realize, much to his surprise, that teasing Virginia Gennaro was a lot of fun. Dalton had noticed some time ago that she didn't take well to being told what to do, and for some reason, he just got a kick out of baiting her. She always seemed so controlled, so well-ordered and unflappable. He couldn't stop himself from wondering how she'd react if she completely lost control. He'd experienced more than a few sleepless nights since coming to Comfort thinking of ways to provoke her, most of them unabashedly sexual in nature. He should be ashamed of himself for his adolescent musings, he told himself. Still, that didn't keep him from wondering how she'd look in his bed, dewy and naked from their lovemaking, her hair strewn across the pillow opposite his like a radiant flame.

"What are you doing back there anyway?" she asked him, her voice now coming from much closer, immediately on the other side of the screen.

"Trying to save some money," he replied, stashing his lascivious thoughts into a vacant corner of his mind where he could enjoy them again later, when he was alone. "I found a few holes in the screen, but instead of replacing the whole thing, I've been patching them with a little surgical gauze and plaster—much like I'd put a cast on a fractured limb. And oddly enough, I think the patches are going to hold." He smiled a little self-consciously as he added before thinking, "Who would have thought my hospital training would come in handy mending an old theater? You know, I almost left my medical kit at home, but I guess there's a part of me that will never be able to leave pediatrics completely behind."

"Why would you leave your profession behind?"

Virginia's question was punctuated by her appearance at the top of the stairs behind the movie screen, and for a moment, Dalton was unable to respond. The double whammy of her innocently offered query and her strangely reassuring arrival left him momentarily speechless. She was dressed in white painter's overalls spattered with every color he could name, a red T-shirt, equally colorful, and a red baseball cap twisted backward on her head. Her strawberry-blond hair was woven into a thick braid that fell over her shoulder to settle comfortably against her breast. The numerous pockets of her getup held a variety of paint-brushes, bandannas, and art tools he'd be hard put to identify. And for some reason, he discovered much to his dismay, he wanted very badly to kiss her.

Instead he shook his head to push the realization away, and focused all of his attention on moving slowly and carefully down the ladder. For a moment, he wasn't sure what Virginia meant by her question. Then he realized what thought he had spoken aloud and frowned.

"I don't know," he finally replied. Then he hastened to clarify, "I mean, I don't intend to leave medicine behind. I just meant..."

Well, what had he meant? Dalton asked himself. Why had he brought up his medical background when his pro-fession was a topic he'd made clear he wanted to avoid? And why make a comment that might lead Virginia to think he was planning on quitting? Unless, perhaps, somewhere in the dark recesses of his brain, that was precisely what he had in mind?

"Just forget it," he finally said with a decisive wave of his hand. "I'm not planning on leaving medicine behind."

She stared at him thoughtfully, clearly weighing her next question heavily before asking it. "You, uh, you're a pe-diatrician?" she asked, her voice cautious, as if she were fearful of his reaction. "I know you said you don't like to talk about your work, but—" she smiled tentatively, "—you're the one who brought it up."

Naturally she would be curious about his job, he thought, especially now that he'd raised the subject after going to such great pains earlier to avoid discussing it. He also realized that for the same reason, he was responsible for any repercussions he might suffer now as a result. So he might as well come clean and not prolong the agony. To sidestep the topic again would only fuel her curiosity.

"A pediatric surgeon, actually," he revealed reluc-tantly.

"Wow," she said, clearly impressed. "That must be wonderfully rewarding."

"No more rewarding than teaching, I'm sure," he replied, trying to steer the conversation away from himself.

"Oh, don't get me wrong," she told him, taking the final few steps to bring her within a few feet of him. Her smile now was genuinely delighted. "I love working with children. And the knowledge that I'm helping to shape their view of the world is enormously satisfying. But what I do is enhance and, I hope, enrich the life of a child. What you do..." She shrugged, pausing as if to search for the right words. "What you do can be literally a matter of life and death. You're a...a preserver of life, Dalton. That has to bring you tremendous gratification."

For a long time, he didn't—couldn't—reply. He thought about the tiny bodies lying unconscious on the operating table before him, so frail, so weak, and so utterly dependent upon him for their very lives. And along with those memories came an all too familiar sensation—deep down inside him, something twisted painfully. Try as he might to ease the sharp ache, Dalton knew there was nothing, nothing in the world, that would ever soothe his anguish. Before he realized what he was doing, he slowly extended a hand toward Virginia, touching the tip of her braid, rolling the rubber band binding it back and forth between his thumb and index finger.

"Not all of them live, Ginnie," he said softly, his voice breaking on the final word. "Too often, they..." He sighed deeply before repeating almost too quietly for her to hear, "Not all of them live."

Virginia didn't know what to say. Where Dalton had been looking at her with easy humor and more than a little playful lasciviousness only moments ago, now his eyes were filled with a haunted kind of helplessness she knew she was responsible for invoking. Instead of meeting her gaze levelly, he only stared down at the hand rubbing methodically along her braid, as if the woven plait of hair were some kind of talisman capable of keeping the evil spirits at bay. And suddenly, she understood more than she wanted to know. She wasn't the only person in Comfort carrying around memories she wished would be put to rest. And she wondered if the demons scratching at the doors in Dalton's mind were anywhere near as loud or as vicious as the ones trying to tear down her own.

"I . . . I'm sorry," she said softly, though whether apologizing for bringing up his unwanted memories or expressing her sympathy that he was burdened with them, Virginia wasn't sure.

He shook his head silently, as if he'd heard her, but couldn't quite free himself of his musing just yet. He continued to stroke his fingers up and down along the length of her braid, an action that caused the back of his hand to brush softly against her breast. If the gesture had come from another man, Virginia would have indignantly accused him of trying to cop a feel and pushed him away. But she didn't think Dalton even realized the intimate suggestion so obvious in the motion of his hand. Nor did he seem to realize the effect his warm caress had on her already ragged heartbeat.

Ever so gently, she lifted her own hand to tug her hair free of his grasp, tossing the braid with forced carelessness over her shoulder. With his amulet removed, Dalton dropped his hand immediately to his side and turned his attention to her face. But only when she smiled at him did the shadows finally begin to lift from his eyes.

"Well . . ." she began again, injecting more cheerfulness into her voice than she felt. She stretched her arms out wide, throwing her head back in abandon. "Well, I'm here for you. Do with me what you will." She quickly snapped her head forward again, as if considering something new. "But please, do be gentle. It's been a while since I painted anything other than sunflowers, rainbows, doggies, kitty cats and dinosaurs."

Yet still, Dalton did not respond right away. He simply continued to stare at her, as if considering her for the very first time. Finally he smiled back, a smile that was at once happy and melancholy, terribly hopeful, yet not a little fearful. "I'll do my best, Ginnie," he said quietly. "Just try to be patient with me."

She shoved her hands deep into her pockets, not because they were cold, but because she was afraid she might reach out to touch him if she didn't do something right away to prevent such a gesture. She reminded herself that Dalton had telephoned her this week only because he had hired her to do a job for him. What the two of them had was a working relationship. Things such as touching, feeling and caring had no business here. "So, where do you want to start?" she asked him, striving for professionalism, hoping to at least keep her emotions in check.

"The guys working on the ceiling in the lobby still haven't quite finished," he told her, "so I thought maybe you could work in the balcony first. What do you think?"

"Sounds great," she told him.

She strode past him to an opening on the opposite side of the screen, then stepped through it to find herself on the stage in front of it. Before her, the auditorium loomed large and welcoming, its once black walls now painted a dark, rich burgundy. The old, beat-up chairs were gradually being replaced by new ones, and the first fifteen or twenty rows of the theater boasted seating in sapphire-blue velvet. The ceiling above was also blue, a factor that gave her a truly wonderful idea.

"You know what would look great?" she asked when he stepped through the opening to come to a halt beside her.

Dalton followed the line of her vision, scanning the newly painted ceiling. "What?"

"Stars," she told him. "Gold stars. And maybe a wispy cloud or two. With a full moon in silver."

"Are you suggesting I remove the ceiling?" he asked dubiously. "Because I just finished painting it, Virginia. Nearly a month, flat on my back on rented scaffolding, like some Michelangelo I most certainly am not. Scaffolding that, incidentally, I've already returned."

"Dalton..."

"Not to mention the fact that what you're suggesting would wreak hell on my matinee schedule. People tend to prefer their movie theaters dark, you know. Adds to the mystique. Not to mention better picture quality."

She waited with her arms crossed restlessly over her midsection and her eyes rolled heavenward for him to finish his harangue. She was glad his despair had evidently fled, and relieved that he was back to teasing again. But she wished he would choose another target for his playfulness. Having Dalton teasing her made Virginia feel warm and fuzzy inside, something she hadn't experienced for a very long time. If she had any hope of keeping the man at arm's length, she was going to have to see to it that he stopped being so cute.

"I meant I could paint all those things on the ceiling," she told him, knowing full well he already knew that. "It would give the theater a more ... I don't know ... ethereal look."

He gazed at her, his smile finally reaching into his eyes. "You artists and your vocabulary," he said with a shake of his head.

She tried to glower at him, but knew she was doing a pretty lousy job of it. How could she be effective in scolding him when he made her feel so good inside?

"Let's wait and see how much time we have," he told her, his voice becoming serious again. "Right now I want to focus on more specific plans. Now, then, the balcony..."

The two of them discussed possibilities for the balcony as they slowly made their way back out of the auditorium and into the lobby, circling the concession stand to ascend the stairs leading to the upper gallery at the back of the theater. The scent of new paint mingled with what Virginia was certain must be an imagined lingering fragrance of freshly popped popcorn. She inspected her surroundings when they reached their destination, describing for Dalton a number of decorating avenues she might explore.

He nodded politely as she spoke, seeming to entertain each of her suggestions, but when she finally paused to offer him an opportunity to add any input he might think relevant, he only replied, "Do whatever you think works best."

"You don't have anything particular in mind?"

He shook his head. "Not really. Every possibility you've described has merit. I just want this balcony to look terrific. I want it to be special."

Virginia smiled at his request. "Why special?"

Dalton ducked his head almost shyly as he confessed, "Because it's always been kind of a special place for me. I spent a lot of time in this balcony that summer my mom and I lived with Uncle Eddie. This was my last great escape."

He suddenly and deftly moved down to the front row, taking a seat in the very middle. Virginia followed him, making herself comfortable in the chair beside him.

"This was *my* seat," he told her, leaning forward to settle his forearms along the top of the balcony's edge in front of him. He placed his chin on the back of his hands and scanned the seats below. How many afternoons had he lolled away in this very chair, allowing the movie showing to take him away from his cares? Too many, Dalton decided quickly. That summer had been the worst one of his life. Well, one of the worst anyway, he amended hastily.

He and his mother had come to live with his uncle because his father had walked out on the two of them one night while they were both asleep. Zach Cameron had literally stolen away into the night, never to be heard from again. Dalton remembered that his mother had cried a lot during the first few weeks they'd spent in Comfort. Nearly every night, he had awaked in the room next to hers at Uncle Eddie's house, staring helplessly at the ceiling while her sobbing went on endlessly until dawn. He couldn't remember his father very well now. He recalled dark hair and a looming physique, but little else. Except, of course, for the way Zach had constantly assured Dalton he'd never amount to much.

Dalton had spent a lot of time that summer wondering if Zach's assertions were true. And somewhere along the way, he must have decided they were not. Because at some point that summer, he'd made a pact with himself to prove his father wrong. He'd promised himself that someday, he would become an important person. A person who mattered, who had something to offer, who made a difference in other people's lives. And now he supposed, in that at least, he had succeeded. He did have something to offer others—he was one of the most respected pediatric surgeons in the country. Maybe the people he was helping were virtual strangers, but at least he was making a difference somewhere.

Yet he hadn't been able to make a difference in the two lives that had meant the most to him. Penny and Dylan were dead. And try as he had to prevent it, Dalton hadn't been able to change anything there. Where his wife and son were concerned, he hadn't mattered at all. Even his own life in Indianapolis had come to feel empty and ineffective. He was still helping other people, still saving some lives, but his own had become pointless to the extent that he'd had to leave it behind for a little while. Virginia had told him his work must be enormously gratifying. But what was so gratifying about making a difference for others when his actions held no satisfaction for him?

She seemed to sense his restless pensiveness and ended it by asking, "So what is it that makes this balcony so special?"

Dalton turned to her and smiled, setting his troubled thoughts aside. "I had a very . . . fond . . . experience with a girl in this very seat."

She smiled back. "A fond experience with a girl in the balcony. I'm not sure I want to know the particulars."

"It wasn't what you're thinking," he assured her mildly, his gaze wandering back to the cavernous theater. "This experience was perfectly innocent. The girl was sitting down there in the fourth row, in the very center, with some friend of hers. I don't remember the friend very well, but I sure remember the girl."

His expression became dreamy as he continued. "She had a long, blond ponytail tied back with a blue ribbon, and bangs that came down almost into her eyes. I even remember what she was wearing—a tight blue T-shirt and even tighter blue jeans." Dalton turned to smile at Virginia. "Of course, she was only about twelve or thirteen, but at fourteen, I myself thought she had a body that wouldn't quit."

Virginia laughed. "Hormonal little guy, weren't you?"

He nodded shamelessly. "Yes, but if you could have seen this girl..." His voice grew wistful as he went on. "I watched that ponytail all through the movie. I don't even remember what Uncle Eddie was showing that day, because I couldn't keep my eyes off of that girl's hair. After the movie ended and the lights came up, she turned around—*immediately,* as if she'd known I'd been watching her all that time and wanted to read me the riot act— and stared right at me, right into my eyes. All I could do was stare back."

"And then what happened?"

Dalton was still gazing down into the auditorium, as if replaying the episode in his mind. "She turned to her friend and said something, then both of them looked back at me, then they started to leave. I wanted desperately to talk to her before she got away, so I jumped up from my seat and tried to make my way downstairs as fast as I could, stepping on feet, shoving people out of the way. I didn't care. All I wanted was to talk to this girl."

"And did you get to?"

Dalton nodded. "Sort of."

"Sort of?"

He nodded again. "Just as I came bursting into the lobby, I caught sight of her ponytail disappearing into the women's room. So, being the suave, debonair fourteen-year-old that I was, I staked myself outside the door. But she didn't come out. I stood there like an idiot for about fifteen minutes waiting, but she never came out. Finally her friend stuck her head out the rest room door and said, 'She wants to know what your name is.' So I told her. Then the friend ducked back into the women's room for a minute. I heard giggling, then the friend's head poked out again. 'She wants to know how old you are,' the friend asked. So I told her that, too. Then the friend went back into the rest room, and there was more giggling. This went on for a while, with the friend pushing open the door every now and then for a new question and answer sequence, until I started to get pretty tired of it and decided to get a few answers of my own.''

''So what did you do?'' Virginia asked.

Dalton rubbed his beard restlessly. ''Well, finally, the next time the friend stuck her head out the door, I grabbed her and pulled her outside, back into the lobby with me.''

''Oh, Dalton...''

He turned to look at Virginia then, smiling. ''It seemed like the right thing to do at the time. Anyway, I sat the friend down on a bench and started asking my own questions. 'What's her name? How old is she? Does she have a boyfriend?' etcetera, but the friend clammed up, and wouldn't say a word.''

''Loyal to the end, was she?''

''Evidently.''

''So then what happened?''

His smile broadened. ''When the girl realized I had no intention of freeing her friend or leaving the theater myself, she came out of the women's room. I'll never forget how gorgeous I thought she looked. All dressed in blue, with those huge blue eyes... You know, I think I still have dreams about her to this very day.''

''Do you?''

He nodded. ''I believe I do.''

A moment of silence ensued. Virginia waited with a smile for Dalton to continue, and when he didn't, asked, ''What did she say to you after that?''

Dalton's lower lip thrust forward in what Virginia would have called a pout in a lesser man. "She didn't say anything to me. She turned to her friend and said, 'Come on, whatever the friend's name was—I forget—let's get out of here. This guy's a jerk.'"

"Oh, she didn't. That must have broken your heart."

"She did, and it did. But the friend came to my rescue and said something like, 'Oh, he's not so bad. He has nice eyes.' I thought that was awfully nice of her, considering the way I'd manhandled her. But the girl wasn't impressed. She spun around on her heel, that ponytail swaying back and forth, and started to make her way out of the theater. With no regard for her friend, I jumped up and ran after her. I think I was trying to reach for her shoulder, but my hand automatically gravitated toward her hair, and I wound up with a fistful of ponytail instead. She jerked around at my touch, an action that of course just resulted in me pulling her hair. And naturally after that I didn't stand a chance."

"Naturally."

"So when the friend caught up, the two of them turned their backs on me and started to walk away. In a last-ditch effort to impress the girl, I reached for her again, but again, my hand went to her hair. This time I came away with a trophy, though."

"A trophy?"

"I yanked the blue ribbon out of her hair," Dalton concluded the story. "At the time, I thought what I did was an accident. But thinking back now, I can't help but wonder if I intentionally went for her ribbon, just so I would have a keepsake of the event."

Virginia laughed out loud. "Oh, Dalton, you're too much."

But he just turned to stare dreamily out at the auditorium again. "Yeah, I'll never forget the girl in the fourth row."

"The Fabulous Fourth Row," Virginia corrected him with a huge grin, still chuckling.

He turned his head to face her again, his expression puzzled. "What?"

"It's not just the fourth row," she clarified. "It's The Fabulous Fourth Row. Best seats in the house. Natalie and I used to sit there all the time. Even when we were kids."

Dalton's face went a little pale. "You did?"

She nodded. "In the very center."

"Really?"

She nodded again.

"That was you?"

Virginia sighed, nodding a third time. "That was me."

He looked at her doubtfully. "No, it wasn't . . . was it? You're pulling my leg. Aren't you?"

She eyed him thoughtfully. "That blue ribbon you mentioned, do you recall if it had a small, white rose pattern embroidered through it?"

He nodded, his expression growing more and more sheepish by the second. "You know, I believe it did."

Virginia leaned forward, too, settling her elbow on the balcony's edge, her chin cupped in her hand. She was enjoying her ability to make Dalton uncomfortable. She liked being the one to tease him for a change. "I remember that day so well," she told him. "I thought you were so cute. You had all that curly hair, and a wonderful smile. But I've always remembered your name as being Donald."

"Don-Donald?" he sputtered. "All these years I've been remembered as a Donald? What amounts to the greatest memory of my adolescent life means so little to you that you didn't even have my name right?"

Virginia couldn't help but laugh. Why, he sounded absolutely indignant. She nodded in response to his statement, nibbling her lip to feign deep thought. "Could be that Natalie got your name wrong to begin with, though. Did I . . . did I really call you a jerk?"

Dalton nodded vigorously. "Yes, you did."

She lifted her shoulders in an embarrassed shrug. "I'm sorry. I only said it because I was nervous."

"Don't worry about it. It was a long time ago. I got over it. Eventually." He shook his head at her in wonder. "So that was you. The woman of my adolescent dreams has come back to me."

"Evidently," she repeated his assessment of some moments earlier.

"You, uh, you were a blonde when you were a kid?"

"It didn't start turning red until I was in high school."

"I see. And you don't wear bangs anymore, huh?"

Virginia shook her head. "I let them grow out after college. But you know, that *was* my favorite hair ribbon you filched. My mother was never able to find another one like it."

Now it was Dalton's turn to smile. "Gee, I feel terrible. Is there anything I can do to make it up to you?"

She thought for a minute, until she came up with what she deemed a suitable penance. "You could buy me dinner at the Iris when we finish up here tonight. And then maybe afterward, we could go to a movie."

He waited for the mental warning sirens that always seemed to accompany an invitation from a woman. However, much to his surprise, he heard none this time. Why not? he wondered. Why didn't he feel threatened the way he usually did when a woman asked him out? Was it because Virginia had already made it clear that she was even less interested in a personal relationship than he was? Or was it because he was beginning to think a personal relationship with her might be exactly what he wanted, what he needed?

No, that wasn't it at all, Dalton assured himself. He just felt comfortable with Virginia, and knew she was comfortable with him. They were two people who had much in common—a passion for movies, a love of an old theater, a memory of a shared adolescent flirtation that each held dear. More than that, though, they were both people who were trying to cope with a painful experience from their pasts, neither willing to share the particulars of those experiences, but both hoping the other might try to understand. And maybe that was all that was really important. They were each reaching out, both seeking comfort and willing to offer it. And what could possibly be dangerous about something like that?

"All right," he finally said. "You've got a deal. But I get to pick the movie."

Virginia nodded her agreement. "Fair enough."

"And first you're going to have to earn it. We have a lot of work to do, so we may as well get started." He rose from his seat, glancing at his watch as he did so. "It's three-thirty now. Think you can wait on dinner until eight or nine? Then we could catch a late movie."

"Sounds good to me," she told him. "I haven't been to a midnight movie in years."

Dalton chuckled. "Yeah, they'll probably throw us out because we're so old."

"Speak for yourself," she sniffed indignantly. "You're as young as you feel."

He rubbed at the stiffness in his legs as he made his way up the aisle toward the balcony stairs. "In that case, better call Sunny Acres Rest Home and book me a room."

"Oh, stop complaining and get to work," she chided him. "Now, where can I find a ladder?"

"You know the theater so well, you tell me."

As it was, Virginia did in fact discover exactly where Dalton kept the painting supplies, and found her way quite capably around the old theater. His last view of her before he retired to the projection room to repair a crack in the ceiling featured a wonderfully rounded, overall-encased, paint-splattered derriere bending over a can of black enamel. After that, he decided it might be better if he just steered clear of her for the rest of the afternoon.

Unfortunately, keeping her out of his line of vision didn't necessarily mean keeping her out of his thoughts. All too often, his adolescent memories of an afternoon twenty-two years ago overlapped with his more recent recollection of the beautiful woman painting the balcony. But what surprised Dalton most of all was the discovery that, despite the passage of those twenty-two years, his feelings for Virginia didn't seem to have changed one bit. She still made him feel giddy and aroused, still caused him to want things he had no business wanting.

He shrugged, trying to remain as matter-of-fact as he could under the circumstances. At least now he understood why Virginia made him feel like an adolescent again. What bothered him most was that, despite the fact that he was now a full-grown, thirty-six-year-old man with more than two decades of experience since that day under his belt, he still couldn't control his libido anymore than he had then. Because even a fourteen-year-old kid couldn't possibly feel as lascivious as Dalton had since meeting Virginia Gennaro. He only hoped the condition was temporary, a result of simply having gone too long without any kind of intimate contact with a woman. Surely after spending more time with her, his desires would begin to ebb.

And once he went home to Indianapolis, he'd probably be feeling like his old emotionless, distant self again in no time. Then everything would be fine. He could go back to being numb, back to being cold, and work himself into an early grave. After that, maybe, just maybe, he might find some peace of mind.

Chapter Six

"I told you we were too old for a midnight movie."

Virginia gazed blandly at Dalton from across his kitchen table and expelled a restless breath of air. "Well, you were the one who chose *Friday the Thirteenth Halloween Nightmare in the Last House on the Left on Elm Street, Part Two.* What did you expect?"

She sipped her brandy languidly, shaking her head in wonder at the way their productive afternoon and peaceful evening together had degenerated into a number of uncomfortable, tension-filled lapses of silence. After spending a very enjoyable, leisurely dinner together, the couple had journeyed onward to the MovieTime Multiplex in search of an appropriate film to top off the evening. Unfortunately, being a Friday night, the multiplex had been packed, many of the seats already sold-out. And when Virginia had confessed that she loved scary movies, Dalton had suggested a dubiously titled one indeed. Reminding herself that she had agreed to let him choose the film, she had followed him into the theater as if she were a lovesick date, settling in close with her bucket of buttered popcorn and soda, only to be assailed by one corporeal dismemberment after another once the lights went down.

And as if such depictions of mangled bodies hadn't been difficult enough for her to stomach, in an effort to turn her attention away from the grotesque displays of mayhem on the screen, she had focused more fully on the crowd surrounding them, an activity she soon discovered to be a rather big mistake. A mistake because she and Dalton had been surrounded by more than a few teenagers in love. Teenagers who spent the better part of the movie locked in physical struggles unlike anything she'd ever witnessed before. Virginia could well remember necking at the movies. But the activities of some of those kids had made her awkward adolescent fumblings seem like the sloppy, harmless kisses of a toddler. She still wasn't sure what had caused her more anxiety—the R-rated violence unfolding on the movie screen, or the NC-17 behavior of the couple right in front of her.

Dalton gazed back at Virginia, lifting his own drink to his lips before commenting. "You said you liked scary movies."

"Scary, not gory," she clarified.

"Well, I thought it would be as good as *Friday the Thirteenth Halloween Nightmare in the Last House on the Left on Elm Street, Part One.* I was wrong, okay?"

Virginia had been about to sip her own brandy, but instead settled the cut-glass tumbler back down onto the table. "You thought part one was *good?*" she asked incredulously.

He stared back, stunned that she would disagree. "Well, of course. Didn't you? Technically it was near perfect. The acting was remarkable, the direction bordering on magnificent."

"Dalton, that movie stank. It was violent, misogynistic—"

"But not gory," he was quick to point out.

"No, it wasn't a spatter film, if that's what you mean. The director didn't focus on bloodletting and body-chopping. But that movie was still plenty gory in its implication."

He sipped his brandy again, eyeing her cautiously. Scarcely half an hour into the movie, Virginia had jumped up and whispered her intention to leave, wanting nothing more to do with the bloody display on the screen. And because they had both seemed far too wound up to go home and go to bed, Dalton had suggested they come to his house for a nightcap and conversation, something to soothe their nerves and chase away the monsters roused by the film. Now he was beginning to wish he'd just driven her home and dropped her off at her doorstep. That way he wouldn't be sitting here wondering what it would be like to have Virginia in his arms.

Throughout the movie, he'd been utterly distracted by the gymnastics of the couple seated in front of them, and not because their antics were so impressive. No, all Dalton had been able to do was cast himself in the young boy's role, the object of his own sexual exploration, one Virginia Gennaro. Even now he had to force himself to push such carnal curiosity away. Instead he tried to focus on the argument at hand.

"You know what your problem is, Ms. Gennaro?" he asked her suddenly.

Her voice was tight when she replied. "No, but I'm sure you're about to tell me."

He nodded. "You just don't appreciate good cinema."

Her eyes widened in disbelief. "You have got to be kidding. That's a low blow, Dalton. And completely untrue. I am more cinematically literate than you could ever hope to be."

"Oh, please..."

"I am."

"You are not."

Virginia started to disagree with him again, but at the realization of how immature they were beginning to sound, she caught herself. Why were they fighting? she wondered. What had brought on all this anger? They were sniping at each other like...like...well, like two adolescents who were overcome by a sexual attraction they could do nothing about. Adolescents in a dark movie theater for example. Hmm...

"I probably should be going home," she announced suddenly. "It's getting pretty late."

"No, don't," Dalton said just as suddenly. He quickly recovered by adding, "I mean, it's not that late. And you haven't finished your drink. Let's...let's go into the living room. I've got a fire all ready to set in the fireplace."

"Well..." Virginia hedged. "It is kind of drafty in here."

"The fire will only take a minute to get started."

"All right," she conceded, telling herself her acquiescence was only a result of the fact that she *was* a little chilly, and not because Dalton was looking at her with such utter longing.

They adjourned to his living room, a huge room with a twelve-foot ceiling. The furnishings were somewhat sparse, worn and outdated, as could be expected of a rental property, the only light in the room provided by a solitary floor lamp in a far corner. But the house itself had a lot of character. It wasn't a good deal different from the one Virginia shared with her mother only a few blocks away. Of course, Lana Gennaro had crammed that house to near overflowing with the remnants of a loving family, having moved there herself as a bride more than forty years ago. Where Virginia's own house was cluttered with photographs, books and other memorabilia, Dalton's temporary residence seemed a little lonely. Like Dalton himself, she thought.

In no time at all, the fire flickered to life beneath his skillful hands, and Virginia moved closer to be near it. Her action brought her to sit beside him on the worn Oriental carpet, the two of them leaning back against the sofa. For a long time, neither said a word, but only watched the flames in the fireplace as they leapt higher, grew brighter and became warmer.

"I'm sorry I snapped at you," he said softly, breaking the silence she had begun to think might go on forever.

Virginia smiled, nudging his shoulder playfully with hers. "That's okay. I'm sorry I snapped back."

He turned to smile back at her. "Don't worry about it."

"I don't know what's made me so short-tempered lately," she said as she shifted to stare at the flames once again. "I haven't been sleeping well. Maybe that's it."

Dalton studied the fire again, too. "I haven't been sleeping well, either."

"Maybe there's something going around."

"Maybe so."

The fire popped and snapped as they sat before it, a fat log shifting to hiss out a stream of smoke and throw a brief spate of sparks toward the screen. Virginia and Dalton sipped their brandy in thoughtful silence for some moments more before his voice invaded the quiet room again.

"I know I promised not to ask, and I know you said you don't want to talk about it, but would you mind so awfully if I asked you about your marriage?"

When she turned to face him, Virginia's expression was wary, but not altogether unresponsive. "Only if I can ask you why you'd want to know."

He nodded. "That's fair."

She took another sip of her drink while she waited for him to elaborate. When it appeared he would not, she said, "All right, then. Why would you like to know?"

He studied her for a moment before answering, as if he wasn't quite certain how to reply. "To be honest, I'm not really sure. I just...it seems important to me for some reason. Several weeks ago, when we ran into each other at the play, you and I pretty much decided we wanted to be friends. So maybe mine is a friendly curiosity. The thought that you suffered a...an unfulfilling marriage makes me wonder if the experience has had some lingering effect on you."

Virginia arched her eyebrows thoughtfully. "But of all the other things we could talk about, Dalton, my marriage is last on the list."

He shrugged restlessly, as if he again didn't know how to reply. "I don't understand my curiosity any more than you do. Maybe it results from the fact that lately... lately I've been thinking a lot about my own marriage."

Her eyes widened in surprise. "You're...?" She didn't even want to think it, let alone put voice to the question. "Are you... married?"

He was quick to shake his head. "Not anymore."

"You're divorced?"

"Widowed. For a little over two years now."

"Oh, Dalton."

Her heart twisted in confusion at his declaration. On one hand, she felt sorrowful at the knowledge that he had once loved a woman enough to join his life with hers forever, only to have her stolen from him at such an early age. But part of Virginia felt a little jealous, too. Jealous to realize there was a huge chunk of Dalton's life of which she had no knowledge, which she'd never shared. It was crazy, she knew. She had met him scarcely two months ago. But in many ways, she felt as if the two of them had known each other for years. The fact that he had experienced such a tragedy without her there to help him through it felt odd somehow. She was so certain she could have been a comfort to him then. In many ways, she had suffered a similar loss.

Although her husband hadn't been taken from Virginia at a time when she wanted to be with him for all eternity, she nonetheless mourned his loss almost as if he had died. Because the Dean she had once known and loved no longer existed. He was as dead to her as Dalton's wife was to him. Even before their marriage had erupted in its final tragedy, she had already been going about the motions to leave him. He had become a stranger to her, a bitter, abusive man completely unlike the one with whom she had fallen in love as a teenager. That stranger had taken her husband from her, and he had taken her child. For that reason, Virginia could very well understand the pain Dalton must have experienced after his own loss.

She curled her fingers softly around his solid forearm as she said, "Dalton, I'm so sorry."

He shrugged a little, but continued to stare silently at the fire.

"Why didn't you tell me sooner?"

Again, that odd, one-shouldered shrug. "It's not something I like to talk about, either."

Virginia inhaled deeply, expelling the breath slowly. She squeezed his arm gently before letting go. "Then maybe neither one of us should bring our marriages up again."

Dalton nodded. "I just... I wanted you to know, Ginnie. That I'd been married, I mean. It seemed important that you know."

She nodded. "I understand."

She understood, Dalton thought. Hell, she didn't understand the half of it. Why hadn't he told her the rest of the truth? Why hadn't he told her about his son's death as well? Maybe because he still couldn't fully face the loss of Dylan, he decided. He hadn't quite dealt with the fact that his son, his seven-year-old son, had preceded him to the grave.

He ran a big hand restlessly through his hair, his fingers curving over his head and down his neck, completing a circle to rub both bearded cheeks.

"You know, you do that a lot," Virginia said suddenly.

Her voice roused him with a start from his reflections. "Do what?" he asked when he turned to look at her.

"Rub your beard," she told him, lifting her own hand to her cheek in a mimic of his gesture.

"Do I?"

She nodded.

"I hadn't noticed. Must be because I haven't had it for very long. I guess I'm still not used to it."

"Could I—" she began, stopping herself before completing her question.

Dalton smiled at her obvious uncertainty. "Could you what?"

Virginia bit her lip anxiously, but dropped her hand back into her lap. She was appalled at what she'd been about to ask him. "Never mind."

Turning to face her more fully, he asked again, "What? What is it, Ginnie?"

She glanced up at him from beneath long, pale lashes, her blue eyes glistening as they reflected the dancing light of the fire. Then, as if she'd been caught doing something she knew she shouldn't, she lowered her gaze back to the fingers clutching her drink.

"Come on," he encouraged her. "There's something you want to ask me, so ask."

She seemed to screw up enough nerve then, because she set her glass down resolutely on the hearth and turned her body to face his more fully. "Can I..." she began again. "I mean, would you mind if..." At his silent urging, she finally finished, "May I touch your beard?"

Dalton knew it probably wasn't a good idea to encourage such an intimacy, but he was damned if he was able to put his reluctance into words. Instead he felt himself nod his head, heard himself say quietly, "Go ahead."

Virginia reached a hand tentatively forward, her fingers crooked ever so slightly as they approached. At first her touch was scarcely detectable, so softly did she run her fingers over the silky strands of hair. That initial exploration seemed to make her bolder, however, because her gentle caress gradually became more insistent. Her fingers tangled in his beard, her palm cupping his jaw with infinite care.

Dalton felt himself come undone bit by bit at her tender gesture, his heart taking up an unsteady thumping like some out of control tattoo. Helplessly, he closed his eyes with the hope that shutting out the vision of her tentative, innocent curiosity might somehow alleviate the exquisite tension roused by her softly journeying hands. But closing his eyes only enhanced her touch more keenly, and fueled the wild sensations burning through his body to burst into an incandescence unlike anything he'd ever known. And when he felt the soft pads of her fingertips rake softly across his lower lip, he felt himself slowly coming apart at the seams.

He hadn't experienced such a gentle touch from a woman for more than two years. And now, having Virginia caress him in such a way felt like the most natural, most beautiful kind of dance.

"Oh, Ginnie," he bit out raggedly, trying unsuccessfully to stifle a groan.

He circled her wrist with strong fingers and halted her exploration before she could send his libido spiraling into some bottomless abyss. But instead of pushing her hand away, he brought it forward again to linger against his lips, his warm breath dampening her fingers as he pressed a small kiss against the pad of each one. When he finally forced himself to open his eyes, it was to find her gazing back at him, languidly, almost salaciously, her own lips parted slightly, as if silently pleading with him to kiss her. Before he was able to stop himself, Dalton leaned toward her, dropping their entwined hands into his lap, pressing his mouth gently against hers.

It was a kiss that seemed to go on forever. When he felt the softness of her skin, the warmth of her mouth against his, he could no more have stopped himself from venturing further than he could stop the sun from rising. He leaned into her more closely, then more closely, and then more closely still, taking as much from Virginia as she would allow. As he came closer, she moved back, until the two of them lay side by side on the Oriental rug before the fireplace.

Virginia was too dazed to realize how precarious their positions had become. She only knew that one minute she'd been getting lost in the feel of her fingers tangling in the soft hair decorating Dalton's warm cheek, and the next he was leaning in to kiss her. Yet instead of pushing him away, as she knew she should, she had welcomed the touch of his lips against hers, had reveled in the glorious sensations roused by that single, affectionate caress. So she had kissed him back. Dalton was the first man she had kissed in five years. And all the closely guarded emotions, all the tamped-down desire, all the unfulfilled passion she had been fighting to keep reined for that length of time suddenly burst forth like wild horses bent on seeing freedom.

She had forgotten how wonderful it felt to be so close to another human being. Had forgotten how easy it was to lose herself in the arms of another, and how welcome such a release could be. So instead of telling Dalton to stop, to leave her alone, she embraced him more insistently, pulling him even closer. Because deep down inside, Virginia realized with no small amount of terror that she never wanted to let him go.

His kisses grew more feverish then, more demanding. She gave what he requested, silently pressing him to meet some of her own needs as well. Their tongues met and joined in a frenzied need for fulfillment, then parted, each striving to taste more deeply of the other's unique flavor. Then, as if trying to dominate her, he rolled until she was lying half beneath him. They clung to each other before the fire, the heat surging from their bodies rivaling that rising from the flames. The fingers that had wrapped around Virginia's wrist now pushed their hands above her head, while Dalton flattened his other palm against the sweater stretched taut across her abdomen. He rubbed his body sinuously along the length of hers, as if the pressure might somehow alleviate the tension she felt building at the juncture of his thighs. Crooking his elbow until her head rested on his forearm, he cupped her breast firmly with his free hand and kissed her more deeply, as if restating his authority.

Virginia allowed him his domination for only a moment, then rolled until she was lying atop him. She shifted until she could rise on her knees to gaze down at him, looking for all the world like a woman bent on having things her way. Her action seemed to pull them both out of their delirious states, because for a moment, all movement stopped, all struggling ceased. The two of them simply stared at each other, gasping for breath, groping for some sense of order in a situation gone completely beyond their control. She was straddling him, her hair cascading over her shoulders and around her face like a flaming russet fireball, her chest rising and falling irregularly, one hand bunching a fistful of fabric at the neck of his shirt. Dalton gripped her waist fiercely with both hands, as if he'd intended for her to sit astride him this way forever.

He was the first one to move. Slowly, gradually, he released Virginia, straightening her sweater where he'd begun to bunch it up in an effort to touch her more intimately. She, too, turned loose of Dalton, removing one hand from his shirt and the other from his belt buckle, where she couldn't remember having placed it to begin with. Yet still, they could only stare at each other in silence. Still, they could only wonder how on earth things had progressed the way they did.

When a cedar log in the fireplace snapped loudly, both of them started, and only then were they able to abandon their fantasies of what could have been to focus on the awkwardness of their reality.

"Oh, God, I can't believe that happened," Virginia said quickly, her voice low and raspy, and quieter than she'd intended for it to be. She scrambled off of Dalton and threw herself into the far corner of the sofa. The light of the fire barely reached her there, which was just fine with her. At the moment, in the darkness was exactly where she wanted to be. "I'm so sorry, Dalton. I don't know what got into me. I just...I...I—"

"Virginia," he interrupted her, lifting a hand to stop the flow of words he knew to be forthcoming—words she might regret later, words he probably didn't want to hear. His own voice was steadier than hers, but nonetheless every bit as bewildered. "Don't apologize. I should be the one to do that. I was the one who kissed you."

She shook her head. "Oh, no you weren't. I kissed you."

He, too, rose slowly from the floor, seating himself on the sofa as well, as far away from Virginia as he possibly could. She duly noted his gesture and tried to ignore the piercing ache that throbbed fretfully in her heart at the clear indication that he wanted so little to do with her.

"All right then, we kissed each other," he finally stated decisively.

She ran a shaky hand through her hair and drew her knees up before her. "Boy, I'll say we did."

He inhaled a deep breath before continuing, releasing it with as much patience as he could manage. "Now then," he began quietly. "We have two choices here. We can either talk about this, or we can just go along as we were before and forget it ever happened."

She eyed him frankly. "I don't know about you, Dalton, but I don't think I could ever forget what just happened here."

"Fine. Then we'll talk about it."

As if his words were a cue to do otherwise, neither said anything further. Silence loomed between them for several long moments, until Dalton stood to stir the slowly dying fire to new life. His deed accomplished, he returned to his seat on the sofa, where he continued to say nothing. Virginia watched the flames and kept her knees clamped together, occasionally brushing nonexistent lint from the front of her sweater. Finally, when he could no longer tolerate the tension burning the air between them, he surged to his feet again and began to pace.

"There's a perfectly logical explanation for why this happened," he said, invoking a tone of voice he used when presenting an occasional lecture on pediatrics to medical students.

Virginia nodded agreeably. "No doubt there is. So, what is it?"

He paused in his pacing to look at her, then immediately began the restless back and forth motion again. "Both of us were married for several years, and we've both been alone now, without . . . you know . . ."

"Sex?" she supplied helpfully.

He nodded. "Sex," he repeated a little gruffly. He cleared his throat nervously before continuing. "We've both been without ... sex ... for a long time. It's only natural that we'd be drawn to each other on a ... a physical level, and that things between us might get a little bit out of control. Especially after ... after ..."

"After what?" she asked softly.

Dalton abandoned his pacing to fall into his seat once again, tilting his head to rest on the back of the sofa so he could stare into the darkness between himself and the ceiling. "God, after watching those two kids sitting in front of us at the movie try to consume each other all night. What a couple of acrobats."

Virginia chuckled nervously, outrageously happy that the two of them were able to find humor in something, even in the endeavors of the overly amorous couple at the multiplex. "They were something, weren't they?"

At the quick agreement, his laughter joined her chuckles. When he turned his head to look at her, she was smiling at him, then she, too, burst out laughing. For long moments they simply let themselves go, enjoying a socially acceptable release for the tension still building inside them. He held his sides as ripple after ripple of amusement bubbled inside him, and he laughed even more as he watched Virginia wipe away a few tears herself. Eventually they were able to get themselves under control again, and Dalton shook his head as he palmed the last of the moisture from his own eyes.

"Oh, boy," he gasped. "I needed that."

As Virginia's chuckles slowly subsided, she nodded and said breathlessly, "Me, too."

He moved closer, sliding an arm across the back of the sofa behind her. Suddenly she didn't feel like laughing anymore. The look in his eyes spoke of a profound desire he'd held in check for too long, mixed with a keen sadness he kept quelled deep within himself. And she knew what she saw only reflected what he must see in her own eyes. All the humor and high spirits left them then, to be replaced by a looming solemnity that seemed to rise from nowhere and stretch to forever. She could tell that Dalton had something on his mind, and frankly, she wasn't at all certain she wanted to know what it was.

"I guess it would be pointless to deny that I'm attracted to you, Ginnie," he said softly, lifting his curled fingers to gently stroke her cheek.

Tiny bursts of heat exploded beneath her skin with every soft caress of his fingertips. She knew her voice sounded weak when she spoke, because that was exactly how she felt. "Likewise, I'm sure you'd never believe me if I told you now that I want nothing to do with you."

"But I'm still not interested in becoming romantically involved," he told her. "Losing Penny cost me a lot. I may never be ready for another entanglement that serious again."

Virginia reached out her own hand with the intention of touching his face, then recalled what had happened the last time she did that, and dropped her hand back into her lap. "And I have no intention of tying myself to another man," she assured him softly. "Ever."

The hand on the back of the sofa tangled gently in her hair, and Dalton gazed into her eyes intently. "But, you know..." He paused, weighing his thoughts carefully. "Maybe we could, if you were interested, I mean, we could..." He shrugged, trying to affect an air of nonchalance. "We could maybe set up some kind of an arrangement that might be mutually beneficial."

Virginia was fairly certain she wasn't going to like what she suspected was coming next. "An arrangement," she repeated doubtfully.

He nodded, still caressing her cheek with the backs of his fingers. "Something that might help us...alleviate some of the tension we always seem to feel when we're around each other. But with no strings attached."

She bit her lip in an effort to keep her anger in check, but was helpless to stop the shiver that meandered through her body with every soft stroke of his fingers. Now she knew how he must have felt when she had touched his beard. No wonder he had kissed her. All she wanted to do at the moment was lose herself in his embrace forever. Surely she must have misunderstood his proposition, she tried to convince herself. He was too nice, too decent. He couldn't possibly be suggesting what she thought he was suggesting. Could he?

Cautiously she asked, "Just what are you proposing?"

Dalton cupped the back of her head with his hand, bunching her hair in his fist. "Well, we both obviously turn each other on," he began slowly.

"Turn each other on," she repeated, her teeth setting on edge as she spoke.

He nodded. "We're both consenting adults. We've both been married, so we obviously know our way around the playground."

"The playground," she mimicked, infecting the word with a tone of disdain.

He nodded again, clearly oblivious to her anger. "There's no reason why we couldn't . . . you know . . ."

Virginia inhaled sharply, rising quickly from the sofa. Because Dalton was unprepared for her movement, and because he was still holding her hair, she felt a brief, painful tug as she leapt up.

"Still behaving like a fourteen-year-old, Dalton?" she snapped at him. She hoped she made it apparent that she was referring to more than the fact that he'd just pulled her hair.

He looked at her askance. "What do you mean?"

"Are you proposing that the two of us sleep together— no, excuse me, we're both adults, I might as well be blunt. Are you proposing we *have sex* just for the hell of it? Just to relieve a little hormonal hyperactivity? That a nice, meaningless, emotionless roll in the sack is just what we both need?"

"Virginia . . ."

"Because if that's what you're proposing, Dr. Cameron, you're way out of line. And I for one am certainly not interested."

She spun on her heel, trying to remember where Dalton had hung her coat when they'd come inside. The foyer closet, she recalled, turning quickly toward the front hall.

"Virginia, wait," Dalton called after her.

But Virginia wasn't interested in hearing any explanation he might have for his insulting offer. She wasn't sure what made her angrier, the fact that he had been shallow enough to make such a proposition, or the thought that he would consider her shallow enough to be amenable to such an agreement. Clearly she had been right in avoiding any intimate contact with the opposite sex all these years, she concluded. Because they obviously hadn't changed a bit since she was a teenager.

She threw open the closet door and snatched her coat from inside, then reached for the front door without even donning the garment. Just as she heaved the heavy front door open, Dalton's big hand flattened against it from behind her, slamming it shut again. Once more, Virginia turned the knob and tried to pull backward, but his grasp was firm, his strength far outweighing her own.

"Let go of the door," she said angrily, still clinging to the doorknob.

"Not until you've given me a chance to explain."

"What's there to explain?" she bit out coarsely, still refusing to turn around and look at him. "You're agreeable to cheap, mindless, meaningless sex and thought I was sleazy enough to find something like that agreeable, too. Now you realize I'm not. And now that we understand each other, things between us should be a lot simpler."

She heard him chuckle humorlessly and spun quickly around to face him. His expression belied nothing of what he might be feeling, but his eyes were as hard and cold as the emeralds they so resembled.

"I have a feeling things between us will never be simple, Ginnie," he said coolly.

"Maybe not," she agreed. "But from here on out, we should have no trouble maintaining a discreet, but effective distance."

Something warm and lively flickered to life in his eyes at her comment. "Speak for yourself," he said softly, taking another step forward to bring his body more fully against hers.

Virginia tugged fruitlessly at the doorknob behind her, trying to ignore the shivery sensations shimmying down her spine at the feel of his warm, hard body pressing so intimately against her own. "Please let me go," she requested quietly.

Dalton shook his head. "Not while you're still mad at me."

She sighed restlessly, releasing the doorknob as she relaxed against the door. "I just don't understand why you said what you did, Dalton. I thought you were different. You seem like such a nice guy. I didn't think you'd be such a..."

"Such a jerk?" he finished for her with a sad smile.

She nodded, searching his eyes for some explanation for his behavior.

He, too, relaxed somewhat, but still kept his hand flattened against the door above her head. "I didn't mean to offend you, Ginnie, and I guess I should have known better than to make an offer like that. You have to forgive me. I haven't been alone with a woman I find attractive, but scarcely know, for more than twelve years. The dating game is a distant memory I never thought I'd find myself playing again. I guess I'm just not sure exactly what the rules are anymore."

She bit her lip anxiously. "You haven't... been with anyone since your wife?"

He shook his head. "I haven't even *gone out* with anyone since Penny."

Virginia nodded in understanding. "I haven't been with anyone since Dean, either."

Dalton supposed he should have suspected something of the sort, but her admission caught him off guard nonetheless. "You haven't . . . for five years?"

She arched her eyebrows philosophically, but shook her head in response, too. "Nope."

He tried to smile reassuringly. "I guess modern society doesn't have much to offer a couple of moral dinosaurs like ourselves."

But Virginia was quick to contradict him. "Really, morality has nothing to do with it. I just haven't met anyone who's meant enough to me, who's been special enough for me to risk—" She stopped herself abruptly when she realized what she had been about to confess.

"Falling in love again?" Dalton concluded quietly.

She glanced down at the floor, nervously twisting her coat in her hands, grateful for his opening. "You know, it's getting pretty annoying, the way you finish my sentences for me all the time."

He laughed. "I guess you and I just think the same way, that's all."

She nodded. The two of them had way too much in common, she thought. If ever a man lived who might make her reconsider her convictions about remaining single, that man was Dalton Cameron. But she just couldn't allow herself to open the door deep down inside her that she had closed five years ago. Because as soon as the lock on that door had clicked shut, she had thrown away the key. And as long as she had anything to say about it, no one would ever breach that barricade again.

"I'm sorry," he said quietly. "I'm sorry I said what I did."

She looked up at him again. "That's okay."

"Can we still be friends after all this?"

Virginia shrugged. "I don't know. Can we? I mean, clearly, there's something at work here that neither of us is especially enthusiastic about pursuing, but something we may not be able to control ourselves. Can we get beyond that? Can we ignore it?"

Dalton studied her closely for a moment before replying. "I'm willing to give it a shot if you are."

She thought about it briefly, then decided that if he thought they could do it, she was certainly willing to make an effort herself. Besides, she confessed reluctantly, she really liked Dalton. He was fun to be around. Surely she could overlook an incredible sexual attraction she had for the man in order to promote a healthy friendship. Couldn't she?

"Okay," she finally said. "We'll just try to put tonight's little fiasco behind us and go full speed ahead with being friends."

His expression was full of relief. "Great."

He removed his hand from the front door, pulling her coat from her now loosened fingers, holding it up to facilitate her putting it on. Then he reached for his own jacket and shrugged into it, silently stating his intention to walk her home. They made the journey in quiet, companionable conversation, and when they arrived in front of her house, they both noted at the same time that Lana Gennaro's bedroom light was on, just as it had been so many weeks ago when Dalton had walked Virginia home after the play.

"I'm going to have a tough time explaining our agreement to my mother," she said. "She had such high hopes for us."

"She doesn't believe in male-female friendships?" he asked.

"Oh, she believes in those readily enough. Just not for her children. Not until her children marry first anyway."

He laughed. "I'm sure she'll understand."

"I hope so."

As Dalton turned to leave, another thought struck him. He would be driving into Indianapolis the following morning, to pick up some supplies for the theater. It hadn't occurred to him to ask Virginia if she'd want to go with him, but for some reason, the thought of not seeing her tomorrow didn't set well with him right now. He turned to find her inserting her key into her front door, and called out her name. When she looked up again, he could tell she was surprised by his desire to prolong their parting.

"I have to drive into Indianapolis tomorrow," he told her. "I don't suppose you'd be interested in coming along, too, would you?"

"But what about the theater? I was going to spend tomorrow painting."

"I won't be there to let you in," he reminded her.

She gave his statement some thought, then settled her hands on her hips in mock challenge. "And just when were you planning on telling me that?"

He knew she was trying to sound petulant, but she failed miserably. "I'm telling you now," he pointed out with a chuckle.

"Oh, thanks so much."

"Look, do you want to drive into Indy with me tomorrow or not?"

"Well, since I'm obviously not going to have anything else to do..."

"Virginia..."

"I'd love to."

Dalton smiled. The trip to the city would last little more than an hour, but having Virginia there to keep him company lightened his spirits considerably. He didn't realize until that moment how much he'd been dreading going alone. He reminded himself that Indianapolis was his home, and that there was no reason for him to be fearful of returning there. But for some reason, his house in Indy no longer seemed real—it was like a place he'd dreamed about, a place almost foreign in his memories. The city itself seemed to hold little for him, he thought strangely. Certainly his job was there, and Indianapolis was where he'd grown up.

But Comfort felt like so much more. After little more than two months, this little community had come to mean a great deal to him, but for the life of him, Dalton couldn't figure out why. Indianapolis had everything a man could want—great night life, some fabulous restaurants, parks, museums, galleries, posh boutiques.... The closest things Comfort had to offer were a little café named after a flower, a town square, a tiny local playhouse and a five-and-dime whose merchandise didn't seem to have changed since 1952. Everything Dalton would ever need was back in Indianapolis. There was nothing for him here in Comfort.

"See you in the morning, Dalton," Virginia called from her front porch, bringing him out of his reverie.

"I'll pick you up at nine," he told her with a final wave.

No, Dalton thought again as he turned to make his way back home, there was nothing for him here. Except for a gorgeous strawberry blonde with willowy legs and a melancholy smile, whose simple presence brought him a peace of mind and serenity of soul like nothing he'd ever known. Friends with Virginia Gennaro, he marveled. That's what he'd said he wanted to be. He chuckled at his own naïveté. As if he could ever hope to keep what they had together innocent. Had he been trying to reassure her with his promise that he'd give their friendship a shot, or trying to reassure himself? Dalton supposed it really didn't matter. Because somehow he was certain they were going to fail miserably in their endeavor.

Still, he added with what he was sure was doomed optimism, it didn't mean they couldn't give it an honest try.

Chapter Seven

"Is that all of it?"

Virginia held the door open as Dalton and Glen Peterson, the proprietor of Peterson's Entertainment Supplies, lugged the last big carton out of the store and pushed it into the back of Dalton's rented pickup truck.

"That's all of it," he told her, taking the clipboard the other man extended toward him. "Popcorn popper, ticket machine, two cash registers, three poster showcases, two soft drink dispensers . . ." He scanned the remainder of the items and nodded his approval before scrawling his signature at the bottom of the invoice. "Now I just wish I knew someone who could fix the projector. I'd really hate to get rid of the original. The fact that so many other fixtures in the theater have to be replaced with newfangled gear is bad enough. At least Mr. Peterson here had a couple of period cash register reproductions, so we won't have any *beep-beep-booping* sounds blowing the ambience of the theater."

"Trixie isn't working?" Virginia asked as she joined him by the truck.

"Trixie?" Dalton asked, glancing up from the invoice with a dubious expression.

She blushed, shrugging a little self-consciously. "Yeah, Trixie. That's what Eddie named the projector."

"My uncle named his projector?"

She nodded.

He handed the clipboard back to Glen Peterson, who expressed his thanks, told Dalton he'd bill him, and disappeared into his store. Then he turned to Virginia with a shake of his head. "No, it, er, Trixie isn't working. And I have no idea how the thing, how she works."

"Maybe I could take a look at her for you," she offered.

He spun around to face her, clearly doubtful she could be of any help at all. "You?"

"Well, you don't have to sound so surprised," she sniffed indignantly. "Eddie taught Natalie and me how to run the projector, because both of his projectionists were notoriously unreliable where showing up for their shifts was concerned. And Trixie has always been about as temperamental as they come."

Dalton smiled at her. "Why didn't you tell me you knew how to run that monster?"

She lifted her chin defiantly. "You never asked."

He straightened, his posture perfectly solicitous as he smiled and asked, "Please, Ginnie, if you have time, might you come to the Palace Theater sometime in the not too distant future and have a look at my... at Trixie?"

She rolled her eyes toward the sky, touching her chin with her index finger as if giving serious consideration to his petition. "Well, I guess I could find the time."

He bowed graciously. "I would be most appreciative."

"Oh, what the heck. I have nothing better to do."

"You're too kind."

"I know."

Dalton opened the passenger side of the pickup truck for her, sweeping his hand dramatically in front of him to silently bid her enter. Virginia inclined her head toward him, hitched up her blue jeans, tugged at her down jacket and took her seat. He closed the door behind her, then crossed in front of the truck to fold himself into the driver's seat. Whimsically she thought he looked like an ad for some men's cologne celebrating the great outdoors in his tight jeans and faded denim jacket over a red-and-black plaid flannel shirt. His hair had grown long since his arrival in Comfort and now hung well below his collar in soft, light brown curls. He'd kept his beard trimmed meticulously close, however, and all in all presented an image of a man who cared about his appearance, but not about societal fashion mores.

She thought back to the night she'd run into Dalton at the playhouse, and considered once again his expensive clothes. He had seemed to feel as much at ease in designer fashion as he did in his informal outfit of today, but for some reason, she still thought his current appearance was more like him. Certainly she liked him better in his casual work clothes. It was yet another reinforcement for her to cling to in reassuring herself that he was nothing at all like her ex-husband. She didn't know why she kept comparing Dalton with Dean. She supposed it was only natural. Perhaps in doing so, she was trying to persuade herself that he would never turn out the way her ex-husband had.

Or perhaps, she thought sullenly, maybe some defense mechanism had switched on inside her, and she was trying to convince herself that despite the differences in the two men, Dalton would be exactly like Dean.

"Where to now?" she asked in an effort to keep her unsettling thoughts at bay. She glanced at her watch. It was only eleven-thirty, still too early for lunch.

"My house," he told her.

His words threw her for a moment, until she remembered that Indianapolis was his home, after all, and certainly the man would have some form of residence here. Yet she couldn't keep the puzzlement out of her voice as she said, "Your house?"

He turned to her and smiled, as if he were as surprised as she was to realize such a thing. "Since we're in town, I'd just like to check on it. A friend of mine—a neighbor—has been keeping an eye on the place, but since I'm here... If you don't mind, that is."

She straightened in her seat. "Of course I don't mind. Why would I mind?"

Dalton shrugged. "No reason."

"So where do you live?"

"North Meridian Street."

"Oh."

Virginia had been in Indianapolis often enough to know that Meridian Street was *the* most wonderful place in the city to live. Block after block of expansive, expensive homes, representing every style from Colonial to Tudor to Renaissance to Victorian, every single house was unique, classy and beautiful. It was the kind of street that always boasted heavy traffic, not just because it was a convenient thoroughfare, but because people simply wanted to look.

And Dalton's house was no different from the others in its exquisite architecture. An exuberant Tudor-style that might have been termed a cottage had it not been for the building's large size, it boasted a two-story bay in front, and narrow casement windows whose leaded panes glittered like diamonds in the early afternoon sun. The front lawn seemed to stretch forever, beneath two huge oak trees that probably covered the grass with shade during the warmer months of the year.

"It's beautiful, Dalton," she said softly as he turned the truck into the driveway.

He pulled to a stop and threw the gearshift into park, then looked through the windshield as if seeing the house for the first time. "I'm thinking of selling it," he told her quietly.

"But why? It's a wonderful house."

He shrugged. "But far too big for one person."

She should have realized that right off, Virginia chided herself. Obviously this must have been the house he had shared with his wife. Now she'd just brought up unwanted memories and made him feel bad. She racked her brain trying to come up with something to say that might make amends for her thoughtless observation, but his voice halted her.

"Penny and I had planned on having a house full of kids when we got married," he said, sounding sad and distant, almost as if he were talking to himself. "Four, at least. Maybe more. She and I were both only children." He sighed fitfully, still staring at the big house. "I don't know what happened. Somewhere along the line we just...ran out of time, I guess." He turned to look at Virginia, the smile he attempted anything but happy. "But then, you and your husband never had children, so I guess you understand."

Dalton's words cut Virginia to the bone, and she struggled to keep her breathing even, her anger under control. She reminded herself that there was no way he could realize how painful, how piercing his remark would be. Because there was no way he could know what had happened. Nevertheless, the reminder of her childless past, her childless present, and an undeniably childless future twisted like a dull knife in Virginia's heart.

"No, Dean and I never had children," she said softly, trying desperately to mask the bitterness she was feeling.

But Dalton must have picked up something from her tone of voice, because his own voice was full of concern when he spoke again. "Did I...did I say something wrong? Did you and your husband deliberately avoid having children? I'm sorry, I just assumed since you taught second grade you liked children...that you would want to have some of your own—"

"Oh, I'd love to have children of my own," she was quick to assure him, hoping her voice was steadier than she felt herself. "You can't imagine how much I would. But..." She inhaled deeply, holding her breath as she wondered how much she should tell him. Finally she concluded softly, "But . . . I can't."

He gazed at her, confused. "You're physically unable? Or you can't because of some personal misgivings?"

It really wasn't any of his business, Virginia told herself. Whatever she chose to do or was capable of doing was simply of no consequence whatever to Dalton Cameron. Yet instead of telling him that, she heard herself reply, "It would be impossible for me to conceive a child. And if by some wild miracle, I did, there's no chance I would be able to carry a baby to full term."

He studied her as he might one of his patients for whom he was forming a diagnosis. Virginia recognized the expression immediately, because she had witnessed the look often enough from other doctors. She'd seen the finest ones in Atlanta, after all.

"I'm assuming that's your physician's conclusion and not your own," he said.

She nodded.

"How long has it been since you've consulted your doctor? Specialists have made considerable strides in the field of fertility in the past few years. There might be some way of treating whatever is wrong."

Virginia shook her head. "There's no cure for what ails me, Dalton," she told him quietly, certainly.

"But—"

She held up a hand to stop him. "Please, couldn't we talk about something else?" She struggled to conjure a smile, then reached across the seat to cover with her own hand still gripping the steering wheel. "I'm sorry I said anything. I'm sorry I brought this whole thing up. Look, maybe it's too late for me to have kids, but you certainly still have an opportunity to see your own dreams of fatherhood fulfilled. I'll bet you find yourself saddled with a passel of kids in no time."

And why did it hurt her to reassure him in such a way? She should be happy for him, relieved that at least one of them might someday achieve the joy a child could bring into a life. But the thought that Dalton would someday experience that ultimate happiness with someone other than herself hurt Virginia even more deeply than her knowledge that she would never become a mother. She told herself she was being silly—that she didn't even want a romantic relationship with the man who sat beside her, or any man for that matter. Even if she could have children, to do so would only mean creating a link between herself and a man again, something she reminded herself she had no desire to do.

But ever since meeting Dalton Cameron, Virginia's dreams and resolutions where her future was concerned had changed. No longer did she find it easy to envision herself living a peaceful, solitary life in her mother's house, finding gratification and solace in the children whose lives she touched through teaching. That had always been such a reassuring, comforting view of her future, a goal she had been so certain she could meet without a fear of ever looking back in regret.

Lately, however, her dreams of the future almost always included the man who had invaded her life so innocently two months ago. And lately, she found herself wishing for something she knew she would never have... a family. A loving mate to come home to at day's end who would offer her a welcoming embrace and share with her his experiences as she shared hers with him. And a child, maybe two. Virginia wished she could have a child. It was a desire she had expressly forbidden herself to feel. But something about Dalton made her yearn for a way of life she had sworn she was past wanting.

Despite his appearance to the contrary, there was something auspicious about the man. Certainly he never showed it, but she could *feel* it—somewhere deep down inside him, there was a chamber filled with a hopefulness and desire identical to her own. Maybe that's why Virginia was so quick to detect it. Because despite the bleakness of his past, Dalton still harbored dreams for his future, just as she did herself. If only she could find some way to tap into them, perhaps there was a chance, however small, that the two of them could help each other.

Dalton shrugged off her apology a little carelessly, but Virginia could tell he felt anything but careless. "Don't say you're sorry. It's not your fault I'm a single man without children, Ginnie. It's no one's fault."

No one's but my own, he thought before he could stop himself. He ignored her assurance that he would someday father a tribe of children, fully aware that no such development would ever occur as long as he had anything to say about it. Instead, he reflected back on that old Spring morning in the Ohio wilderness two years ago. He should have been able to save Penny and Dylan, he berated himself. There must have been something he could have done. If only they'd been more careful. If only he'd seen what was coming. If only he'd acted more quickly. If only, if only, if only...

"Come on," he said as he opened his door to get out. He shook his house keys with an ominous jingle. "We don't have to stay long."

He heard Virginia following him up the walkway and wished he knew what to say to make her feel better. She wasn't responsible for his mood. Hell, this little excursion into his past had been his idea, not hers. Thinking about it now, Dalton decided coming to his house while she was with him probably hadn't been one of his best ideas. Naturally she would be curious about things, and naturally she would want to ask questions. Why had he brought her here? he wondered again. The only thing worse than thinking about Penny and Dylan was talking about them. And now he would be forced to do both.

The key turned easily in the lock, and he pushed the front door open silently. The house smelled a bit stale and dusty, and the slate-tiled foyer felt a little gritty beneath his shoes, but beyond that everything was exactly as he had left it. To his right, the sun filtered through the casement windows in the living room to scatter dappled diamonds of light on the sculpted Chinese carpet, sending dust motes dancing like fairy powder around the Oriental furnishings. To his left, the library beckoned with its dark mahogany paneling and deep-hued Victorian furnishings. Funny, how he'd never paid much attention to the way his home was decorated before, Dalton thought. Penny had always had such exquisite taste. Had he ever even complimented her on it? He couldn't remember now.

"My office is in the back of the house," he said, "behind the kitchen."

It surprised him to realize that he'd had to think for a moment before he remembered where his office was. Strange, since his office was just about the only room he'd ever visited while living here. That and the bedroom for much needed rest. The house had been Penny's domain. And despite the fact that she had also worked fifty- and sixty-hour weeks sometimes, she had been the one who was responsible for making sure the housekeeper showed up and completed her tasks. There had been very little for Dalton to see to around the house. His common practice upon returning home at the end of the day had been to pour himself a glass of wine, reheat whatever Penny and Dylan had eaten for dinner, then retreat to his office to pore over medical journals, patient files and hospital business. Then he would stumble up to bed at some point after midnight, kiss his wife's forehead and roll over for four or five hours of sleep.

God, what kind of life had that been? he wondered now. Had he really lived like such a mindless robot? And was that all he had to go back to when his leave of absence was over in July? He caught a glimpse of Virginia from the corner of his eye and only then recalled that she was there with him. And suddenly his house didn't seem quite so empty, quite so lonely, any longer.

"Come on, it's this way," he said, inclining his head toward the long hallway before them.

She followed silently behind him, but he could sense her intense interest in her surroundings. So he offered a perfunctory tour as they went, identifying each room they passed as best he could, trying not to dwell on how unfamiliar he felt with his own home. His rented house in Comfort felt infinitely more welcoming than the building through which he now strolled. When they reached the kitchen, it, too, was like some forgotten room he hardly recognized. Everything was so neat, so tidy, so...white. Had the kitchen always seemed this sterile? His kitchen in the house in Comfort was anything but orderly, the wallpaper claiming just about every color he could imagine. And the cabinets were dark wood with ornate handles, nothing like the sleek lines of the Scandinavian style here.

"Everything seems to be in order," he said. *I think.* But then how could he know for sure when he'd paid so little attention to everything before?

"Someone left you a note."

Dalton spun around, again almost forgetting Virginia was with him. He smiled at the warm coils of reassurance her presence sent rippling through his body. "What did you say?"

She pointed toward the kitchen table, where a pencil had been tossed carelessly onto a yellow legal pad. She knew it was none of her business, but she couldn't stop herself as she approached the object in question. Ever since entering Dalton's home, she had become even more intensely curious about him than she was already. The furnishings here were so formal, so expensive looking. Certainly it came as no surprise to her that a pediatric surgeon made so much money, and who knew what his wife had done for a living as well, but the house simply did not seem to go along with the Dalton Cameron she'd come to know. He wasn't a formal, expensive man. And as beautiful as his home was, he simply didn't seem to belong here.

"Someone left you a note," she repeated when she came to a stop at the kitchen table.

Dalton strode forward, too, looking over her shoulder to read the message dated nearly a week earlier.

"Hi, Dalton," it read in a broad, round, feminine hand. "Don't know if you'll be stopping by anytime soon, but if you do, give me a call. It's nothing important—just wondering how you're doing. Hope to hear from you before long. Love, Shari.''

Love, Shari? Virginia repeated to herself, feeling a little sick to her stomach. This was the *friend* who was watching Dalton's house? A woman? A woman who was concerned about how he was doing? A woman who wanted him to call her? A woman who dotted the *i* in her name with a little heart?

As if he knew what she was thinking, Dalton cleared his throat indelicately and said, ''Shari signs everything with love, even, I suspect, her bills to the phone company. She's not, um, she isn't—''

His explanation was cut short by the rattle of loud knocking at the back door. Virginia saw him start, as if the sound were the last thing in the world he expected to hear.

''That's probably Shari,'' he said unnecessarily, making his way slowly to answer the summons. ''She, uh, she lives next door.''

''That's convenient,'' Virginia remarked blandly, cursing herself for even caring.

''Yeah, she's been a real peach to watch the place for me.''

''I bet.''

His progress toward the back door slowed, as if he were stalling for time. ''She's divorced . . . three young kids . . . works two jobs. I've, uh, I've always tried to help her out whenever I could.''

''Uh-huh.''

''Patching her radiator or programming her VCR or shoveling her driveway when it snows, that kind of thing.''

''How nice of you.''

''Watching the house has just been her way of paying me back is all.''

''How nice of her.''

''There's nothing more to it than that.''

''I see.''

The knocking sounded again, this time louder.

"I'll just answer that," he said.

"Good idea," she replied.

The woman who entered was the last kind of person Virginia wanted to have worrying about Dalton. She was tall, blond, beautiful and ebullient, and obviously concerned about his welfare. She pulled him immediately into her arms for a warm—but not too demanding—embrace, kissing him briefly on the cheek before letting him go. Worse than all that, though, Virginia realized as she watched the intimate byplay, Shari seemed to be a genuinely nice person. Damn her.

"Oh, wow, look at this beard!" the other woman exclaimed. "You look fabulous!"

Shari ruffled her fingers through the furry growth with a familiarity that set Virginia's teeth on edge. She remembered how hesitant she herself had been about performing such a gesture, and blushed to recall that she had even asked Dalton's permission to do so, for Pete's sake. He must think her the most shriveled of shrinking violets after having had contact with this bright, exotic flower who was his next-door neighbor. Virginia shook her head in wonder that he'd even bothered to speak to her.

"Hello, Shari," Dalton greeted the other woman with a warm smile. "You look pretty great, yourself."

"It's so good to see you," Shari told him, squeezing his arm affectionately. "I came home for lunch and saw a truck parked in your driveway, loaded up with stuff. At first I was afraid somebody was cleaning you out, then I saw all the boxes labeled with movie theater equipment, and I figured it was you. How are you? How's the theater coming? Why haven't you called me? Justin and Micah miss playing football with you. And Brenna has been asking when you're going to have dinner with us again."

Oh, great, Virginia thought. Shari would have to have one of those voices—deep and husky, as if she were speaking from the back of her throat and the depth of her soul. Yet the way the other woman spoke didn't cause her nearly as much turmoil as did what she was saying. She had three children, Dalton had told her. Virginia could pretty much figure out that's who Justin, Micah and Brenna were. Clearly he had developed a very good rapport with the youngsters. And clearly he was close to the entire family if he was accustomed to having dinner with them. She studied Shari more closely, taking in the sophisticated, short haircut, the expensive, dress-for-success suit, the willowy stature tempered by lush curves. Her hips in particular caught Virginia's attention. They could perfectly cradle a good many more healthy, robust children.

Knowing a similar inspection of her own attributes would leave her substantially lacking, Virginia concluded that the best defense was a good offense, and decided to loudly introduce herself to the other woman. After all, she thought morosely, Dalton evidently had no plans to do so.

"Hello," she sang out in a voice that sounded far cheerier than she felt. "I'm Virginia Gennaro. And you're obviously Shari."

The other woman's head snapped around at the introduction, and Virginia could see how startled she was. "Yes, I am," she said with a smile, stepping forward to offer her hand. "Has Dalton told you about me?"

Virginia shook her head as she graciously took Shari's hand. "No. I just saw your note is all."

Shari nodded. "Nice to meet you."

Virginia deflated at the realization that her rival was in no way catty or obnoxious. The other woman was honestly pleasant and had a very nice smile. To compete with her on any level would be fruitless. Then Virginia reminded herself that competition for Dalton was out of the question anyway. Simply put, she didn't want the prize. Did she? No, of course not. Let Shari have Dalton—she was obviously interested. The two of them would no doubt be very happy together. His passel of kids was right there within his reach. But why, she wondered further, hadn't he reached out to grab what could obviously be his? Unfortunately, before she could offer herself an adequate answer, Dalton spoke again.

"I'm sorry I didn't call, Shari," he told her. "I guess I've been so wrapped up in the theater that I didn't realize how much time had passed since I left Indianapolis."

Shari smiled at Virginia one final time, then turned back to Dalton. "I was just getting a little worried, that's all. You left in kind of a hurry, and for so long you've been so—"

She stopped abruptly, and Virginia could have almost sworn Shari glanced quickly over her shoulder as if only remembering she and Dalton were not alone.

"Well, anyway," the other woman hastily continued, "obviously you're fine, but keep in touch next time."

"I will," Dalton vowed. "I promise. So, how are the kids?"

"They're great. But like I said, they miss you a lot. The boys are in school, and Brenna's in daycare, otherwise I'd ask you to come over and say hello. If you're going to be here all day, maybe you... and Virginia, of course," she added over her shoulder, "would like to come over for dinner?"

Some perverted part of Virginia was actually hoping Dalton would say yes. She realized she'd love to meet Shari's kids, but then wondered why she'd want to put herself through so much misery. No doubt Shari's children were as perfect as Shari was herself. She wondered again why Dalton wasn't more seriously involved with his neighbor. Unless of course the two of them were in fact very much involved, and he had simply chosen for some reason not to tell Virginia about it.

"Thanks, Shari, but we have to be getting back."

"Oh, well," she concluded with another dazzling smile, retracing her steps toward the back door. "Maybe next time."

"It was good to see you," he told her as he embraced her briefly one last time. "Tell the kids I said hi. And tell Micah not to forget that new spin I taught him. Tell him to keep his wrist firm."

"Will do. Virginia," Shari said, lifting her hand in farewell.

"Bye," Virginia told her, mimicking the gesture.

And with that, Shari-with-a-heart-over-the-*i* was gone, almost as if she'd simply been a semiconscious vision. All that was left behind was a lingering fragrance of something spicy and expensive, the kind of perfume for which a woman spent more money than she could afford, but sprayed on every body part she could find.

"She's very nice," Virginia said honestly.

Although he stared out the kitchen door behind her, Dalton's thoughts seemed to be on something other than his next-door neighbor. "Shari? Yeah, she's great. Her kids are terrific. Micah's football team at St. Andrew's went to the Toy Bowl this year."

Virginia smiled. "The Toy Bowl?"

Dalton nodded, his own smile mirroring hers. "Missed winning by two points. Poor kid was crushed. I've been trying to show him how to keep more control on the ball, but he's so little, he can barely manage."

Virginia walked over to him, splaying her fingers open between his shoulder blades, rubbing her hand in slow circles over his back. For some reason, he seemed to need comforting. "You're going to be a wonderful father someday, Dalton," she told him softly.

The moment the words were out of her mouth, she felt him stiffen, the muscles beneath her fingertips tensing until they were as solid as rock. When he spun around to face her, his eyes were like ice—cold, hard, unyielding. Her heart plummeted, and her stomach burned with some unknown fire. She shook her head silently, unaware of what she might have said to cause such a complete change in him. A moment ago, he had been speaking fondly of his neighbor's son, almost as if the boy had been his own. Then without warning, his mood had turned bitter. And for the life of her, Virginia didn't know what she'd said or done to inspire the change.

"I'll be in my office," he said harshly as he pushed past her without a second glance. "Give me ten minutes, then I'll be ready to leave."

Dalton was gone before Virginia could ask what was wrong, gone before she could even begin to understand what had so suddenly set him on edge. Not only that, she realized uncomfortably, he had left before she could ask him where the bathroom was. Frankly she wasn't sure she could make the hour-plus drive back to Comfort without using the facilities first. She started to follow him to ask for directions, but at the sound of a door slamming loudly enough to make the glass contents of the kitchen cabinet behind her clink and jingle, she hesitated. Maybe she'd just look for the bathroom herself, she decided. It was a big house. Surely there must be one down here somewhere.

But much to her surprise, a quick search of the downstairs revealed nothing. It must be beyond the office where Dalton had shut himself up, she decided. But there was no way she was going to knock on that door and interrupt him when he had gone out of his way to insinuate she would be unwelcome. Upstairs, then, she decided. But the thought of venturing upstairs when she hadn't been issued an invitation made her uncomfortable. Of course, not being able to answer a call of nature that was becoming more and more persistent made her even more uncomfortable. Surely Dalton wouldn't mind if she just slipped upstairs for a minute. It wasn't as if he'd never had to go to the bathroom himself before. Besides, he might never even find out.

As quickly as she could, Virginia stole up the carpeted steps until she found herself in a long hallway dotted with doors on both sides. Some were open, others were closed. But one of them must be a bathroom. Right or left? she wondered. Well, she'd always been liberal in her thinking, why not left? What a wise woman she felt like when the first room on her right turned out to be the one she'd been seeking. After relieving herself, she gave herself a perfunctory inspection in the bathroom mirror and was disgusted to realize how frumpy she must have looked in her Anderson College sweatshirt and jeans beside the immaculately put-together Shari. Virginia shoved both hands through her long hair and pushed it away from her forehead, sighing in frustration. Her mother had always told her she looked like an angel. Why, just once, couldn't she seem a little more...tempting?

She waved a hand in disappointment at the woman staring back at her from the mirror and reached automatically over to flush the toilet. At the rushing sound of water being sucked loudly away, Virginia closed her eyes in despair. There was little chance now that her journey upstairs had gone unobserved by Dalton. Resigned to the fact that she'd be caught red-handed soon enough, she opened the bathroom door later and strode out into the hallway again. And when she did, she was helpless to avoid noticing the room directly across from her. The door was thrown open wide in welcome, and the sun threw horizontal shadows on the brightly woven rug as it filtered through the blinds. It was only a bedroom, something that shouldn't come as a surprise to Virginia. Yet it surprised her very much.

Because it was the bedroom of a child.

Two easy steps put her in the doorway, and she placed a hand gingerly against the jamb as if to keep herself from pitching forward. The wallpaper was clearly intended for a young boy, with drawings that depicted a variety of sporting equipment known to boys everywhere. The single bed was covered with a red spread, a trio of throw pillows in blue, yellow and green tossed haphazardly at the head. The windowsill was cluttered with juvenile paraphernalia—plastic dinosaurs, a microscope, an autographed baseball in a stand and three small trophies. Beside the window, perched atop a tripod was a very sophisticated-looking telescope that seemed more suited to a science teacher than a little boy. Beside that, two tall bookshelves housed reading material on sports, astronomy, cars and unexplained phenomena.

It was exactly what a young boy's room should be, Virginia thought with a smile. Exactly how she would arrange one for her own son, should she find herself in such a miraculous position someday. Why hadn't Dalton told her he had a son? she wondered frantically. Why hadn't he said a word about him? And where was the boy staying now?

She felt a hand cup her shoulder gently, and when she turned to face Dalton, found him staring past her into the room.

"I didn't tell you about him, Ginnie," he said quietly, as if he'd read her mind, "because my son is dead."

Cold fingers wrapped tightly around her heart at the announcement, and hot tears stung her eyes. She watched as Dalton strode past her, into his son's room, looking around at his surroundings as if he hadn't considered them for a very long time. Finally he sat at the edge of the bed, letting his hands hang loosely between his knees.

"I suppose I should have cleared everything out of here a long time ago. No doubt one of the local children's homes could find a good bit of use for it." He rolled his shoulders in what might have been a shrug had his been a more casual observation. "But I just never seem able to find the time, you know? There's always something else that seems more important."

"Why didn't you tell me?" she asked softly.

He shook his head, reaching for one of the throw pillows at the head of the bed. "I don't know. I wanted to, Ginnie, but I couldn't for some reason."

She nodded sympathetically. She, above all people, understood what it was like to want to remain silent on a topic. "What was he like, your son?" She envisioned a miniature version of Dalton, with curly brown hair and mischievous green eyes, bubbling over with questions about how the world worked, and she couldn't help the sad smile she felt playing around her lips.

"He loved baseball, cheeseburgers and gazing at the stars," Dalton told her quietly. "His name was Dylan, and he was seven years old when he died." When he turned to look at Virginia again, his eyes were bright with unshed tears. "And unfortunately, Ginnie, that's about all I can tell you about my son. Because despite the fact that I was the boy's father, I scarcely knew him at all."

"Oh, Dalton," she whispered, entering the room slowly, almost reverently, to take a seat beside him on the bed. "I'm so, so sorry. I don't know what to say. I... How long ago did it happen?"

"Almost exactly two years ago," he told her. "I lost him and Penny at the same time. We were camping in Ohio. Both Penny and Dylan loved to canoe, but the river wound up being much rougher than we realized. We hit some rapids, and the canoe capsized. Penny and I managed to grab hold of a low-lying branch, but Dylan disappeared almost immediately. Penny let go and went after him, then I let go and went after her, but... but I slammed into a cluster of rocks, and somehow my legs got caught. When I tried to twist free, I broke one leg, and then fractured the other...."

He shook his head, still staring blindly out at his son's bedroom. "Everything happened so quickly. One minute I saw Penny's head—she was so close to Dylan—then the next minute, both of them were gone. Just gone. As if they'd never been there at all. I don't know how it happened. We were all wearing life jackets, but somehow... I just don't know how it happened."

The cold fingers wrapped around Virginia's heart squeezed tighter, robbing her of breath and warmth. For a long moment, she didn't—couldn't—speak. No amount of condolence or compassion seemed adequate enough to comfort him, and frankly, how was she supposed to do justice to the memory of two people she'd never even met? Only Dalton could help himself work through his grief, she thought, something he clearly hadn't managed to do, even after two years. What could she possibly say that might help him?

"The worst part of it was," he went on relentlessly, as if she hadn't spoken, "that weekend was supposed to be a renewal of sorts. I had been working so many hours at the hospital, and Penny was a C.P.A. with a big local firm and had just landed a huge account, so she had been dedicating most of her time to her job, as well. Dylan hardly saw either one of us. Hell, he knew more about his baby-sitter than he did his parents. So the three of us took this trip to kind of get to know each other again. To try to be a family for a change. That was the first time, Ginnie, that I ever made time for my family while I was married. I'd never been there for either one of them before that weekend. And when I finally made myself available . . . I failed them."

"It was an accident, Dalton."

The words sounded lame and poorly chosen, even to Virginia's ears. Still, she added, "You can't blame yourself. There was nothing you could do to prevent the outcome."

He shook his head. "I should have been able to help them. There must have been something I could do."

Virginia draped an arm across his shoulders in an effort to bring him closer, emotionally, if not physically. "I'm sorry," she repeated, feeling helpless and anguished and angry at a fate that would allow such a tragedy to occur.

Dalton surged to his feet and paced the length of the room, then spun around to gaze at her in accusation. "Dammit, Virginia, why do you always apologize for things that aren't your fault?" he bit out angrily.

"Dalton, I—"

"You had nothing to do with their deaths," he raged on, ignoring her attempt to explain. "You weren't there, you have no idea what happened. For God's sake, you didn't even know them!"

"But—"

"What were you doing snooping around up here in the first place?" he demanded further, his voice booming like a cannon in the otherwise silent house. "If you wanted to know more about me, all you had to do was ask. You didn't have to go creeping around my house in an effort to uncover my deepest, darkest secrets."

"Dalton, you're upset—"

"You're damned right I'm upset! Upset that a woman whose friendship I valued, a woman I thought I could trust, would turn out to be a shallow, meddlesome enough busybody to go searching through my house!"

"I wasn't searching your house," she defended herself meekly. "I had to go to the bathroom. And when I said I was sorry, I was just trying to help...."

"Help?" he repeated incredulously, thrusting both hands through his hair in frustration. "You want to help me, Virginia? Then remind yourself that my past, my life, is absolutely none of your business. Better yet, from here on out, just stay the hell out of my life completely!"

And with that he stormed out of the room, leaving Virginia well and truly alone. She heard his heavy step take the stairs two at a time, then heard a door slam loudly somewhere within the bowels of the house. A single tear spilled from the corner of her eye, and she palmed it away automatically. She had only been trying to help him to talk it out, she reminded herself. She hadn't meant to be snooping around. And she hadn't meant to find out about Dalton's son. She hadn't meant to hurt him. With a final, deep breath, she rose from the bed and exited, turning one final time to view the bedroom.

It was a bright, happy room, the domain of what must have been a very bright, happy child. Dalton had said his son was seven years old when he died, the same age as many of her students. Seven years old, she reflected. A time when children were full of energy, inquisitiveness and laughter, well on their way to becoming strong-willed adolescents. They needed a considerable amount of attention, the answers to a variety of questions. They were thoughtful, caring and curious. Dylan had been torn from his father's life at a time when the young boy had just begun to show hints of the man he would someday become. In many ways, she supposed, Dalton had lost more than his son. He'd lost a good portion of himself, as well.

And that was probably why he was still hurting so much, Virginia thought further. Perhaps he was mourning the loss of more than he realized. She should be patient with him, and forgiving. He hadn't been striking out at her with his angry words, he'd been trying to deflect that anger from himself. It was a self-preservation mechanism housed within every human being. She should know that as well as anyone. After all, Virginia reminded herself, she had been forced to cope with her own share of anger after Dean had attacked her—anger at her husband, anger at herself, anger at the doctors who had been unable to mend her, even anger at her friends and family for not being there to rescue her when she had needed them most. Human psychology was often an ugly game, she reminded herself. She shouldn't take Dalton's reaction personally.

But she did. She was a woman who prided herself on understanding human nature, yet she was quick to find blame with herself when situations concluded with a less than happy ending. She should have known what to say to Dalton that would have made him feel better. She should have been able to understand more fully, and help him through his pain. Instead she'd propelled him away, let him go off by himself without even trying to console him.

Maybe he was right, Virginia thought. Maybe he'd be better off if she just left him alone. After they arrived back in Comfort, she decided as she turned to make her way downstairs, that was exactly what she would do.

Chapter Eight

"Miss Gennaro, Miss Gennaro! Bryan is drawing a dragon on top of his house!"

Virginia tried to hide her smile, adopting the standard-issue teacher's bland expression as she glanced up from grading her fifth period class's work to consider her sixth period class. "Now, Candace, you know we don't discourage others from drawing what they like," she reminded the little girl. "If Bryan wishes to include a dragon in his drawing of the house where he'd most like to live, then Bryan may certainly do so."

"But why would he want an old dragon?" Candace demanded petulantly.

"Well, maybe Bryan can tell us." She turned her attention to her other pupil. "Bryan? Can you explain to Candace why you're drawing a dragon on your house?"

Bryan continued to color furiously with a green marker as he spoke. "If we have a dragon on the house, he can breathe fire down the chimney and into the fireplace, and then we won't have to pay heating bills. My dad says the heating bills are sky high.''

Virginia couldn't help but smile at that. "See there, Candace?'' she said to the girl seated beside Bryan, who still scowled at her classmate's art work. "Bryan has a perfectly good reason for adding a dragon to his house.''

Candace reached for a pink marker and said triumphantly, "Then if Bryan gets a dragon, My Pretty Pony is gonna live in my backyard.''

"I think that would be wonderful,'' Virginia told her with a nod of approval. "Now then, let's see how everyone else has drawn the house where they would most like to live.''

Just as each of the children put down their markers and began to lift their brightly colored pictures into the air for her inspection, a shrill bell rang to announce the end of the day. The eighteen children in the classroom scrambled to gather their belongings, stuffing their supplies into book bags and backpacks, hoisting their burdens in effortless haste, with high hopes of escaping a few moments early so they could enjoy their weekend for a few moments longer. Virginia called out a weekend assignment amid the hustle and bustle, knowing that come Monday morning one or two of her students would swear she had designated no such homework.

Let's see, she thought as she watched the children file out with quickly offered farewells, who would it be this time? Probably Kevin Galworthy and ... Amanda Phillips. They had been the first two out the door. She made a mental note to ask the two for their assignments first come Monday and closed her grade book to gather her own things together. Why shouldn't she get an early start on her Friday, too? Natalie would be meeting her for lunch in a half hour, then the two of them were going to take in a new romantic adventure at the multiplex.

Virginia tried not to think about her last visit to the movies two weeks ago and the way the evening afterward had progressed. Nor did she dwell on the day that had followed it, when she and Dalton had exchanged a few more than heated words and spent a disastrous afternoon driving back to Comfort from Indianapolis in complete and utterly uncomfortable silence.

When she shoved the last of her papers and books into her satchel, Virginia looked up to find one of her students still seated at one of the six round tables dotting the term, his head bent close to his chest, his hands spread open wide over his drawing. Stephen Brewer was new to her class this quarter, and she didn't know the boy well. She was aware that he had recently moved to Comfort with his grandfather, but knew little else about him.

"Stephen?" she called out quietly, moving from behind her desk to approach him. "Class is over. You can go home now."

The little boy shook his head. "But, Miss Gennaro, I didn't finish," he told her guiltily. "My picture's not done yet."

"That's okay, Stephen. You can finish it in class on Monday, how will that be?"

But still the boy did not move. He only continued to sit with his eyes cast downward, his hands splayed open across the paper covering a good portion of the table before him.

"May I see how much you have finished?" Virginia asked him.

He started to shake his head again, then reluctantly removed his hands from his project, doubling them up in his lap. The page before him was empty save four straight lines that formed an irregularly shaped square. She was puzzled. He must have been sitting here for almost an hour doing nothing while the other children chatted amiably and drew to their hearts' content.

"I don't live in a house," Stephen explained quietly.

"That's okay," she told him, seating herself somewhat awkwardly in the child-size chair beside his. "You didn't have to draw your own house, just the kind of house where you'd like to live. A lot of the children at school don't live in houses. Tracy lives in a trailer with her aunt and uncle, and John and Louis and Denise all live in apartments with their moms. David and his parents live in a duplex. Do you know what a duplex is?''

Stephen shook his head.

"It's a building that's divided into two homes, so two families can live in it.''

When the boy finally looked up at Virginia, his eyes were filled with tears. "But I don't live in any of those things," he said quietly. "Me and Grandpops live in Mrs. Hovecamp's boarding home. We only have one room, and we eat dinner every night with everyone else who lives there. Mostly they're all old people, like Grandpops.''

She smiled reassuringly. "Well, Mrs. Hovecamp's is a house, isn't it? A great big house with green shutters and a backyard big enough to play lots of games. When I was a little girl, I used to play croquet in Mrs. Hovecamp's backyard all the time. She's a nice lady, isn't she?''

Stephen nodded. "She makes good lemonade.''

"She sure does. And do you know something else?''

He shook his head again, but smiled a little.

"In the spring and summer, when the weather is warm, the window boxes on Mrs. Hovecamp's house are full of red geraniums. No one else in Comfort grows geraniums as nice as hers. She's the geranium queen around here. Everyone's always jealous because their houses never look as nice as Mrs. Hovecamp's does.''

"Really?''

Virginia nodded. "I'd say you're awfully lucky to live there.''

"You think so?''

She nodded again, more vigorously this time. "You know what you could do Monday in class?''

"No, what?''

"You could draw Mrs. Hovecamp's house for the house where you'd most like to live.''

"I could even do it this weekend," Stephen offered as his smile grew a bit broader. "She said I could do my homework on her dining-room table anytime I wanted to.''

Virginia smiled back. "I bet she'd even make you some lemonade if you asked nicely and said please."

"I bet she would, too."

Stephen twisted his face into a thoughtful expression for a moment, then asked, "Miss Gennaro? How do you draw ger...geran...?"

"Geraniums?" she supplied helpfully.

He sighed in relief. "Yeah."

She selected a red marker from the plastic pens scattered across the table before him and removed the top, then drew a series of curlicues that vaguely resembled the flower in question. "Mmm, something like that," she told the boy. "But maybe Mrs. Hovecamp will show you a picture of how her house looks in the summer, and you can see for yourself."

"I'll ask her," Stephen said, his smile now broader than she had ever seen.

He began to place his markers meticulously back into the flat, yellow box that housed them. When he had completed the task, he gathered his books as well, stuffing all of his belongings into an aged, exhausted backpack before standing up to hastily don a well-weathered jacket. Lastly, and with infinite care, he rolled up the unfinished drawing on the table and tucked it down between his coat and shirt.

"Thanks, Miss Gennaro," he said quickly as he sped toward the door.

He halted only a moment at the sight of a tall, brown-haired, bearded man who leaned leisurely in the doorway, a man who made Virginia's heart race erratically when she noted him at the same time. But Stephen seemed undisturbed by the man's presence, and breathed a "'Scuse me, mister" as he went racing by. And that left her to be alone with Dalton Cameron.

She wondered how long he'd been standing in the doorway. She hadn't seen him at all since their return from Indianapolis, despite the fact that she was supposed to be painting the theater for him. When he had ordered her out of his life completely, she had assumed he would find someone else to finish the Palace decoration for him, something he must have done, because he certainly hadn't inquired into her whereabouts of late. Now as he stood staring into her classroom, dressed in black corduroys and a thick, charcoal-colored sweater, his black overcoat spilling down around him like a storm cloud, he reminded Virginia of a bad omen. All she could do was wonder what he wanted and wish he didn't look so damnably attractive.

"Hi," he said softly, his voice a bit gruffer than she remembered.

"Hello," she answered coolly. She was still stinging from the effects of their last encounter, and wasn't sure she was ready to be anything more than polite to him.

"Nice kid," he remarked, looking down the hallway after Stephen. "I know how he feels. I felt a little displaced myself sometimes when I was his age. My father moved us around a lot, whenever he lost his job. Which was pretty frequently."

Virginia wasn't sure how to comment on his revelation—mostly because he seemed not to require a response. So she rose from her seat and returned to her desk, where she went back to gathering her belongings. She pretended not to notice the sound of his boots scraping across the tile floor as he slowly entered the classroom, nor the fragrance of the cold, windy outdoors that surrounded him when he drew nearer. Instead she snapped her satchel shut, then turned to the cabinet behind her desk to retrieve her coat.

"You're, uh, you seem to be pretty good with kids," he said as he situated himself comfortably on the edge of her desk—the edge she would have to pass in order to leave.

"Well, isn't that handy, since what I do for a living pretty much revolves around teaching them," she muttered sharply.

She thrust her arms into the sleeves of her coat, grabbed her satchel by the handle and prepared to leave. As she took a single step forward, however, Dalton stretched his long leg up to plant his foot firmly against the chalk tray along the bottom of the chalkboard. Because Virginia's desk was tucked into a corner of the room against the wall, and because she now stood behind it, his action effectively barred her from leaving without removing his leg by force. No doubt he realized that, she thought. For some reason, he apparently wanted her to be a captive audience.

"Is there something you wanted?" she asked impatiently as she gazed at the leg blocking her path.

Once again, she was wearing what Dalton had come to think of as her teacher clothes—a long flowered dress with a prim lacy collar. He recalled the slender, well-formed legs he knew were hiding underneath and sighed imperceptibly. Who would have thought a second-grade teacher could be so unbelievably arousing? He watched as she bunched her long hair in one hand and freed it from beneath her coat, the tresses shimmering with the colors of a sunset as they danced around her shoulders. He noted the full, near perfect lips lightly stained with plum-colored lipstick and the natural blush of pink softening her cheeks. But her eyes were what drew him most. The color of the ocean at its most dangerous depths, her eyes caught his gaze and gripped it with the tenacity of a powerful electric surge.

Was there something he wanted? Dalton repeated her question to himself. No, not much. Just for time to stand still so that he could stand here and gaze upon the beauty of Virginia Gennaro forever.

"I wanted to apologize," he said softly.

She had been struggling to put on her mittens, but her hands stilled in their endeavor at his quietly uttered request. "Apologize for what?" she asked evenly, her voice barely touched with an edge of resentment.

She might be great with kids, Dalton conceded, but she was lousy when it came to pretending to misunderstand. Maybe she was only being polite, he told himself. That would be just like her. Courteous to a fault, even when some thoughtless bastard had run roughshod over her emotions.

He had been unfair to her two weeks ago, terribly unfair. And he'd had thirteen days to regret the ill-chosen words he'd hurled at her when they'd visited his house in Indianapolis. But how could he have told her about the feelings he still carried around two years after the deaths of his wife and son? How could he describe the guilt, the anger, the regrets? Virginia Gennaro was a nice woman who lived in a nice town and taught nice kids and had a nice life. Yes, she'd experienced a bad marriage, but how could her ghosts be anywhere near as haunting and frightening as his own?

Instead of being a husband to his wife and a father to his son, he'd been a virtual stranger to them, because he'd worked so relentlessly to become a success. And when he'd finally taken it upon himself to try to make it up to them, he'd lost them...just like that. And now he would never be able to go back and make amends. He'd never be able to hold them and tell them all the things he wished he'd said. Had he ever told Dylan he loved him? Dalton didn't think so. And now his son would never know that he had been loved dearly by his father. Because now he was gone forever.

How could Virginia ever understand the anguish his loss had caused him? How could she even begin to comprehend the scope of his emotions when she'd never suffered a tragedy comparable to his own? How could her simple, unhappy marriage even begin to compare to what he had lost himself? She couldn't possibly understand, Dalton told himself. But that didn't give him any right to turn on her the way he had.

"I'm sorry for...for what happened when we were in Indianapolis. I had no right to speak to you the way I did. I overreacted. And I'm sorry if I hurt your feelings."

"There's no need to apologize," she assured him, returning her attention to her mittens. "You didn't hurt my feelings."

"Then why haven't you been at the theater for the last two weeks?" he demanded, unable to mask his disappointment that she hadn't been around.

"Because you told me—let's see if I can remember the exact phrasing—" She feigned thoughtfulness as she bit her lip and gazed toward the ceiling with one eye closed. "You told me that from there on out, I should just stay the hell out of your life completely. Was that about the gist of it?"

Dalton nodded reluctantly. "That was pretty much exactly the gist of it."

"Then I'm afraid I don't understand. I assumed that by staying away from the Palace, I was fulfilling your edict. Has my avoidance of you somehow been incomplete? Believe me, I've done my best to follow your instructions to the letter."

He sprang up from her desk and surged forward, clamping his hands on her shoulders in one less-than-gentle motion. When her eyes met his, they were startled and full of heat, offering him every indication that she was willing to do combat with him. He forced his fingers to relax somewhat in their grasp, but he did not release her completely.

"Dammit, Virginia, you've been more than effective at avoiding me," he bit out. "That's the problem."

She watched him silently, obviously unwilling to bend in any way that might make his apology a little easier to offer. With a helpless sigh, he rubbed his hands up and down the length of her upper arms, uncertain whether the gesture was meant to reassure her or himself.

"I didn't mean it," he said softly. "I was angry when I told you I wanted you out of my life."

"You were angry at me," she reminded him.

He shook his head. "No. Not at you. At myself."

He released her then, leaning back against her desk, wrapping his arms around himself as if to keep himself from falling apart. With his legs stretched out before him, his feet crossed at the ankles, he still blocked her path sufficiently enough to keep her from fleeing until he could make himself heard. He groped for words that might somehow explain his behavior of two weeks ago, but all he could say was, "Maybe I haven't...handled...Dylan's death as well as I originally thought."

Virginia, too, leaned back against her desk, settling her satchel on the floor near her feet. It was a posture that put her in close contact with Dalton, a gesture that indicated she was willing to talk. Score one point for him, he thought. Now if he could just make her understand.

"Maybe you haven't," she agreed quietly.

His eyes met hers evenly as he added, "But I'm doing the best I can."

Virginia nodded. "It takes time, Dalton. You'll never be over it completely."

"I know."

"Just don't fight your feelings. Don't try to hide them. If you keep pushing them down below the surface, you'll only wind up burying them so deep inside that their only way out will be to eat away at you until there's nothing left. Whatever grief you still feel, you have to let it out, let it go."

He smiled at her, but it wasn't quite a happy one. "You sound like you're speaking from experience."

Virginia smiled sadly back. "Just trust me on this one, okay?"

He nodded, but didn't press the issue. Instead he only told her, "I've missed you."

Something in her eyes flickered to life at his confession, some unidentifiable something he was afraid to question.

"I've missed you, too," she said.

He studied his surroundings in an effort to avoid looking at her. Frankly he still wasn't sure what to say to her, still wasn't sure what he was feeling. The classroom was small and brightly lit, its walls decorated with colorful drawings in splashes of red, blue, yellow and green depicting a variety of images. The tables, the bulletin board, everything was lower to the ground than it would be for adults. Virginia spent her days in this pint-size world, he reflected. A woman who loved children but couldn't have her own, yet surrounded herself with constant reminders of what she was missing. He couldn't understand that. He was beginning to realize that the reason he'd originally requested a leave of absence from the hospital had little to do with his uncle's movie theater and more to do with the fact that he just wasn't sure anymore whether he could pursue a career in pediatric surgery.

Ever since Dylan's death, every patient Dalton lost made him feel as if he was losing his son all over again. In an effort to battle such a reaction, he'd smothered his emotions down deeply inside him until every reminder of children left him feeling cold and empty inside. And that wasn't a good way for a children's doctor to feel.

He pushed the thought away, turning to Virginia. "I brought a peace offering," he said suddenly, hopefully.

Her smile broadened, taking on a happiness Dalton was relieved to see. Maybe she wouldn't stay mad at him after all.

"What kind of peace offering?" she asked.

He stuffed his hand into his coat pocket and extracted a thin length of pale blue ribbon, embroidered with white flowers, rumpled and crinkled from having been stored for twenty-two years at the bottom of a shoe box in his closet. He pulled it taut between both fists, then let the ribbon fall loose in one hand as he ran the thumb and index finger of his other hand along the fabric to straighten it.

Virginia's heart took wing as she watched him. "You kept it all these years?" she asked softly, reaching for the free end of the ribbon when he released it.

Dalton still gripped the other end in his fingers. When she caught the ribbon in hers, he slowly began to wind his end around his hand, gradually bringing her hand closer. When his fingers were nearly completely wrapped in blue, he flattened his palm against hers and studied her face, wishing he could tell what she was thinking. Her eyes were as blue as the ribbon he held, but nowhere could he detect a hint of what she might be feeling. There were things he wanted to say to her, things he wanted to make clear. But for the life of him, he didn't know where to begin.

"This is how I felt that day when I was fourteen," he finally told her quietly. "You had me wound up in a knot, and all I wanted to do was be close to you. In a lot of ways, Ginnie, that hasn't changed at all in twenty-two years. What scares me now is that I'm old enough to know better, but I still can't seem to help myself where you're concerned."

His words surprised her, he could tell. She no longer looked at him with curiosity and wonder, as she had virtually since the day he'd met her. Now she was watching him as she had that night at his house when the two of them had capitulated to emotions left too long in check. Now Virginia was gazing at him with longing and desire. Dalton knew he should discourage her, knew he should put an end right here and now to what he had reluctantly started. But he also knew something else. He knew he wanted nothing more than to explore the odd friction that was pulling him toward her as if they had become two ionized poles. To resist would be to go against the laws of nature, he told himself. So why should he even bother?

"Dalton," she began softly. "I wish you wouldn't say things like that. You confuse me."

"I don't mean to," he said. "Truly, I don't. I just . . . I haven't been able to stop thinking about you for the past two weeks. I know it's crazy, I know it's wrong—"

"It isn't wrong," she assured him, raising her free hand to cup his jaw. His beard was soft and silky, the skin beneath warm and vibrant. "And it isn't crazy," she said further, as she leaned forward to press her lips briefly against his.

When Dalton tilted his head to kiss her back, Virginia retreated, ending the kiss as quickly as she had instigated it. He watched as she dipped her head to her chest, then released the ribbon and ran her hands anxiously through her hair.

"Or maybe it is wrong," she mumbled softly. "Maybe it is crazy." Her eyes met his again as she added, "But for some reason, it doesn't feel like it."

Dalton straightened, then reached forward to tuck the blue ribbon into the breast pocket of her coat. Virginia's heart pounded wildly behind her rib cage at the soft brush of his fingers against her, remembering that one wild moment at his house when he'd cradled her breast so carefully in his hand. She wished she could rewind all the time they had spent together in Comfort, and replay every frame in slow motion. She wished she could reedit a few of the scenes, too, so that the two of them might have gotten off on better footing, and so that each might have understood from the beginning what motivated the other.

But life wasn't a movie, she told herself. Once the scene was played, there were no second takes. Certainly there was something between her and Dalton that didn't show signs of going away. But he was still coping with a tragedy that had left him unwilling to risk the part of himself he'd once opened to love. And she had decided that the only way to cope with her own painful experiences of the past was to avoid reliving them. And that meant not getting involved again.

She sighed hopelessly. They were two people who had a very real chance of finding something wonderful, something healing, and something permanent together. Yet neither one could afford the risk factor involved in such a chance. If for some reason a relationship between the two of them didn't work out, neither might be able to deal with the loss again.

"Maybe we should just forget about what happened in Indianapolis," Dalton said quietly.

Virginia emitted a single, humorless chuckle. "Forget Indianapolis, forget about what happened at your house two weeks ago. If we keep forgetting what happens, Dalton, we're not going to recognize each other on the street soon."

The fingers lingering at her pocket shoved a handful of her hair over her shoulder in a gesture that was familiar and affectionate. As soon as he realized what he had done, Dalton snatched his hand back, stuffing it into his pocket as if to punish it for its transgression.

"I just meant," he tried again, "that maybe we could start all over again." Before she had a chance to reply, he hastily added, "Could I maybe persuade you to come back to work for me?"

She pushed herself away from the desk and bent to pick up her satchel, silently indicating it was time for them to leave. "I don't know," she hedged, striving to recapture the playfulness of their earlier encounters. Maybe he was right. Maybe they should just try to start over again. "You're a pretty grumpy boss, Dalton. And you're only paying me minimum wage, after all. I'm not sure the aggravation is worth it."

She was teasing him, Dalton thought, relief washing through every cell in his body. That had to be a good sign. His spirits rose a little. "But you're the only one who knows what I want," he said. Quickly he clarified, "For the theater, I mean." Then another thought struck him. "And you promised to help me with Trixie." There, that ought to do it, he decided. Virginia was nothing if not loyal to her commitments.

"Hmm, I don't know."

His conviction began to waver. "Okay, then, how about if I grant you a lifetime pass to the Palace Theater once it's reopened?" he offered.

Her smile this time was undeniably delighted. "Now that's a deal that has real merit."

"So you'll come back to me? To the theater I mean?" God, he sounded like he wanted her back only for personal reasons, he marveled. And of course, he assured himself, that wasn't true at all. Yes, he wanted to return to their earlier friendship, but that wasn't his *primary* reason for needing—or rather wanting, he corrected himself quickly—her back. He wanted her back because no one else in town had the vaguest idea how to paint the theater. And no one else knew anything about the projector. The fact that Virginia just happened to be nice to have around hardly played into his apology and invitation to return at all. Didn't it?

"So can you start this evening?" he asked, hoping he didn't sound *too* enthusiastic.

His question seemed to catch her off guard. "Well, um, actually I sort of have plans this evening."

"Oh."

The one-word reply sounded petulant and disappointed, even to Dalton's ears. Virginia had plans? On a Friday night? Plans that didn't include him? Idiot, he berated himself. Of course her plans wouldn't include him. He was the one who had ordered her out of his life, after all. But that didn't mean she had to go running off into the arms of someone else, did it?

Someone else, he repeated to himself. Someone *else?* What the hell did that mean? She hadn't been in *his* arms to begin with. Well, except for that one night after the movie, he reminded himself, feeling his blood pool in some very dangerous places as a result of the warm memories tumbling through his brain. But that had been a mistake, he assured himself quickly, pushing the memory away. He and Virginia had both thought so. What difference did it make to him if she found something to do with someone else? Why should it matter? But dammit, it did matter. As much as Dalton hated to admit it, the thought of Virginia with another man stuck in his craw like a rusty spike.

She started to explain. "It's nothing etched in stone. I could always tell—"

"No, that's okay," he interrupted her with a wave of his hand. Frankly he didn't want to know the details. If she told him the guy's name, it might be someone he'd met since coming to Comfort, someone he recognized. And if it were someone he recognized, he'd never be able to meet the guy again without wanting to strangle the creep. "You don't owe me an explanation," he assured her. "If you can't work, you can't work."

She looked as if she might continue with her explanation, but he raised his hand again to ward her off.

With a sigh of resignation, she simply concluded, "How about tomorrow then?"

"Tomorrow will be fine."

"I can come early in the morning if you want."

Oh, sure, he thought. Like she was really going to feel like rolling out of bed at the crack of dawn after partying all night with some jerk who would only be after one thing from her.

Stop it! Dalton commanded himself. This was getting ridiculous. He was behaving like some teenage stud who had just pinned his best girl. Virginia was an adult woman with adult needs and an adult sense of responsibility. It was none of his business what her private life involved. None of his business who she saw in her spare time. It was just that simple. But simple could in no way describe the tumult of emotions swirling around inside him like volcanic magma about to erupt.

"Tomorrow morning would be great," he said, injecting a calmness into his voice that he didn't feel. Then he remembered that he had an appointment in the morning and said, "But I won't be getting to the theater myself until around ten, so don't worry about showing up early."

She frowned fretfully. "Darn. I was hoping to get an early start. I think I could pretty well finish what's left of the balcony in one day if I begin early enough. Oh, well."

Without a second thought, Dalton reached into his pants pocket and extracted a ring of keys. "Here," he said as he wriggled one free and extended it toward her. "Here's the key to the Palace. Go as early as you like."

Virginia reached gingerly for the key, fingering it uncertainly. "Really? You don't mind? You trust me?"

He eyed her hopelessly. "Of course I trust you, Virginia."

She knew he was only referring to the theater, knew his trust didn't necessarily encompass any other facets of his life. Still, she found herself wishing he could trust her completely in everything. Because more and more lately, especially after their exchange of this afternoon, Virginia found herself wanting to trust Dalton. To trust him with her safety, her life...even her love. He might just be the one, she thought as she took the key he offered her. He might just be the man who would allow her the opportunity to trust, to love, again. If only he would give her the same chance. If only he might learn to trust, to love her, too.

"Thanks, Dalton," she said softly. There was more she wanted to tell him, more she wished she had the nerve to say. But instead, when she spoke again, it was only to offer with a smile, "I'll stop by the bakery and pick up some breakfast for us. I'll be there for you when you arrive."

She would be there for him, Dalton repeated to himself as they made their way out of her classroom and into the cool, early April afternoon outside. If only she weren't speaking about tomorrow morning alone. If only he could think of some way that would allow Virginia to be there for him forever.

The following morning, Dalton found that Virginia was true to her word. The moment he entered the theater, he knew she had already arrived. Although he could detect no outward sign of her presence, he just knew somehow that she was there. There was a welcomeness about the place he didn't normally feel when he was there by himself. Despite the love he had developed for the Palace Theater, being alone in the cavernous building didn't feel quite right. It was a place meant for hundreds of people, not a solitary man. Yet by the simple addition of one other person, the theater felt better. More natural. More . . . right.

He strode across the lobby to the manager's office, which now actually resembled a manager's office. The stained, yellow cinder block had been plastered over and painted in the same mauve hue as the lobby. The shelves above his new desk boasted booking schedules, ledgers, film books and a variety of histories and biographies of Hollywood and its inhabitants that he had rescued from the bottom of a closet at his house in Indianapolis when he'd gone in search of Virginia's hair ribbon. He wasn't sure why he had brought them all here, when he wasn't planning on staying himself, but he hadn't been using them at home, and maybe someone might find use for them someday. He tossed his mail into the In box for review later and shrugged out of his coat, tossing it casually onto a hook behind the door.

Then he went to find Virginia.

Although his sneakered feet made no noise on the balcony stairs, Dalton made no effort to hide his arrival. Not until he topped the final step and stood at the balcony entrance, and found her sitting atop a tall ladder in her painter's clothes of some weeks before, pressing a stencil flat against the wall as she brushed sapphire-blue enamel over it. When he realized she hadn't noted his arrival, he started to greet her and identify himself, but something stopped him. Virginia, despite being completely wrapped up in her task, he noted with a broad smile, was also singing a song.

"You say you're tired of bein' in that minority," she sang out softly, "responsible for wars, crime and poverty, who statistically speaking will be dead before me, you men might rule the world, but you ain't happy."

She discarded the stencil into a small tray to search for another, accompanying herself with a little air guitar as she did so. Then she began to sing again.

"Now you say you wanna be more like me, and get in touch with your sensitivity, learn to do crochet and calligraphy, you got a bad case of uterus envy."

She dropped the second stencil as soon as she found it, and instead picked up two paintbrushes, then did a little drum solo on the top of the ladder. Dalton couldn't hold in his laughter any longer, and let loose with a rousing roar of it.

Immediately Virginia spun around, so quickly that she almost tumbled from the ladder. She dropped her paintbrushes to grip the top of the ladder fiercely with both hands, steadying herself as best she could while being completely overcome with embarrassment. She watched as Dalton walked toward her with slow, measured strides, feeling herself blush more furiously with every step he took. His laughter had finally calmed to a few scattered chuckles by the time he reached her, and he bent to retrieve her paintbrushes from the floor and return them to her.

"Please," he said with a smile. "Please just tell me that you just wrote the music, and were not the lyricist for that song."

She smiled back a little nervously, trying to quiet her jumpy heart rate. She curled her fingers around the paintbrushes he extended to her as gingerly as she would touch two snakes. "Actually the one who wrote the music was Marsha Delancey, our keyboard player. She conducts the Comfort Symphony now. I, uh, I was in fact the lyricist for 'Uterus Envy.'"

He laughed again. "Boy, you were a real man-hater back then, weren't you?"

She shook her head vehemently. "Not at all. 'Uterus Envy' is a punk anthem in every sense of the word. It's a song that made a legitimate social statement about its time. Back in the mid-seventies, men were beginning to get in touch with their feminine sides. I was just, um, trying to help them along, that's all. Frankly I still haven't figured out where they went wrong."

Dalton nodded doubtfully, but continued to smile. "I see."

"Oh, what would you know about it?" she accused him playfully from her lofty perch. "You were probably the biggest jock on campus. You wouldn't know your sensitive side if it mugged you in a dark alley."

"Yeah, I played football at IU," he verified, still grinning. "Starting lineup. And I was good, too. What of it?"

She shook her head at him with mock disappointment. "It figures."

He took another step forward until there was no room left between himself and the ladder, no room left between his broad chest and her red high-top sneakers. He circled her ankles with his hands, holding her captive as he asked, "And just what's that supposed to mean?"

Virginia bit her lip. Now she'd done it. In addition to stenciling the balcony, she'd also managed to paint herself into a corner where Dalton was concerned. Just what had she meant by her remark? she wondered. She had been looking at him in his tight, paint-spattered sweatshirt and khakis, thinking what an incredibly solid, wonderfully sexy physique he had when she'd made her ill-advised comment. But she could hardly tell him that now, could she?

"Just that, um..." she began nervously, looking everywhere except at Dalton. "Um, I just meant that any man who looks like you do, must have been very... athletic in college."

"Who looks like me?" he repeated in a suggestive murmur. He tugged gently on her ankles until he freed them from the top rung of the ladder, an action that caused Virginia to sway in her seat. She dropped her paintbrushes to the floor again in order to steady herself, but this time Dalton showed no sign that he intended to pick them up. Instead, he only stepped slowly, carefully, up to the third rung of the ladder himself, and circled his waist with her legs before asking further, "And just what does *that* mean?"

His gesture brought Virginia very close to him. His face was parallel to her chest, but he still tilted his head back to gaze up into her eyes. Instinctively she circled his waist more tightly with her legs, telling herself the gesture was simply meant to help keep her balanced on the ladder. And when she turned loose of the ladder to settle her hands firmly on his shoulders, that, too, was an action she promised herself was only intended to help steady herself.

However, when she felt herself leaning forward, dipping her head toward his, she wasn't quite able to convince herself that her primary concern was her equilibrium. Because kissing Dalton would surely be the most dizzying experience she could ever have. Nevertheless, despite a position that was growing more and more precarious by the moment, she found herself doing just that.

"I just meant," she began to answer his question quietly, her mouth nearing his with every breath she took, "that you look very..."

"Very?" he encouraged her, tilting his head back farther in anticipation of her own actions.

"Very..."

Whatever adjective she had intended for Dalton became lost as she brushed her lips softly against his. And as soon as their warm mouths made contact, he turned the tables on her. Where she had been the one who started the kiss, he evidently intended to be the one who would finish it for them.

He raked his clawed fingers slowly up along her legs, pausing to knead the tender flesh at the backs of her thighs. Virginia gasped at the insistent demand evident in the motion of his fingers, a gasp he turned to his advantage by slipping his tongue into her mouth. Immediately she was overcome by a fire in her midsection that threatened to rage out of control. But instead of trying to smother the flames, she only urged them higher by meeting Dalton's exploratory caresses with a few of her own.

Her response seemed to inflame him as well, because the hands at her thighs pressed onward, cupping the soft swells of her derriere as he lifted her from the ladder and pulled her more fully into his arms. Virginia was only half aware that she was floating through the air and down toward the ground. She felt Dalton stumble gracelessly into one of the nearby chairs, pulling her into his lap as he did so. For long moments, they only curled their bodies into each other, touching, tasting, reveling in the emotions they had denied for too long.

Virginia rubbed her hands over Dalton's beard, tangling her fingers in the curly hair at his nape before venturing lower to stroke his shoulders and chest. She felt his hands all over her, first tugging her hair free from its braid to weave the long tresses through his fingers, then journeying more boldly forward. One strap of her overalls had become unbuckled somehow, and he reached lower, to the hem of her T-shirt, bunching the red fabric in his hand and pushing it aside to allow himself entry. His fingers were warm as they strummed her ribs, then rose higher to gently cup the lace-covered swell of her breast. He groaned aloud when he discovered his prize, then kissed Virginia more deeply as he stoked his thumb tenderly over the soft mound.

She, too, uttered a quiet sound of surrender at his gentle touch, turning instinctively in his arms to facilitate his endeavors. As she did so, she shifted her hand from the hard, solid expanse of his chest to dip it underneath his sweatshirt. Virginia nearly fainted at the hard, hot contours of corded muscle her fingers encountered. But instead of retreating, she slipped her hand lower, over the solid length of him pressing insistently against the restraint of his trousers.

If she had thought him solid and strong before, she now knew he was so much more. Cupping him possessively in her hand, she could only want more of him, want him in the most intimate way. Her touch seemed to make Dalton reconsider his actions, however, because he suddenly seized her wandering hand in his and pulled her away. Yet still, he kissed her deeply, still he held her close.

Finally, when Virginia could no longer tolerate the spirals of heat and electricity pounding through her veins, she broke away from him.

"Do you know what you're doing to me?" she gasped raggedly.

Dalton stared back at her wildly, as if he were as lost in their embrace as she was. "I have a vague idea," he told her, his own breathing anything but steady.

"Why?" she asked further, thinking the query a very good question. "Why are you doing this to me?"

He shook his head slowly, obviously as confused as she was, too. Tangling his fingers in her hair again, he tipped her head forward until her forehead rested lightly against his own. "I don't know, Ginnie. I just don't know."

"Dalton, I..."

Virginia wasn't sure what she had meant to say. Something encouraging perhaps, something hopeful. But hopeful was the last thing she was feeling right now. Right now mostly what she felt was confused. Because sitting here with Dalton, kissing him, holding him, touching him, felt so wonderful, so natural, so right. But how could that be? she wondered. How could he generate such responses in her when she had been so certain she would never want to experience that closeness with a man again?

For five years, she had been so certain no man would ever mean enough to her to make her risk the peace of mind and philosophical resolution she had struggled so hard to gain after Dean had robbed her of her happiness. She had convinced herself there wasn't a man alive she would ever trust enough to surrender her heart to him again. Yet here she was, handing her heart to Dalton on a silver platter.

Because somehow, as she gazed into his stormy green eyes, she knew she had been wrong. Wrong about everything. She could scarcely believe it, even as the realization slowly dawned upon her, but somehow, somewhere along the line, she had managed to fall in love with Dalton Cameron. How it had happened, or why, or when, she didn't know. But the warmth and giddiness that rippled through her every time she saw him or thought about him could only indicate one thing. She was in fact in love with him. More in love than she'd ever been in her life.

And now what was she going to do? He was a man battling the ghosts and guilt of having lost his wife and son, a man who had assured her he was in no way ready to commit to a woman again. He was a man who wanted a house full of children. And despite having so much to give to him in the way of love and devotion, children were the one thing Virginia could never provide for him.

What am I going to do? she repeated to herself.

She didn't realize she had also spoken the words aloud until Dalton shifted in the chair to curl his index finger below her chin, tilting her head back to stare into her eyes before he replied, "Well, for starters, you could kiss me again."

He rubbed his lips lightly across hers, flattening his palm against her cheek and burying his fingers in the hair at her temple as he did so. Virginia's turmoil doubled as quickly as her heart rate at the tender caresses, and for one wild moment she allowed herself to enjoy the warm, rapid-fire sensations. His beard and mustache tickled her already sensitized skin, and she smiled against his mouth.

"What?" Dalton asked softly as he pulled away again. "What's so funny?"

"Your beard," she said quietly, skimming her fingertips over the soft strands. "It tickles."

He smiled, lifting his own hand to cover hers and press it more intimately against his cheek. "Does it?" he asked. "I could shave it off if you want."

"No," she cried quickly, her eyes widening in distress. "No, don't. I like it. It's just that I'm not used to it, that's all. I've never kissed a man with a beard."

Dalton studied her face closely, taking in the bewilderment in her eyes he knew reflected what must appear in his own. Her cheeks and mouth were reddened by what was probably a combination of his beard and her embarrassment, and he wished he could think of something to say that might make everything between them all right. But what could he possibly say, when he had no idea how to explain the morass of disorder tangling his thoughts? How could he describe for her what he was feeling when he didn't even know that himself?

What on earth had made him kiss Virginia like that? he wondered. All he could remember now was coming upon her in the balcony to find her in a thoroughly carefree state of mind, a state that was completely lacking inhibitions. She had thought she was alone, so her guard had been down. Dalton couldn't remember a time when there hadn't been some kind of barrier she'd erected between the two of them. Since meeting her, she had affected an air of distance, however slight, that had simply expressed her unwillingness to become involved with him or anyone else. Not that she had been aloof or standoffish, he allowed. Just the slightest bit . . . uninterested.

But this morning he had seen a new side to Virginia. With her singing and playing of imaginary instruments, he'd seen a playfulness, a sense of the absurd he hadn't detected in her before. And he liked it. Although he'd already realized she was fun to be around and laughed a great deal, this new knowledge of her ability to be so uninhibited had tugged at something inside of him he'd forgotten he was able to feel. She'd made him feel warm again. Capable of laughter. How could he resist such a temptation?

For the first time in two years, Dalton had glimpsed a brief, surprising vision of what his life *could* be like, how it could be different, more enjoyable. For a moment, he completely forgot about his lonely house in Indianapolis, forgot about his demanding career and empty life there. For a moment, all he saw was the abundance and bounty, the wealth of life that Virginia Gennaro could offer. So he'd reached out for her, for all the warmth and laughter she could provide. He'd kissed her. And kissed her again. And when she'd kissed him back with such undeniable desire of her own, he had only wanted her more.

But now he told himself he must close the window on that vision of Virginia. Slam it shut and throw a heavy drape across it. There was no way he could take advantage of all she had to offer him. It wouldn't be fair to simply take from her without ever giving anything in return. Because as much as he might want to, he had nothing of himself left to give her. He'd been tapped dry of his emotions more than two years ago, and nothing could ever refill him. She'd already experienced one unhappy marriage, and she deserved so much more than he had to offer her. She deserved happiness. She deserved a man in whose emotions she could feel secure. And happiness and security were things Dalton knew he could never provide for her. How could he, when he knew he was never going to feel secure or happy, truly happy, himself again?

"Virginia, I..."

He what? Dalton wondered. Boy, he'd really managed to muck things up this time.

"Dalton, don't worry, I understand."

He looked at her again, watching in amazement as her expression changed from intimate desire into something that resembled a kind of melancholy resolution. "You do?" he asked softly. "That's funny, because I'm not sure I understand this myself."

She disengaged herself from him and stood, discreetly tugging her clothing back into place before sitting down in the seat next to his. She reached over and clasped his hand in hers, pulling it over the armrest to cradle it in her lap.

"It's like you said at your house that night. We've both just been alone so long, and for some reason, there's this strange attraction between the two of us. An attraction that neither wants, but one we can't seem to battle very well."

"Are you so certain that's all there is to it?" Because Dalton sure as hell wasn't so certain the case was so simple with him anymore.

She nodded. "Of course. What else could it be?"

He opened his mouth to answer her, but the only sound that emerged was a soft sigh. So instead of replying, he simply lifted his shoulders in a half-felt shrug.

Virginia nodded her comprehension, yet felt anything but understanding.

"So what are we going to do about it?" he asked her further.

This time it was her turn to shrug. Because for the life of her, she didn't have the vaguest idea. "We could try to ignore it. Pretend this never happened," she suggested half-heartedly.

He shook his head. "We tried that already, after that night at my house, remember?"

How could she forget? Virginia wondered miserably. "Well, then…" She thought for a moment. "We could try to stay out of each other's way."

"That's not likely to happen while we're both going to be working on the theater together," he pointed out.

"Maybe we could work in shifts."

He shook his head. "You see, Virginia, the problem is I don't want to ignore you. I don't want to forget about you. And I don't want to stay out of your way."

His voice had lowered to a soft, sultry caress, and she shivered at the exquisite sensations shimmying down her spine as a result. "Then wh-what do you want?" she stammered quietly.

The hand she held in her lap reversed the position until her own hand was enclosed in his. After a quick squeeze, Dalton brushed his fingertips gently across her palm, an action that elicited a few more shivers from Virginia, then withdrew his hand completely. When her eyes met his, there was no need for him to answer her question out loud. He wanted to make love to her, she realized with no small amount of amazement. His desire was as clear as a summer day. Unfortunately so were his intentions. She could tell immediately that although he wanted her, he would not seek satisfaction for his longing.

"I... I guess I should get back to work now," she said suddenly, rising quickly from her seat and pushing past Dalton into the center aisle of the balcony before he could stop her. "I still have a lot to do if I'm going to finish up here today as I promised you."

But before she could completely retreat, Dalton circled her wrist with strong fingers to prevent her from returning to her work. "Virginia," he said softly.

His voice, so quiet, so solicitous, stopped her more quickly than his physical strength ever could. He sounded confused and disconcerted and... hopeless. She had no choice but to turn around and meet his gaze.

"Would it be safe to assume we've left things between us just a tad unfinished?" he asked.

She nodded helplessly. "I think that's a safe assumption, yes."

He nodded. "Good. Just so we understand each other."

She couldn't help but smile. "Oh, sure. No problems there, no sir."

Dalton rose from his seat, too, following her as far up the center aisle as the last row. Once there, they parted ways, she to her right and he to his left. And as Virginia climbed the ladder to complete the project she had begun, Dalton descended the balcony stairs feeling as if he'd just started something he had absolutely no way of ever finishing.

Chapter Nine

Despite his assurances to the contrary, Dalton did in fact seem to avoid Virginia for the next several weeks. She showed up to do her detailing nearly every evening and weekend, usually to find him working in a part of the theater completely removed from wherever she was working herself. Often she came across him poring over paperwork at his desk or conveniently on his way out to run some errand. On those occasions, he would lift his head and hand to offer her a perfunctory greeting, then immediately return to whatever he was doing, citing a problem with the booking schedule or a face-off with the plumber.

His reluctance to see or talk to her was more than a little disconcerting for Virginia. Twice now she had kissed him, and twice had been offered a glimpse of what it might be like to give herself completely to the man. There was no doubt in her mind now that she had fallen in love with Dalton, and the knowledge that he might never feel the same way stung her deeply. If only there were some way she could help him work through his feelings for his wife and son, she often found herself thinking. If only she could help him envision a future for the two of them as clearly as the one she was beginning to see herself.

But inevitably, she would be forced to remind herself that, even if she could inspire him to look toward a renewed future, Dalton's vision of such a future would include something her own did not. Children. He'd made no secret that he wanted them. He'd already lost one, and knew the acute pain that accompanied the loss of a child. Virginia understood that pain, too, to some extent. Although she'd only been twelve weeks along when she'd lost her baby, she'd already come to feel a deep and abiding love for the child. She'd made plans. She'd made preparations. And she understood the desolation that came with having those plans dashed and destroyed. In that, at least, she comprehended Dalton's grief completely.

She knew she was crazy to set herself up for more pain. She told herself that every day. But she couldn't stop wanting him, couldn't stop needing him. And the knowledge that his emotions didn't run as deeply as her own left Virginia feeling as if she were lacking something somehow. The fact that he could so easily rouse such a reaction in her after years of convincing herself that she was all right also made her feel a little angry. Angry at Dalton for being so damnably attractive. Angry at herself for letting him get to her in such a way.

Now as she put the finishing touches on her mural behind the concession stand, she heard him hammering at something directly above her in the projection room. Every time she lifted her detail brush to touch up a delicate line or fine-tune a tiny particular, something metallic and annoyingly loud clattered to the floor, or Dalton shouted some creative expletive she'd never encountered in her work as a second-grade teacher.

She shook her head, studied the mural, then glanced down at her watch. It was nearly ten-thirty, and she was coming to a good stopping point. She decided she would just finish the last two art-deco styled letters in the word

Palace that appeared on the painted rendition of the marquee outside the theater, and then she could go home for a nice long soak in the tub.

After carefully completing the *C*, Virginia dipped her brush into the paint again to dab the last bit of color on the *E*. Just one more tiny stroke and she would be done...

"*Dammit!*" she heard from upstairs. The shout was followed by what sounded like a hammer being hurled against a brick wall. She jumped, and the paintbrush in her hand went skidding outward to the left, then back to the right, so that suddenly, her art-deco *E* looked like a top hat with two Viking horns.

"Dammit yourself," she muttered through clenched teeth, lifting a paint-spattered rag to rub away the offending letter before it dried. She tossed her paintbrush into a coffee can half-filled with mineral spirits, trying to tune out the string of unintelligible complaints that followed Dalton's initial outburst. When it appeared he had no intention of halting his derisive commentary anytime soon, she slammed the coffee can down on the tarpaulin below her with a thump hard enough to send some of its contents spilling over the side and onto her fingers. Wiping her hand on her overalls, Virginia blew an errant strand of hair out of her eyes, and mumbled to herself, "That does it. This has gone on long enough."

She stomped across the lobby and pushed open the projection room door with a mighty heave, trudging up the stairs with deadly intent. When she reached the landing, she stood at the entryway to the projection room with her feet planted firmly apart, her hands doubled into fists at her hips. Dalton lay sprawled on the floor at the base of the huge projector, an open toolbox beside him. He apparently hadn't heard her come up, which was no surprise to Virginia, because he was again pounding irregularly and loudly on something she was sure he had no business pounding.

"Do you mind?" she shouted in a voice she hoped rivaled the volume of his own some moments ago.

He started at the booming question that came from no-where, banging his forehead soundly on the metal casing of the projector as he lifted his head to discern the origin of the query. Virginia took some satisfaction in the knowl-edge that she'd startled him so. Until he wriggled out from beneath the projector and glared at her. Until she saw how angry he was. And realized the anger was directed at her.

"What the hell are you yelling about?" he shouted back. "Jeez, you could have given me a concussion."

She gathered herself together again and glared right back at him. "If you ever expect me to finish the work you hired me to do," she stated in a low, careful tone of voice, "you're going to have to do me one favor."

He rubbed at a place on his head just behind his hair-line, streaking a smudge of black dirt across his forehead as he did so. "What's that?" he asked warily.

Virginia inhaled deeply and yelled, *"Shut . . . up!"*

His hand stilled its motion, but he didn't remove it. He gazed at her blandly from beneath slightly curled fingers, giving her the bizarre impression that he was saluting her. Having said all she wanted to say, she spun around to go back downstairs, but Dalton's command halted her.

"Stop right there."

She hesitated, but wasn't quite able to gather her nerve enough to pivot around and face him. Instead, she only stood silently at attention with her back to him. For a long moment, he didn't speak, then she heard him toss some-thing back into the toolbox with a muffled clank, followed by what she thought sounded like a deep, impatient sigh.

"You're not going anywhere, Ginnie."

She couldn't remember the last time he'd addressed her with the familiar, affectionate nickname, and hearing him do so now caused her no small amount of turmoil. Finally she spun slowly around and met his gaze. "Oh, no?" she asked skeptically.

He shook his head slowly, meaningfully. "Not until you tell me why you're so mad at me."

Gee, where should she begin, Virginia wondered. She mentally listed the reasons. Let's see, she thought, she was mad at him because he'd been so wonderful, mad at him because she'd been helpless not to fall in love with him. Mad because he'd aroused in her feelings she had banned from her heart. Mad because he made her want things and dream of things she had expressly forbidden herself to desire. Mad because he would never love her back.

But after a moment's silence, all she said aloud was, "I'm mad because you messed up my *E*."

He narrowed his eyes at her, his eyebrows drawing downward in confusion. "I messed up your *what*?"

"My *E*," she repeated impatiently. "You know, *E*. A, B, C, D... *E*."

Dalton was certain he must be misunderstanding, that his bump to the head must have just disoriented him a little. Surely what Virginia was telling him made sense somehow. He just had to stand here for a moment and let the fuzziness in his head clear, and ponder her outrage, her indignant posture and fiery eyes. Surely there was some cogent, simple reason for her to sing the first part of the alphabet song as she had. Any minute now, a perfectly clear understanding of the situation would dawn on him.

"I... I'm afraid I don't understand," he said a moment later.

She rolled her eyes heavenward. "My *painting*," she told him irascibly. "My mural of the theater. With all your thundering and slamming around up here, you made me mess up."

He slapped a hand to his forehead in a gesture of mock censure. "Oh, *that* E," he said indulgently, as if he should have realized exactly what she'd been referring to all along.

His lips trembled at the corners, threatening to smile, an action he battled fiercely. A smile would only serve to destroy the lousy mood he'd been striving to keep alive for weeks, ever since the last kiss he and Virginia had shared in the theater balcony. Since then, Dalton had been feeling edgy and uncomfortable about something, lying awake most nights in an effort to pinpoint exactly just what that something might be. Now as he studied Virginia in her baggy, messy painters' clothes, in all her righteous indignation, he knew precisely what the something was that had been bothering him. It hadn't been some*thing* after all, but some*one*. Virginia Gennaro.

And now of course, he had to laugh at himself, because the realization came as no surprise at all. Of course he would be bothered by his preoccupation with Virginia. That last kiss had been one of the most enjoyable experiences he'd had in a long time. Even more enjoyable than the first one, because it had lacked the awkwardness of the first time. That second kiss had been more natural than the first, somehow, more...right. The problem was, Dalton still had no idea what he was doing.

"I'm sorry if my work up here was disturbing you," he said. "But Trixie is giving me a hard time."

Virginia frowned at him. "I don't blame her, with the way you're treating her. She's a sensitive bit of machinery, Dalton. You have to be gentle. Patient. You have to treat her with respect."

He wondered briefly if they were still talking about a movie projector, then decided it didn't matter. Allegory had never been his strong suit. He didn't much cotton to people who didn't speak frankly.

"She won't respond to me," he said. He cocked his head to the side in confusion for a moment, sure he had just told himself he was done speaking in symbolic terms. "And I don't know what to do to get back on good terms with her."

Virginia tilted her head back to stare at the ceiling and muttered, "Men. They just don't get it." Then she approached the old projector, and laid a comforting hand on the big saucer that would accommodate the first reel of a major motion picture.

"You have to forgive him, Trixie," she said softly. "He's new in town." To Dalton, she added, "Do you have a flashlight?"

He reached behind himself and pulled the instrument in question from his back pocket, extending it toward her, handle first. Virginia tried to ignore how warm the metal handle had become thanks to its intimate position in Dalton's back pocket, and instead switched it on and turned the beam toward the place where he had removed a perfectly square plate to reveal the projector's inner workings. A rainbow maze of plastic-coated wires looped and wound through each other, and below them a series of metal dots and dashes winked back at her in the light. Although not a new sight for her, it was one she hadn't viewed for over a decade, and she tried to remember exactly what she might be looking for.

Trixie's moody, but she's a nice gal, Eddie's rusty voice came back to Virginia from twelve years ago. For a moment, she could almost feel the old man looking over her shoulder. *You just gotta know when to stroke her and when to give her a good, swift kick in the tuckus. Mostly, though, you gotta remember that the red wire feeds the green wire, which feeds the blue wire, got it? Red, green, blue. Like reverse alphabetical order. Forget about the yellow wires. They don't do nothin'. Least, I ain't figured out what they do.*

Tucking the flashlight beneath her chin so that it threw a perfect circle of light into the compartment, Virginia went to work. With a few deft maneuvers, she twisted the wires around until they were connected in the way Eddie had instructed her so many years ago.

"Try her now," she said when she withdrew her hands, snapping off the flashlight and handing it to Dalton.

He looked utterly skeptical, but flicked the main switch to the On position anyway. Immediately Trixie began to click and hum and rattle, a sound so familiar and so nearly forgotten to Virginia that she laughed out loud. Dalton stared at the projector incredulously, then he, too, broke out into a smile. With the turning of another switch, the projector's light sputtered to life, and on the other side of the auditorium, a huge, white rectangle of light burst into being on the movie screen.

"You did it," he said with a chuckle. "I don't know how you did it, but you did it."

He came around to the other side of the projector and clapped his hands on her shoulders in congratulations. "She works. I can't believe it, but she does." He leaned forward and kissed Virginia quickly, innocently on the mouth. "Thanks, Ginnie," he said. Then he seemed to realize what he'd just done, and his eyes sobered. When he leaned forward again and took her mouth, he was anything but chaste, and anything but brief.

Virginia was completely unprepared for it. One minute the two of them were reveling in their success, and the next, she was caught up in a hot, ravaging desire unlike anything she'd ever known. He limned her lips with his tongue, then darted deep inside to taste her more completely. Her knees buckled at the intimate, demanding touch, and she felt herself crumple to the floor. Dalton moved right along with her, catching her to his chest before moving both their bodies into a horizontal position. He cradled her head on his forearm as he moved his body over hers, rubbing himself sinuously against her. Helplessly she wound her arms around his waist and pulled him closer, too delirious to give her actions a second thought.

For a long time they lay on the floor of the projection room, their kisses becoming more demanding, their explorations bolder, with every passing moment. Only when Virginia felt Dalton curl his fingers over the tender flesh of her breast did she finally begin to realize how far they had gone, and how fast.

"Stop," she said as she tore her lips away from his.

Her chest rose and fell in ragged rhythm as she struggled in vain to slow her pulse. Dalton lifted his head to stare down into her eyes, but his big body held her pinned to the floor.

"Why?" he demanded roughly. "You were enjoying it as much as I was."

Although she couldn't deny the truth in his assertion, she knew a verbal acknowledgment would only prolong their current, uncontrolled behavior, something that would undoubtedly be a mistake.

"Dalton, look where we are, what we're doing. This isn't the place for it."

"This is the perfect place," he countered. "This theater is a place that's important to both of us." He smiled fondly as he added, "It's where we first met, remember? Why shouldn't we make love here?"

Virginia squirmed beneath him. "Because it has a concrete floor," she grumbled. "A cold, hard concrete floor." There, that was as good a reason as any, she thought.

But Dalton's eyes only grew darker, more impassioned as he said, "Then you can be on top."

Her pulse rate doubled at his roughly uttered suggestion, an agonizingly clear image of what he proposed blazing itself to the forefront of her brain. It was the position they had been in when they'd called a halt to their lovemaking at his house weeks ago, and she was terrified to realize how arousing the thought of reestablishing that posture was now.

"No," she whispered. "It isn't right. Not like this, Dalton. Not just yet."

He looked at her for a long time, taking in her disarrayed hair and rumpled, paint-spattered clothes, focusing on two dots of black paint near her lip. She smelled strongly of mineral spirits and her floral perfume, a combination he found oddly appealing. "If not now, then when?" he asked hoarsely. "Because I can't take this much longer. I am going to make love to you, Ginnie. And soon."

His words invaded her muddled thoughts like a warm balm. She should be offended, she told herself. He was making assumptions and assertions he had no right to make. But she couldn't deny them. She didn't want to. She was as anxious as he to make love. But not on a cold, concrete floor, in an ancient movie theater full of ghosts.

"We'll know when the time is right," she finally told him. "Somehow, we'll know."

He nodded almost imperceptibly, but didn't remove himself right away. Instead he smoothed a hand over her hair and down her cheek, brushing the backs of his bent fingers along the sensitive skin of her jaw and throat. He tipped his head forward to kiss her one more time, then rolled away from her and sat up, reaching a hand out to help her follow.

Virginia took his hand and rose to a seated position as well, eyeing him cautiously as he did so. "Can I ask you a personal question?" she asked suddenly.

He seemed as surprised by her query as she was herself, but nodded. "Sure."

"Are you involved—intimately, I mean—with your next-door neighbor?"

At first Dalton was extremely confused. His next-door neighbor in Comfort was Mr. Eustis McGroarty, a grizzled old man of indeterminate years, who did nothing but grumble and accuse him of trampling his rosebushes. Any suggestion that the two men might be involved in *any* way was disturbing. But intimately? Absolutely not. Then he realized Virginia was referring to Shari back in Indianapolis, and relief filled him.

"Of course I'm not intimately involved with Shari," he told her. "What kind of a question is that?"

But instead of answering Dalton's question, she demanded further, "Why aren't you?"

He stared at her in disbelief. "You think I *should* be involved with Shari?"

"Well, she is very attractive, don't you think?"

He shrugged. "I guess so. Yeah, she's all right."

"And she seems to like you."

Virginia noted a slight twitch at the corner of his eye as he responded, "She and I get along okay, I guess."

Forcing herself to push onward, determined to find an answer with which she could be completely satisfied, she continued, "And she's got three great kids you obviously get along with very well."

His expression continued to be wary as he said, "Yeah, so? What's your point?"

"Well, it just seems to me, Dalton, that the two of you would make a perfect couple. Add her kids into the picture, and you'd have the perfect family. I just can't figure out why the two of you haven't gotten together, that's all. It seems kind of... odd to me."

"Odd," Dalton repeated blandly. "Odd." He stood and went over to the projector, which was still running, and switched it off. "What's odd, Virginia," he said softly when he turned around again, fixing her gaze intently with his, "is that you're trying to foist me off on another woman after one of the most pleasant gropes I've ever experienced."

She felt herself color at his frankness, but refused to look away. "All I'm trying to do is put things into perspective," she told him. "Like why you keep throwing yourself at me, when I have so little to offer you, when you could have the family of your dreams in Indianapolis."

Dalton wanted to be outraged by her statement, but unfortunately had to admit there was a grain of reason in it. Why was he so irrevocably attracted to Virginia, a woman who lived almost a hundred miles from his home, who clearly had no desire to pursue a permanent relationship, who was physically unable to have a family, when Shari had let him know on more than one occasion that she was more than available for all of those things? He liked his next-door neighbor, liked her a lot. She was a nice person, easy to talk to, fun to be around. Her kids were terrific. But there hadn't been the tiniest spark between them as far as Dalton was concerned. Not once could he remember a time when he'd even wanted to kiss her.

And then there was Virginia, a woman for whom he'd felt an immediate awareness, an immediate desire. What was it in her that reached him when other women had left him cold?

"I don't know, Ginnie," he replied honestly. "You're right. Shari's terrific. But there's absolutely nothing between us beyond a nice, casual friendship. I don't...I don't *want* her. I don't feel a need for her. You, on the other hand..."

He approached her again, extending his hand to help her up. She took it reluctantly, boosting herself as he pulled her toward him. The double action caused her to pitch forward more quickly than she had planned, and she wound up back in his arms again, feeling edgy and warm and unwilling to let him go.

"You on the other hand," Dalton began again, "make me feel things I can't even begin to describe."

Virginia gently disengaged herself from him, and moved slowly back toward the door. With one final glance over her shoulder, she began to turn away again, but as they had before, his words stopped her.

"When the time is right, Ginnie."

It was all he needed to say. Soon enough, she thought, they would have to submit to the desires burning them both up inside. Soon enough, they would be making love.

Chapter Ten

The three weeks that followed flew by in a blur. All too soon, April became May, giving Virginia and Dalton little time to worry about their personal relationship, because they worked at double-time speeds to complete the finishing touches on the theater. For the grand reopening, he planned a celebration reminiscent of a Hollywood premiere, complete with spotlights outside and an invitation-only, black-tie guest list. Together, they worked frantically to make sure everything would be just perfect for the affair, and together they succeeded admirably.

By reopening night, the theater looked wonderful. As Virginia stood in the lobby, pondering her surroundings, she couldn't help but compare it to the Palace Theater of her youth. Gone was the aura of decline and neglect that had been so prevalent back then. Gone, too, were the dark, dingy colors and harsh lighting that had made the lobby then seem stark and overbearing. Now the lobby fairly gleamed in its new attire, the soft mauve walls and pale blue recessed lighting evoking a genteel quality the old building had lacked before. Even the carpeting, a diamond pattern in sapphire and amethyst, added to the richness and elegance inherent in the theater now. Potted palms scattered around the lobby completed the look. She felt as if she had stepped back in time some sixty years and was awaiting the premiere of Cecil B. DeMille's latest epic.

Dalton exited his office then, dressed in a white dinner jacket and dress shirt, his black trousers perfectly pressed and pleated, a black bow tie knotted expertly at his throat. Virginia couldn't help but sigh. There wasn't a single leading man in Hollywood who could compare in looks or demeanor. Nothing would please her more than if the two of them could star together in a feature-length lifetime.

She gazed down at her black velvet gown, tugging up a spaghetti strap that kept threatening to fall down. The dress was authentic enough for the occasion—it had belonged to Virginia's grandmother, and was on loan from Lana. Her mother had also dug deep into an old jewelry box and discovered a pair of huge rhinestone earrings that virtually covered Virginia's ears with the extensive starburst pattern. A matching brooch was pinned at the top of her dress discreetly between her breasts, and it caught the light to explode in a prism of sparkling color.

Dalton approached her slowly, ogling her shamelessly from head to toe as he came. "You look magnificent," he said as he took her hand in his. "And I don't care what they say... snoods should never have gone out of style."

She automatically lifted a hand to the strawberry-blond tresses caught up in black netting that was studded with rhinestones and topped by a black velvet bow. The snood had belonged to Lana, too, and Virginia had almost foregone wearing it tonight. But she'd liked the effect when her mother had finished arranging the accessory for her, and at Lana's encouragement had decided to wear it after all. Now Dalton's praise only added to her enjoyment of having dressed so formally for tonight's grand reopening.

"You don't look so bad yourself," she replied, skimming her thumb and forefinger along the length of his lapel. She straightened his tie, even though it was already perfect, and smiled. "Bogie and Cary have nothing on you."

He raised his eyebrows and smiled. "Why, thank you. That's quite a compliment."

She nodded. "You bet it is. There aren't many men alive who are more attractive than Humphrey Bogart and Cary Grant."

"And you, my dear," Dalton said, pulling her playfully into his arms, "put Veronica Lake to shame."

She inclined her head slightly to acknowledge the compliment. "Really?"

He studied her face for a long time before responding, then bent his head to press a soft kiss at her temple. "Really," he whispered as he drew away. He framed her face in his hands as he added, "You are quite possibly the most beautiful woman I've ever seen, Ginnie. And having spent a good portion of my life in dark theaters, I've seen the best of them."

She covered his hands with hers, turning her head slowly so that she could place a soft kiss first on one palm and then the other. His eyes widened at the intimacy of the gesture, and he tilted his head slowly toward hers. But just as he was about to kiss her, the entrance door into the lobby rattled and shook as someone outside pounded loudly to gain entry.

"We'll finish this conversation later," he said softly as he pulled away.

Virginia nodded again silently. She wondered if Dalton was feeling as muddled and feverish as she, wondered if the longing and desire swirling frantically inside her mirrored anything he might be feeling himself. She wondered if he was thinking what she was thinking—that tonight, for some reason, would be the perfect occasion for the two of them to make love.

She watched as he went to unlock the door, thinking that no man alive could do justice to a white dinner jacket in quite the same way that he did. He threw her one final, wistful gaze as he turned the key and opened the door, then pushed it open to allow in the two very early arrivals.

Virginia smiled when she saw her mother and brother. Lana was dressed to the nines in a blue-beaded number and heels, while Evan looked edgy and annoyed in his dark suit, clearly unwilling to be at the reopening. Where Virginia had inherited her mother's slender, delicate Scandinavian features, Evan Gennaro was every inch his Mediterranean father's son. With his thick black hair and dark complexion and eyes the color of bittersweet chocolate, he resembled his sister about as much as a Studebaker did. Yet the two siblings were a handsome couple, as Lana took pride in pointing out to anyone who would listen. Her children might be single, she often grumbled, but not because they weren't attractive.

"Oh, Dalton, you look wonderful," Lana gushed as she entered. "We just had to come early. We couldn't wait to see the place."

"She had to come early," Evan corrected his mother. "If it had been left to me, I'd be home watching the Cubs."

Lana frowned at him. "Oh, Evan, lighten up. We don't even live in Chicago." She turned to Dalton, resurrecting her smile. "This is my son, Evan, Ginnie's brother. I don't think the two of you have met."

Dalton extended his hand to the other man, wondering why he seemed so angry. Virginia's brother sized him up from head to toe before shaking his hand, and even then the gesture was wary.

"Hello," Evan said quietly. "Pleased to meet you."

Funny, Dalton thought, he didn't sound pleased. "Likewise," he replied anyway.

Evan strode away and Lana moved in to express her amazement at the changes Dalton had wrought with the theater.

"This place used to be such a dump," she said with a shake of her head. "Now it looks like a...like a...well, like a palace. It's going to be such a pleasure coming to movies here again. On behalf of the entire town, I thank you."

Dalton smiled. "You don't know how happy it makes me feel to hear that. I hope everyone in Comfort feels the same way you do."

"Oh, they will," she assured him. "You've put so much into this place. It's just a shame that you're not planning on staying here to run the theater yourself."

Her words caught him off guard. He had forgotten that in a matter of weeks he would be returning to Indianapolis permanently. For some reason, the realization didn't set well with him. He was surprised to discover that he would greatly miss this little corner of the world. Comfort had been more of a home to Dalton than anyplace else he'd ever lived. He tried to reassure himself that in Indianapolis, he'd only be a little over an hour away, close enough to visit almost anytime he wanted to. But the thought did little to ease his mind.

Virginia came forward then to stand beside her brother, kissing him briefly on the cheek. "It was nice of you to come to the reopening, Evan," she said as she linked her arm through his. "You'll make Natalie a very happy woman tonight."

He grimaced. "I don't even want to think about what it would take to make Natalie Hogan happy. I'm not here because of her." He turned his back on his mother and Dalton, his voice lowering to a near whisper as he added, "I'm here because Mom threatened to come over and cook for me every night next week if I didn't show up at this stupid reopening."

"Well what's so terrible about that?" Virginia demanded. "Mom's a terrific cook. And God knows nutrition has no place in the Evan Gennaro diet. You could probably use some home cooking."

He stared down at his sister as if she were from another planet. "Ginnie, I have a couple of dates next week with some very intriguing women. The last thing I need is Mom hovering around."

"*Some* dates?" she repeated. "With a *couple* of women? As in more than one?"

Her brother nodded. "I'm no English major, but last I heard, *women* was plural for *woman*."

She shook her head at him disapprovingly. "You're hopeless, Evan. Absolutely hopeless."

He smiled back at her, a smile Virginia recognized as his dangerous one. "No, Ginnie, I'm hopeful. If you saw these two women, you'd understand why."

She frowned. "I'll try to be as gentle as possible when I break the news to Natalie."

Evan's back went up at the mention of the other woman's name. "This is none of Natalie's business, and I'll thank you to keep my personal comings and goings to yourself."

"Why do you dislike Natalie so much?" she demanded.

"I don't dislike her, she just..."

"What? She's intelligent, articulate, has a great sense of humor. And she's beautiful."

"God, don't you think I know how beautiful Natalie is?" he snapped suddenly.

Virginia raised her eyebrows in surprise. "Well, that's the first I've heard about that."

Evan ran a restless hand through his hair, then shifted his shoulders uncomfortably. "Natalie just... she rubs me the wrong way, that's all."

She was about to press the issue, but her brother interrupted her before she had a chance.

"So what's the story with this guy, Dalton, Ginnie? Mom can't seem to talk about anything else lately. Are you and he... you know... serious?"

"If you're wondering whether or not we've slept together, Evan..." She shook her head in mild wonder at the way he twisted up his features at her bluntness. Brothers were so unwilling to face facts when it came to their sisters' sexuality. She tried to be understanding as she concluded, "The answer is no."

The relief on his face was undeniable, and Virginia couldn't help but smile. Her big brother had always been overprotective. But after what had happened with Dean,

Evan had gone out of his way to check up on her. She supposed that, like her mother, he felt more than his share of anger at her ex-husband. Certainly Evan had made it clear what he would do to Dean if he ever saw the other man again. She shuddered in spite of herself. It wasn't a pretty picture.

"Don't worry about me, Evan," she said softly. "Dalton is different from Dean. He's kind and gentle and very, very sweet. He'd never hurt me."

"We all thought Dean was pretty great once upon a time, too, if you'll remember. And look how that turned out."

She hugged her brother fiercely. "Don't worry" was all she said again before releasing him.

Shortly after that, Dalton's newly hired employees began to arrive, most of them students from Anderson College. The ushers were dressed in short royal blue jackets decorated with gold braid, their black trousers sporting a stripe of blue down along the sides. The cashier and concession workers wore identical black trousers, with crisp white shirts and black bow ties. Virginia thought everyone looked marvelous in the attire. With all its new trappings, the theater even felt different. Somehow, she knew the Palace was pleased by the turn of events, and somewhere, she was sure Dalton's uncle, Eddie Schneider, was nodding his complete approval.

She recalled a conversation she'd once had with Dalton in which he'd expressed his confusion about why his uncle had willed him the Palace upon his death five years ago. At first Virginia had thought Eddie must have done so because his nephew loved movies as much as Eddie had loved them himself. But now she understood a little better. Eddie must have known somehow that Dalton's affection for the Palace would ultimately lead him to fix her up, and knew that his nephew had the financial funds to do so. In short, Eddie had known he would take care of the old place. And of course, being the kind of man he was, Dalton had done just that. He was a man who was devoted to the things and people he loved, whether he realized that or not. Certainly Eddie had seen that in his nephew. And of course, Virginia did, too. Now if only she could convince Dalton of his capacity to love again. But how on earth could she manage that alone?

Within the hour, and little by little, more guests began to trickle in. In no time at all, the lobby of the theater began to fill with people, all of them dressed in the finest attire they owned, excited and buoyant that the long-awaited re-opening of the Palace had finally arrived. And as the hour neared seven, the time assigned to the showing of *Casablanca,* the crowd began to wander into the auditorium. Only when Dalton was about to close the doors behind them did one final guest come barreling into the lobby from outside—Natalie, almost out of breath and nearly out of time, but looking stunning in a form-fitting, silver sequined gown.

"Am I too late?" she asked breathlessly, clutching the hem of her dress in both hands and lifting it above her knees to run forward.

"You just made it," Virginia told her, chuckling at the sight her best friend created. "Dalton's just getting ready to go up and start the first reel now."

She was about to offer to show Natalie to the seat Lana was saving for her in The Fabulous Fourth Row, but she saw her brother emerge from the men's room at that moment and got a wonderfully wicked idea. "Oh, Evan," she sang out loudly. "Look who's here. Natalie. Why don't you show her to her seat. You know, the one Mom saved between her seat and yours?"

The expression on her brother's face was murderous, but Virginia only smiled. Then she saw him turn his attention to Natalie, his eyes lingering on the length of well-shaped calf still visible beneath the hiked-up hem of her gown. Immediately Natalie realized where his gaze had strayed, and she dropped her dress back into place, blushing furiously at the fact that she had been witnessed in such disarray by the one man she wanted to find her irresistible.

"I know how unpleasant Evan can be sometimes," Virginia said to her friend in an aside she didn't bother to hide. "But it would mean so much to him if you'd sit beside him at the movie tonight."

Natalie's smile was dazzling as she gazed at Evan. "I'd love to."

Virginia watched her brother approach with the wariness of a jackal, then she pushed him toward Natalie until the other woman could tuck her arm possessively beneath his. As the couple walked away, Evan shot his sister one final, killing look, then followed his escort helplessly into the darkened auditorium. Her mother would be proud of her, Virginia thought with a smile. Perhaps she was her mother's daughter after all.

"All set to get this show on the road?"

She heard Dalton's voice from behind her, and spun around to find him smiling at her. This was the moment he'd been building up to for four months, a moment she had helped him achieve. It gave her more pleasure than she would have guessed to realize she had been an integral part of an undertaking that was obviously bringing him such joy. The two of them had worked so well together, and the Palace had turned out beautifully thanks to their efforts. If only there were some way they could rebuild their future as effortlessly as they had this old theater. And if only the future would be as wonderful, as full of delight, as the Palace was now.

"I'm more ready than you know," she told him with a smile.

Dalton bent to kiss her quickly, chastely on the mouth, then pushed open the door to the projection room behind him and climbed the stairs. Virginia followed close behind, until the two of them stood on each side of Trixie, staring through the viewing window at the crowd below. Soft murmurs rose from the room along with the aroma of freshly popped popcorn. Dalton touched a switch on the wall to his left, and the scarlet velvet curtains began to slowly part across a freshly whitewashed movie screen.

Then the turn of a dial brought the house lights down gradually until the auditorium was settled into darkness.

He nodded to Virginia, who flicked the switch on the projector, and both of them watched in wonder as the huge saucers turned, looping the celluloid film up and down and around before feeding it into Trixie's innards. Another switch threw a small rectangle of light through the viewing window, a rectangle that grew and grew as it spread out over the crowd until a huge white light splashed to life across the movie screen at the opposite end of the room. The sound of an orchestra swelled up at the same time from a number of speakers throughout the auditorium, followed by flickering black-and-white images that were larger than life.

"We have achieved film," Dalton said with a huge grin. "The Palace Theater is in business again."

"Congratulations," Virginia whispered happily.

His gaze met hers over the top of the projector, and she was helpless to look away. "I couldn't have done it without you, Ginnie," he told her quietly. "Thanks."

She shook her head slowly. "You don't have to thank me for anything, Dalton. I'm the one who should thank you. For bringing so much back into my life."

His expression became a little confused as he asked, "What do you mean?"

"The theater," she said quickly, trying to recover herself. She hadn't meant to speak so frankly. "You've brought the Palace back to Comfort. This place has always been a special place to me. For years I . . . I've felt as if I lost a part of myself. And now you've given it back to me. I should be thanking you."

"No, Ginnie, you're wrong. Whatever was missing in your life, you brought it back for yourself. You were as instrumental in recreating the Palace as I was. You love it as much as I do, and it's only right that we did this together. I wish . . ."

His voice trailed off, and he didn't finish whatever he had been about to say.

"What?" she asked him softly. "What do you wish?"

But Dalton only shook his head and remained silent. He had almost told her he wished the two of them could go on together, could tackle some new project that needed fixing. His life, for example. He wished Virginia might help him refurbish that. But such a wish would be impossible to grant. There wasn't enough paint and plaster in the universe to patch the empty places inside of him. Even the sturdiest hammers and nails couldn't rebuild all that had been destroyed.

But maybe Virginia Gennaro could, a little voice inside piped up unbidden. *If only you'd give her a chance.*

But Dalton wouldn't listen. Virginia couldn't know how deeply he was hurting inside, couldn't understand the magnitude of his grief. How could she help to rebuild something she didn't know the first thing about?

The two of them watched the first movie in silence, then headed back down to the lobby for the fifteen-minute intermission between films. After the second feature ended, the two descended again to say farewell to all who had attended the evening's affair and send the last of their workers home. When the last of the well-wishers had left, Virginia turned to find her mother exiting the auditorium, followed closely behind by Evan and Natalie. The couple still had their arms linked as they had before, but the gesture seemed more familiar now for some reason, less strained.

"Well, that was absolutely wonderful," Lana said as she took Dalton's hand in hers. "I haven't had that much fun at the movies since Eddie showed a double feature of *My Man Godfrey* and *Bringing Up Baby.*"

"I have both of those scheduled for August," he told her with a smile.

She nodded her approval. "Then I'll be seeing you in August."

"Oh, no, I'm afraid you won't," he told her. "I'll be going back to Indianapolis at the end of June."

"Oh." Lana didn't even bother to hide her disappointment. "Well, maybe you'll change your mind."

"No, I—"

"Thanks, Dalton," Natalie interrupted him before he could complete his denial. "We had a great time."

Evan, too, expressed his happiness at seeing the theater up and running again, shaking Dalton's hand this time with what seemed like genuine pleasure. Then he settled his arm comfortably around Natalie's waist—voluntarily, Virginia noted—and the two of them exited the theater behind Lana.

And then Virginia turned to find that only she and Dalton remained.

"I think it's safe to assume that the evening was a smashing success," he said softly, locking the exit doors before pulling down the shades to indicate the theater was now closed.

She nodded. "Boy, I'll say it was. You're going to have crowds on your hands every night at this rate."

When he turned around again, he only stood for a moment watching her, the expression on his face revealing not a clue as to what he might be feeling or thinking. Just when the silence was about to drive Virginia crazy, he moved, striding quickly past her without a word, headed in the direction of the manager's office. Curious, she followed along slowly behind, halting just short of reaching the door when she heard a crisp, clear *pop*.

She smiled. There wasn't another sound in the world like that of a champagne cork leaving the bottle in a festive rush. She peeked around the office door and saw Dalton splashing a generous amount of the pale gold liquid into a long-stemmed glass, purposely pouring too much so that the foam bubbled up to the rim, and down over his fingers. Immediately Virginia sprinted forward and pressed her lips to the rim of the glass, laughing as she drank in what she could of the excess. After the threat of overflowing seemed no longer imminent, and before she realized what she was doing, she began to lap lightly at the champagne that still dripped from his fingers.

The touch of her warm tongue mingling with the cold champagne spilling over his hand made Dalton's insides explode in a riot of sensation. He placed the bottle on his desk, and with his free hand curled his fingers below her chin, to tip her head back until he could lose himself in her eyes. Without looking away, he removed his other hand from her loosened grasp, blindly setting the glass of champagne down beside the bottle. Then without giving Virginia or himself time to consider what he was about to do, he bent his head and took her mouth with his, kissing her as he had never kissed her before.

All the passion, all the longing of more than two years roared to life inside of him when he touched his lips to hers. If he had thought their earlier kisses had sent him spinning out of control toward disaster, this one would surely be the end of him. He didn't know why he needed so desperately to feel her closeness then, or feel it more completely than he ever had before. He only knew that one minute he and Virginia had been going about the motions to end the evening, and the next he'd realized he simply didn't want the evening to end. Suddenly, he realized with no small amount of fear, he wanted nothing more than to make the evening last forever.

He deepened the kiss then, pulling her into his arms to twine their two bodies together. She responded by wrapping her arms possessively around his neck, urging him closer, then closer still as she kissed him back with a fierceness and longing that rivaled his own. Two hearts hammered an identical ragged rhythm, two mouths celebrated the ultimate sensual experience, two minds linked together in united joy. Dalton felt himself pitching forward, taking Virginia with him, bending her over his arm as he kissed her more fully. One hand at her waist snaked upward to yank loose the snood, freeing her hair until it spilled down his arm like a red, raging river. He tangled his fingers in the silky tresses, cupping his palm at the back of her head, pushing her mouth more insistently against his.

Virginia felt dizzy and delighted, outrageous and out of control. Everything was happening so quickly, so spontaneously. She'd had no way to prepare, no warning for what was to come. This kiss was nothing at all like the others she and Dalton had shared. Before, she had always felt some degree of restraint within him, a clear indication that the kiss would go no further than a simple, if mind-scrambling embrace. Now that restraint was gone. Nothing in his posture implied that he had any intention of reining himself in should things progress too far. He wouldn't be stopping at a kiss this time, she realized vaguely as she felt his lips at her temple, then her cheek, then her throat. She rejoiced in the anticipation of what would come next.

The arm circling her waist grew taut as she felt his other hand leave her hair and caress her back, then move forward to pause at the base of her rib cage. Dalton pulled away to gaze into her eyes as his fingers crept upward, stroking each rib as if playing a celestial harp, curving over her breast to palm the peak to life. Then his fingers reached higher, thumbing the strap of her gown down over one shoulder. His eyes lowered to the creamy expanse of skin revealed above the top of her dress, his hand following to stroke over the warm flesh. Virginia could feel her pulse quicken beneath his fingertip as he dipped into the small hollow at the base of her throat, and closed her eyes helplessly when he placed a warm kiss there.

Dalton had never smelled anything as sweet as the soft skin beckoning him close. His tongue flicked over the warm skin he had just kissed, then his hand strayed to the rhinestone brooch pinned between her breasts. Gently he removed it, then lowered his mouth to kiss the soft swells of her breasts rising ever so slightly above the black fabric. When he splayed his hand open across her back, he encountered her gown's zipper, and he moved his hand upward until he found the metal clasp closing it. Bit by bit, he drew the zipper downward, feeling the soft velvet come away above his hand. When her back was bared nearly to the waist, Dalton hooked his index finger beneath the strap of her gown and slowly, oh so slowly, began to draw it down her arm. Virginia sighed almost imperceptibly as he did so, her eyes darkening as her pupils grew large with wanting.

Beneath the black gown, she wore a black strapless brassiere, something lacy and translucent and utterly arousing. Dalton bent his head forward to taste her through the filmy fabric, touching the tip of his tongue to the tip of her breast with infinite care.

"Oh, Ginnie," he groaned as he forced himself to pull away. His eyes were languid and dark when they met hers, his mouth parted as if he intended to taste her this way forever. "You make me want things I shouldn't want."

"Why shouldn't you want them?" she asked him breathlessly, feeling bolder than she ever had before. "There are things that I want, too, Dalton. And I'm tired of denying myself. Tired of telling myself no. If I want things...if I want you...then why shouldn't I have you?"

His eyes darkened even more at her declaration, and the hand cupped below her breast flexed to gently squeeze the tender mound. "I want you, too," he whispered roughly. "God help me, I want you so badly. But not here, not like this. When I make love to you, Ginnie, I want to be in my bed, in my house, where I can take my time and not overlook a single thing."

Virginia was scarcely coherent enough to answer, yet managed to murmur, "But your house is in Indianapolis, Dalton. And it's so big, so empty. If we have to go there, we might never find each other."

Once again, he had forgotten that Comfort wasn't his home. And for tonight, if never again, he wanted it to be. "My house here," he clarified. "Please, Ginnie. Come home with me tonight."

Immediately she nodded her agreement, threading her fingers through his hair to bring his lips to hers one final time. "Yes," she said after she kissed him. "Let's go home."

He smiled at her, but Virginia could see he wasn't entirely sure about what they were planning to do. She didn't blame him for being uncertain. She was more than a little frightened herself. But nothing in the world would change her mind. Making love with Dalton felt like the most natural thing she'd ever do. And perhaps, just perhaps, if they made love, he might come to understand that what the two of them had created together over the past few months could overcome any obstacle the fates threw in their way. She was so certain of that herself. Why couldn't Dalton feel the same way?

After tonight, she promised herself. After tonight, maybe he would.

Chapter Eleven

They arrived at his house in record time. Dalton had stashed the open bottle of champagne in the silver ice bucket where it had been chilling all night, had gathered it and Virginia into his car and had driven through the dark streets of Comfort like a pro. Now as they stood facing each other at opposite ends of his living room, he suddenly felt awkward and uncertain. His earlier passion still simmered just below the surface, but somehow he had clamped a lid on it too tightly, and was unable to set it free.

Virginia seemed to sense his uneasiness, but didn't press him. Wordlessly she strode to the coffee table and pulled the champagne from its resting place, the ice rattling against the silver bucket as it shifted the only sound in the otherwise silent room. She refilled the glasses they had hastily emptied at the theater and held one out for Dalton, then sipped idly from her own. She smiled at him, and suddenly the anxiety that was clenching his heart began to ease its hold.

"Did I tell you how beautiful you look tonight?" he asked softly, still not quite ready to approach and accept the glass she offered him.

Her cheeks grew pink at the question, and she shifted her gaze to study a worn spot on the carpet. "Yes," she replied quietly. "Yes, you did. Thank you."

He closed the distance between them in three easy strides, extending his hand slowly to close it over hers when he reached for the glass of champagne. Without releasing her, he asked, "Did you mean what you said earlier tonight? That you . . . want me?"

Virginia tried to tug her fingers from beneath his, but Dalton took the glass with his free hand and wove her fingers with his own to prevent her escape. When she looked up to meet his gaze, her eyes caught the soft light in the living room, throwing back an unmistakable reflection of desire.

"Yes, I meant it," she told him. "I know it sounds crazy, but I think I've wanted you from the moment I laid eyes on you. I just wasn't willing to admit it. To you or to myself."

He nodded. "I feel exactly the same way. There's something about you, Ginnie. I don't know what it is, or why I picked up on it so immediately, or why I want you and no one else, but . . ." His voice trailed off, and he shrugged his confusion. "You've made me feel alive for the first time in more than two years. And I don't want that feeling to end. Not just yet."

Virginia wanted to assure him that the feeling didn't have to end at all, that it could go on forever if he'd only allow it to. But the time for talking was over. They had waited so long, had battled so many obstacles to finally arrive where they were now. They had too many wants that needed fulfilling, too many desires that demanded satisfaction to worry about anything else right now. She sipped her champagne one final time, then set her glass on the coffee table. Dalton did likewise, swallowing nearly half the contents of his glass before putting it down to join hers. Then, as if both had heard some unspoken instruction, they came into each other's arms.

What began as a tentative, exploratory kiss gradually escalated to a fierce demand. The moment their lips touched, time dissolved away to nothing, and they were back to the passionate embrace they had forced themselves to end only a short time ago. Dalton felt Virginia's hands circle his neck, her fingers entwining themselves in the curly hair at his nape, and he hooked his own hands at the small of her back, pulling her closer toward him. And when he felt the soft contours of her body pressing so intimately against his own, he felt himself go a little wild.

The hands at her waist splayed open and rose higher, caressing every inch of her they encountered as they went. When Dalton felt the warm skin of her back above her dress, he fumbled for the catch of her zipper, then slowly drew it downward, recalling again how soft, how warm, how tender Virginia had felt beneath his fingertips before. The black velvet fabric of her gown slowly opened, exposing another kind of velvet for him to explore. He lifted his hands to the straps of her dress at her shoulders, lifting them until the two thin strips of cloth fell away. The dress pooled in a dark heap at her waist, exposing the ivory skin of her torso and the scrap of black lace covering her breasts that he had only glimpsed earlier.

He pulled away, his gaze skimming down over her body and lingering at her breasts, at the way the pale skin rose in two perfect arcs above the black lace. He was helpless to do anything but stare. She was exquisite. Incredible. The most beautiful sight he'd ever beheld. And she was his. If not forever, at least for tonight. He knew he shouldn't allow himself the pleasure, knew he didn't deserve to be this happy, if even for a little while. But Dalton also knew there was no way he could deny himself, no matter how hard he might try.

"Dalton, you're embarrassing me," she said softly as she crossed her arms shyly over herself.

Immediately he pulled her arms away again, settling them behind his neck. "No, don't be embarrassed," he told her. "I'm sorry, Ginnie, I just haven't... You're just so... I just can't seem to keep my eyes off of you."

She snuggled close to him, luxuriating in the feel of the rough fabric of his dinner jacket rasping against her sensitive flesh. Two could play this game, she decided then. She hooked a finger through one loop of his bow tie and tugged gently, freeing the length of silk from its bond. Slowly she pulled the tie away from his collar, then began to unfasten the gold studs in his shirt one by one, tossing each over her shoulder as she went. The casual scattering of *click... click... click* as each stud made its landing on the hardwood floor caused Dalton to smile. But that smile disappeared when she raked her fingernails softly over his bare chest and shoulders, shoving away his shirt and jacket in one easy move.

Virginia's breathing became ragged and unsteady when she encountered the hardness, the strength, the sheer power of his body. Fully clothed, the man looked potent. But once those trappings of civilization fell away, he was magnificent. She had felt the contours of his muscle before and had known his physique would be well formed and solid. Yet she hadn't realized what kind of raw awareness his naked form would arouse in her. The pale brown hair on his face only hinted at the dark swirls decorating his chest, a virtual plain of masculinity that swept from one side of his torso to the other, narrowing only slightly as it approached his waist.

As if helpless to stop themselves, her fingers tangled themselves eagerly in the curls on his chest, lingering in their exploration to touch every inch of him. She recalled vaguely that her husband had been clean-shaven and had sported no hair on his chest. Virginia rejoiced in Dalton's obvious differences, loving the fact that his body varied so completely from her own, yet had been formed to be so utterly complementary.

She felt the dress at her waist slip lower, curving over her hips like an exotic sarong. Instinctively her fingers skimmed lower to cover Dalton's belt buckle. When her eyes met his, she saw two green flames flickering with an unknown fire. For a long moment, neither of them moved or spoke, then he tipped his head forward in an almost imperceptible nod, and Virginia pulled the length of leather free. The button of his trousers protested at first, or perhaps she was simply growing too weak to accomplish her task. When her struggles became more insistent, his hand covered hers to still the movement, but didn't remove her fingers entirely. Unable to tolerate even this small distance that had come between them, she leaned forward, touching the corner of his mouth gently with the tip of her tongue before limning his lips completely.

Dalton closed his eyes in an effort to ease the jolt of electricity her tender touch sent shuddering throughout his nervous system. The heat of her body was a powerful surge against his. The soft lace of her brassiere became a torturous instrument when she pressed herself more intimately against him, rubbing herself like a cat who's found a friend for life. Her hand at his waist shifted a little when she stood on tiptoe to kiss him, and he flexed his fingers more insistently against hers, pushing their hands lower, back and forth along the hard ridge that strained against his trousers.

He felt her go limp in his arms as he continued the caress, heard her breath catch before she emitted a small groan of desire. Only when he felt as if the intimate touches would send him over the edge did he remove their hands, then clamped his arms around Virginia and bent forward, taking her mouth with his in a searing kiss.

"Upstairs," he whispered roughly when he pulled away. "Right now."

She nodded helplessly, clinging to his shoulders to keep herself from hurtling off into some unknown abyss. She had intended to walk beside him as they climbed the stairs, their arms entwined, their bodies perfectly matched step for step. But with one swift, easy gesture, Dalton swept her up into his arms, and carried her toward the staircase and up the stairs before she even had a chance to react. The next thing she knew, he was settling her gently at the center of a huge four-poster bed in his darkened bedroom, the only illumination provided by the bluish white light of a street lamp outside.

And then he was beside her in the bed, kissing her again with all the need and demand of a man who's been too long without satisfaction. She didn't have time to feel worried or anxious, didn't have time to wonder if what they were doing was right. It must be right, she told herself. Because nothing had ever felt more wonderful.

His touch was everywhere. The soft silk of his beard tickled her in places that had never been ticklish before, and his lips warmed and aroused every inch of her. The black velvet dress disappeared somehow, leaving Virginia in her lacy black underthings instead. For a moment she thought those would disappear, too, then she rolled to her back and opened her eyes to find his silhouette towering over her like a looming specter. Light filtered in through a window behind him as he came up on his knees between her legs, giving him the appearance of a dark shadow. The shadow came closer then as Dalton bent forward, his big body pausing only inches shy of touching hers, and her pulse pounded in her ears as she waited to see what would happen next.

A touch. A simple touch, what might have been a harmless gesture if offered by someone else. But the feel of his fingertips skimming lightly over her face and throat made Virginia come unwound. His hand went lower then, thumbing the hollow at the base of her throat, then dipping lower still, his fingers pausing at the slight cleft between her breasts rising from a deep V in her brassiere. Her breathing became raspy as he ventured farther, pushing away the lacy fabric as he went. The cool night air kissed her breasts as they were bared to the darkness, then Dalton bent his head to taste them, to warm them once again.

His mouth closed over her hungrily, pulling and tugging and demanding, as if trying to slake an impossible thirst. His hand circled her other breast, alternating palming the soft mound and fingering the rosy peak to rigid life. Virginia could only lay still and let wave after wave of sensation ripple through her, could only tangle her fingers in his hair and hold him close, and hope that he never, ever stopped.

How had she lived for five years without this kind of intimacy? she wondered vaguely. And then she realized that even during the happiest moments of her marriage, she had never felt this close to Dean. The emotions Dalton roused within her were new and unfamiliar. She hadn't been prepared for that. Although she had acknowledged the fact that she loved him, she hadn't realized the depth of that love, the all-encompassing scope of that love. Nothing in her life had felt the way loving Dalton did. And for the first time she understood that losing him would be more than painful. It would be crippling, inconsolable, devastating. She couldn't make love to him and let him go. She just couldn't. Somehow she had to make certain they stayed together forever.

Her thoughts then gradually began to approach delirium, because Dalton chose that moment to focus his attentions elsewhere. The hand on her breast ventured lower, his mouth following closely behind. Virginia's brassiere did in fact disappear then, as did her panties and stockings. After that, things became a little fuzzy and incoherent, probably because her temperature rose to feverish heights. For a long time, she only wandered in and out of a semiconscious ecstasy, growing ever nearer an explosion of sensation like nothing she'd ever felt before.

And then Dalton was beside her again, turning her to face him, kissing her as he urged her fingers down toward his waist. When Virginia encountered the waistband of his trousers, she pushed petulantly at the fabric in a fruitless effort to remove the obstacle. With his help, the two succeeded in their task of disrobing him as well, and only then did she fully begin to appreciate what a truly perfect human form could be.

Dalton was magnificent. As she closed tentative fingers around the long length of him, Virginia sighed with complete delight. But after only a single stroke of her hand, he pushed her over onto her back, nearly climbing atop her to still her motions.

"It's been a while, Ginnie," he bit out a little raggedly. "I may not be able to hold out much longer. I'm sorry, I—"

"Shh," she whispered with a dazed smile, touching two fingers to his lips. "You've already given me things no one else ever could. It's been a while for me, too, remember? But I don't recall a time when I've ever felt this good. I—" She stumbled over the word "love" and replaced it with "want" instead, then pulled Dalton close to kiss him once again.

Apparently satisfied with her answer, he came to her then, entering her not with the raging, demanding thrust she might have expected under the circumstances, but with a slow, careful, tentative motion. For a moment, neither moved, only luxuriated in that one simple gesture of closeness neither had enjoyed for so long. He kissed her deeply, his mouth and hips both pressing more intimately against her to reach as far inside her as he could before withdrawing to repeat the action again. He tried to move slowly, tried to prolong their joining as long as he could. But having Virginia so close after having wanted her for so long hastened his lovemaking.

Yet she stayed with him, her own culmination joining his, and they both cried out as they reached that sensual apex together and fell eagerly into the slow descent beyond. Afterward, their bodies slick with the sheen of perspiration, and sensitized beyond feeling, they lay silent, clinging to each other to keep the morning at bay, letting the night time envelop them into its dark, erotic mystique.

Sometime before dawn, Virginia opened her eyes to the most wonderful awakening she'd ever known. Dalton lay behind her, spooning her warm body against his, his hand cupping her breast with a familiarity brought about by numerous episodes of lovemaking. His beard tickled her neck and ear as he kissed her. She smiled, stretching her body languidly, marveling at the exquisite achiness tightening places she'd never known to ache before.

"What time is it?" she asked sleepily.

"I don't know," he murmured in reply. "And frankly, I don't care."

She rolled over in bed to face him, her smile growing broader. "My, but don't we sound grumpy this morning. What's the matter? Didn't you get enough sleep last night?"

He gathered her close, kissing her hair, her temple, her cheek. "Mmm... What I didn't get enough of last night was you."

After one final kiss, he settled her against him, wrapping one arm around her shoulder as he tucked her head into the hollow created between his own shoulder and jaw. "Won't your mother be worried about you not coming home last night?" he asked softly.

Virginia chuckled. "Are you kidding? She's probably having champagne for breakfast. I think she's disappointed every time she comes downstairs to find that I *haven't* spent the night with a man."

He rubbed his cheek thoughtfully against the top of her head. "Boy, mothers sure have changed a lot over the years."

She sighed, reveling in the warm closeness of waking up beside a man she loved so dearly. "My mom just wants me to be happy. She knows that I'm a grown woman with relatively good judgment, and she trusts me not to place myself in a dangerous situation."

The irony of her words stung her, even as she spoke them. Sometimes falling in love could be the most dangerous activity a person could undertake. It was a lesson Virginia had learned all too well, one she hoped desperately she would never have to study again.

She felt Dalton laugh. "I guess I should be flattered that Lana doesn't suspect me of being a knife-wielding maniac."

Before she could stop herself, Virginia replied, "There are other dangers besides the obvious ones, you know. And those are the ones that can be most deadly."

He stiffened almost imperceptibly beside her, and there was a moment of silence before he replied, "I'm the last person you need to tell about that."

At the dangerous calm and absolute soberness she heard in his voice, Virginia turned her head to face him. The playfulness and easy affection they had enjoyed only moments ago had fled, to be replaced by a solemnity she didn't understand. Then she finally realized he was thinking about his wife and son. He hadn't understood that she was talking about her own marriage. He had simply assumed she was speaking of his own past tragedy.

"I'm sorry, Dalton," she apologized hastily. "I didn't mean that the way you think. I wasn't talking about your own experience."

He relaxed somewhat, but didn't relent completely. "Then what were you talking about?"

As unwilling now as she'd been before to speak of the particulars of her marriage, Virginia bit her lip to keep from spilling out all the anxiety and emotion she was feeling inside. Instead she only shook her head, silently pleading with him to let the subject drop.

Unfortunately he didn't seem too willing to cooperate. Because instead of switching to a new topic, Dalton set her away, reaching for his watch on the nightstand beside him. She looked across the faint darkness and saw the luminous dials angled into the position of 5:25. Almost angrily, he tossed the timepiece back to its resting place, then straightened his legs out before him and crossed his arms over his broad chest. She felt him retreat from her as clearly as she would have had he risen from bed and left the room entirely.

"What are you thinking about?" she asked quietly, even though she was fairly certain she didn't want to hear his response.

For a moment, she feared he wouldn't reply, then he sighed raggedly and ran a restless hand through his hair. "What do you think I'm thinking about?"

Virginia sighed, too, folding her body into a ninety-degree angle as she leaned her back against the headboard. "Your wife," she replied softly. "And your son."

He nodded. "You know, it's probably just as well that you brought the subject up."

"I didn't mean to, Dalton, I—"

He held up a hand to stop her. "No, honestly, Ginnie, it's all right. I suppose I was being overly optimistic in hoping that we might prolong this...this..." He flexed his fingers open, as if trying to pull a word out of thin air, then closed them into a tight fist again. "Our time together," he concluded quietly. "But it would probably be better if we just cleared the air right now."

"Cleared the air?" she asked, confused.

He nodded, but didn't look at her. "What happened tonight, although enjoyable and enormously satisfying..." He paused, glancing at her quickly before turning away again. "It shouldn't happen again, Ginnie."

A cold fist clenched her insides, driving the air from her lungs in a fitful *whoosh*. She told herself not to panic, reminded herself that she had been prepared for a reaction such as this one. But at some point during the night, she had begun to think they had moved beyond barriers and obstacles to find a freedom and openness they could enjoy together. In his willingness, even eagerness, to make love to her, he had seemed to put the past behind him and look toward a future with her. She had begun to assume that in time things between them were going to be all right. But obviously she had been grossly, sadly mistaken.

She forced her voice to be calm and steady as she asked, "Why shouldn't it happen again?"

"Because, call me old-fashioned, but what happened between us last night was an experience that shouldn't be shared by two people unless they're in love, that's why."

Virginia bit her lip, wondering how much she should reveal to him. Be honest, she told herself. Drastic times called for drastic measures. And what could be more drastic than honesty?

"At least one of us *was* a person in love last night," she said quietly. "And she still is this morning."

He shut his eyes tightly at her announcement, snapping his head backward to land against the headboard with a less than gentle thump. "That isn't what I need to hear right now," he told her.

Her mouth twitched with a mixture of sadness and uneasy happiness. "Well, that's too bad. Because I do love you."

"Ginnie, you can't," he told her, his eyes still closed, his head still tipped back.

She arched her eyebrows in surprise. "What do you mean, I can't? It's too late, Dalton. I love you. I can't help it. Emotions aren't things that you can turn on and off at will. You can't control how you feel."

He finally opened his eyes, turning his gaze on her with a steady, predatory gleam. Enough early-morning light had crept into the room from outside for her to see that he looked distant, indifferent and completely cold. "Yes, you can," he said quietly, coolly, even, Virginia thought, a little angrily.

She shook her head. "No, you can't."

He emitted a single, mirthless chuckle, his lips stretching into a smile that was anything but happy. "Sure you can. I've been doing it for years."

She narrowed her eyes at him, drawing the sheet up around her in an effort to chase away the chill she felt creeping into every fiber of her being. This wasn't the Dalton she knew and loved. This man beside her in bed was a complete stranger. She felt as she had so many years ago when she'd first seen changes in Dean. Maybe she'd been wrong about Dalton after all, she thought as a thick lump of ice formed from nothing in her stomach. Oh, God, what if he was about to turn on her, too?

"Don't look at me like that," she whispered, unable to keep the fear out of her voice.

As soon as she uttered the request, he complied, his expression changing from one of utter disregard to complete concern. "Ginnie, what's wrong?" he asked. "Why are you so frightened?"

She relaxed when the old Dalton returned, but couldn't quite console herself about the stranger she had glimpsed for only a moment. "You . . . you startled me for a minute, that's all," she said softly. "With all that talk about manipulating your emotions."

"I'm sorry," he said. He still didn't understand her sudden, fearful reaction, but he sighed deeply, and then tried to explain. "There's something I have to tell you, Ginnie, something you should know about me," he began again, his voice quieter and calmer this time. "But I'm not sure where to begin."

She reached across the bed, touching her index finger briefly to his lips, then dropped her hand onto the mattress between them. She couldn't imagine what he might tell her about himself that she didn't know already, but she said, "Maybe the beginning would be a good place."

When his eyes met hers they were resolute and melancholy. "All right. I'll go back to the beginning. Even back before I lost Penny and Dylan."

He took a deep breath, as if trying to fortify himself for what he had to reveal. When he spoke again, his voice was low, level and oddly detached. "You have to try to understand how difficult it is to do what I do for a living. To perform surgery on an adult human being is stressful enough—to know that you may well be the one factor keeping that person alive.

"But a child, Ginnie, a child who hasn't even had the opportunity to experience and enjoy life yet . . . you can't imagine how it feels to know you hold the preservation of that child's life literally in your own hands. And too many times, my hands, my expertise, haven't been enough to keep those children alive. Every time I lose a patient, I feel like a failure, as if I'm somehow responsible for that loss of life. The sense of helplessness, of defeat, of depression that comes along with that feeling ... It can be numbing, almost dehumanizing in its effect."

He opened his hand on the stark-white sheet that lay across his lap, as if searching for something he once held dear and had lost somewhere along the line. When Virginia placed her own hand against his, he squeezed it briefly, then released it, setting it aside.

"Long ago," he began again, "I learned to retreat to a place inside myself that numbed the pain after experiencing losses like those. Eventually I became so good at it, and my distancing became such second nature, I took it home with me every night after work, erecting a wall between myself and my family that none of us was ever quite able to breach. I wasn't as close to Penny and Dylan as I should have been, as I wish I could have been." He turned to gaze at Virginia completely as he told her, "And the same thing would only be true if I became involved with you."

"But that isn't true at all," she was quick to contradict him. "When you first came to Comfort, you were a bit distant and standoffish, but you've changed completely over the past four months. You're accessible, warm ... affectionate. And unless you've been faking all that, Dalton, you're not the same man you were before."

"But don't you see?" he demanded anxiously. "That's only because I've been here, removed from the demands of the hospital. Once I go back to Indianapolis, once I go back to medicine, all that will come to an end."

"But how do you know that?"

"Ginnie, you don't understand. You don't know what it's been like to lose my family the way I did, you can't comprehend the anguish, the helplessness, the hopelessness. For the last two years, I've been eaten up with guilt, replaying over and over again in my mind how many times

I could have shown Penny and Dylan how much I loved them, how many times I even could have *told* them. How many ways I could have changed the outcome of that damned weekend when they were killed."

Virginia was about to speak, uncertain what she might say that would console him and reassure him. But Dalton rose from bed, completely ignoring his nakedness, and paced across the room to retrieve his robe from a hook on the closet door. He didn't return to bed then, but sat down in a chair on the other side of the room. He clasped his hands together between his knees, and hung his head in anguish.

"And every time I lose a patient now," he continued softly, "I lose my son all over again. No one could be expected to rebuild his life after all I've seen. Certainly I'm not the kind of person who could. My only hope now is to retreat once and for all to that place inside me where I don't feel anything, where I can hide out and spend the rest of my days trying to nurture what little peace of mind is left in me."

Finally he lifted his head to gaze at her, and Virginia didn't think she'd ever seen anyone look so sad.

"Loving you, Ginnie, would only cause me more turmoil. I couldn't live with the constant worry that someday I might lose you, too."

For a long time, she didn't speak, only echoed all that he had told her in her mind, searching for the right words that might help him make sense of what was happening between them. Unfortunately she could scarcely make sense of it herself. Still, she tried anyway.

"You know, Dalton, a lot of people experience significantly painful experiences at some point in their lives. But if they try, and with a little help from the people who care about them, they can usually manage to overcome the tragedy and leave it in the past where it belongs. A lot of times, they even go on to be very happy."

She was tempted to tell him about what had happened to her during her own marriage, about an experience painful enough to rival his own, and about how she had overcome adversity with the help of people who loved her and eventually moved forward in her life. But looking at him now, seeing him so utterly defeated and unwilling to change his way of thinking, she realized he was in no state of mind to listen to what she might have to say or try to understand her.

"Maybe it would be better if I just left," she announced softly. Later, when the two of them were thinking more clearly, she would try again.

When Dalton said nothing to dissuade her, Virginia died a little inside. Wrapping herself awkwardly in the bed sheet, she rose and collected her scattered clothing, telling herself not to cry as she picked up the crumpled velvet gown from the floor. She had embraced such high hopes for the evening when she had dressed only twelve hours earlier. Twelve hours, she marveled. Only half a day. That's how long it had taken to completely shatter her world.

As she struggled to dress, the bed sheet fell down around her hips. Before she could gather it again and lift it over her, Dalton's hand shot out to wrap around her wrist and halt her action.

"What's this?" he asked as he pulled her toward him. He rubbed his thumb gently over the thin pink line to the left of and just below her navel. "It looks like a surgical scar."

"It is," she said, touching the scar with him. Her voice faltered only slightly as she added, "That's where...that's where the doctors tried to mend me."

Dalton didn't look at her face, but continued to stroke his finger over the small, dark flesh that was her constant reminder of what she would never have. "And just how did you become broken to begin with?" he asked softly.

But Virginia only shook her head silently and tugged the sheet up over her again, forcing his hand away as she did so. As she hastily dressed, she told herself her unwillingness to talk about her past was in no way similar to Dalton's reluctance to deal with his own problems. She had come to terms with her tragedy, had learned to live with it and be happy.

Hadn't she? Of course she had. The problem in their relationship lay with him, not her. She loved him. Readily, unconditionally. And she knew he felt something for her. No one could make love to another human being the way he had to her unless there was some amount of affection involved. Was it love on his part? She wasn't honestly sure. But whatever he was feeling had the potential to be love, she just knew it.

If only she could figure out some way to help Dalton find his way there.

Chapter Twelve

With her work at the Palace completed, Virginia had no reason to visit the old theater, unless she happened to feel like going to a movie. And after the way things ended with Dalton, movies were the last thing on her mind. She went out of her way to avoid him for a week, steadfastly dodging places like the Purple Iris Café and the supermarket near their homes, in addition to the Palace Theater. She hoped allowing him those seven days without her might help him put into perspective the lovemaking they had shared and the incongruity of his ensuing announcement that he would never be able to let himself love her. She hoped he would contact her at some point in the week, hoped that by leaving him alone, he might realize on his own how essential and timeless the bond they had created together had become.

But when he did not call or contact her during that week, Virginia began to wonder if perhaps she had been wrong. She had assured herself that Dalton was already more than halfway to loving her because he had been so tender, so wonderful when they made love. His technique hadn't been the practiced, passionate mauling of a man who wished only to assuage some physical need left too long unsatisfied. What the two of them had shared together had been meaningful, momentous and unforgettable. It had been, in a word, loving.

At least that's what she had considered it. And when it appeared as if Dalton might not see the event in the same light as she, Virginia began to wonder if perhaps the situation called for her taking a more active role. She decided at the end of seven days that it was time to face him again. Maybe the lovemaking they had shared together hadn't been enough to bond them for life after all. Maybe what was necessary now was a bonding of their souls. Perhaps the time had come for her to talk again about her own experiences, her own demons.

Perhaps the time had come for them both to face the ghosts of their pasts.

The Palace Theater was closed on Monday nights, so Virginia chose that night to visit. Somehow she knew Dalton would be there instead of at his house, despite the fact that no films were scheduled to be shown. The theater had become something of a haven for him, she suspected, much as it had been a sanctuary to her in her youth. And when she drove up Monday night to see his sleek, black sports car parked in the center space before the theater, she couldn't help but smile sadly.

The front doors were unlocked, and she pushed one open silently, finding the lobby softly lit, but clearly empty. A further inspection of the manager's office found it, too, vacant. So Virginia entered the theater auditorium, making her way slowly down the left aisle toward the screen in front. Perhaps he was working behind it as he had been before, she thought. Patching a few more holes in the screen when he really should be attending to the empty places in himself.

"Virginia."

She had reached the fourth row of seats when she heard his voice call out her name from behind. She spun quickly around to find Dalton standing at the auditorium door, his hands shoved deeply into the pockets of his faded jeans, a gesture that caused his white shirt to stretch taut across his chest. The defensiveness of his position, however, was contradicted by his posture, his legs spread apart as if he were assuming an offensive stance. Virginia could only stare at him, remembering the way his fingers had felt in the darkness, skimming over the soft velvet of her skin. Suddenly all her well-rehearsed speeches and matter-of-fact philosophy flew out the window, and she could only wonder what she might say that would keep this man from pushing her away forever.

Dalton had seen her from the window of the projection room above, where he had been sorting through another box of photographs his uncle Eddie had stashed on the highest shelf of a closet. It was because he had found a black-and-white snapshot that he wanted to view in better light that he had moved from the closet to a lamp near the projector. The photo depicted a group of four teenage girls standing behind the concession stand with their arms linked behind each other's shoulders, smiling and laughing as if they hadn't a care in the world. At first, what caught his eye was that one of those girls looked like a much, much younger Natalie Hogan, with a short, punkish haircut that had caused him to smile.

And then he had noticed that another one of those girls was Virginia. Her face was in a slight profile, her hair caught back in a ponytail that fell nearly to her waist. She was wearing a T-shirt that sported the Palace logo, and a huge, man-style vest. Dalton had felt the air leave his lungs in a rush as he studied this teenage version of Virginia. He couldn't believe how much she had changed since then. Not only did she appear much younger in the photo but also much happier and much more innocent. But there was something else there, something more...

And when Dalton realized what that something more was, something inside him crumbled, something inside him died.

At first he hadn't realized, he supposed because he hadn't known her before coming to Comfort, save a brief afternoon encounter from their adolescence. But somehow, seeing this youthful Virginia clearly for the first time, and comparing her to the woman he knew today, he saw what that something more in her face was as obviously as he did the photo in his hand.

And then he had glanced up from the photo and through the projection room window, and he had seen the woman Virginia standing in the auditorium, her face in profile much as it was in the snapshot. And he had seen even more clearly the differences in the two countenances, had seen precisely what it was that had changed so over the years.

There was a complete absence of pain in her youthful expression. In the woman, though, was an aching awareness of something terrible. All of a sudden, Dalton recognized in Virginia's face exactly what he felt in his own heart. There was something she hadn't told him, something she was carrying deep inside her that still hurt to this day. He should have detected it right off, he told himself. Because it was something he saw himself every time he looked in a mirror.

And now as he stood at the top of the aisle gazing down at her again, he saw that the look lingered still. She was as beautiful as ever in her baggy khaki trousers and pink T-shirt, her hair swept back and gathered at her nape with an antique silver clasp. But the pain was there, too, he noted, in her eyes, in her face, in the way she held herself, and Dalton felt himself drawn to her as he never had been before.

Virginia watched him come, walking toward her with slow, careful strides, looking as if he were weighing something heavily in his mind. When he reached her, instead of greeting her, he lifted his hand to touch his fingertips momentarily to her cheek, then dropped his hand quickly back down to his side.

"Hello, Dalton," she said quietly, her voice echoing softly in the cavernous room.

"Hello, Ginnie," he replied.

For a long time, neither spoke, but only gazed at each other as if rewinding every experience they'd shared together to replay them in slow motion in their minds. Then Virginia remembered that she had come to the theater for a reason, and she did her best to conjure a smile.

"How have you been?" she asked, knowing the question sounded lame, but having no idea what else to say.

"All right," he told her.

After a brief pause, she added, "How's business?"

"Good. We've been sold out every night."

"That's wonderful. See? I told you everyone in Comfort was looking forward to seeing the Palace reopened. Was I right?"

He inclined his head toward her in something of a salute. "You were right."

Silence followed again, stretching ominously across the auditorium like an unhealthy sigh. Finally Dalton broke it by asking simply, "What are you doing here, Ginnie?"

She shrugged nervously. "To be honest, I don't know. I thought I had a reason to see you, but now... I'm not so sure."

He crossed his arms over his chest, another deceptively defensive gesture. "Why did you come?" he asked again.

She bit her lip anxiously. "I wanted to talk to you."

"About what?"

"About us."

He drew in a deep breath and released it very, very slowly. "I thought we already talked about...us. Last week, at my house, after we..." His voice trailed off, as if he needed as little reminder as she of their last encounter.

She shook her head, his mention of what they had shared together helping Virginia regain her nerve. "No, Dalton, that night we talked about you. What I have to say to you now, what I *need* to tell you... It concerns me."

"I thought you said you wanted to talk about us."

"Once we've talked about me, the two conversations together will equal having talked about us."

He smiled a little. "You have an odd way of figuring your math."

She smiled back. "That's why I teach art."

He chuckled once, but it was a sound lacking in humor. "All right. We'll talk."

He opened his arms to sweep one to his right, indicating she should take a seat. Virginia made her way down the fourth row until she paused before a seat in the very center, then folded herself into the chair. Dalton followed, seating himself immediately to her left, then turned to face her.

She rubbed her hands up and down the sapphire-blue velvet of the new chair and smiled. "It feels different sitting in here now. The seats are a different color, the walls are a different color. Everything seems to have changed."

"Still the same screen," he pointed out. "That's the main part of the theater, and it hasn't changed."

"No, I suppose not," she ceded. "But everything else has."

He nodded, and Virginia knew he realized as well as she that they were talking about more than just the Palace Theater.

"When I was living in Atlanta," she began again, "whenever I had trouble sleeping, I would close my eyes and picture myself sitting right here in The Fabulous Fourth Row. I'd focus on that vast white screen, and somehow that image would comfort me and lull me to sleep. I don't know why it was so effective, but it worked every time."

"Did you often have trouble sleeping while you were living in Atlanta?" Dalton asked.

She squirmed a little in her seat. "Often enough."

"That's where you lived when you were married, wasn't it?"

She nodded, but said nothing more.

"Is that what you want to talk about now, Ginnie? Your marriage?"

This time Virginia was the one to draw a deep breath and release it slowly. "Want?" she repeated. "No, I really don't *want* to talk about my marriage. But I need to, Dalton. There's something about me I think you should know."

"Virginia, nothing you can say will change my mind about the way I feel," he told her before she could get started. "You're a wonderful woman, and I do care for you, but...there's no future for us. I have nothing to offer you. There's nothing left inside of me to give. Losing Penny and Dylan drained me of every last ounce of emotion I have. I'm empty, Ginnie. And there's nothing in the world that could refill me."

She turned to study him for a moment, then said solemnly, "I know exactly how you feel, Dalton. And that feeling *can* change."

He shook his head, but his voice was calm as he said, "How could you possibly know how I feel? Look, I don't doubt that you experienced some pain when your marriage fell apart, that's only natural, but—"

"Some pain?" she interrupted him, throwing the words back as if they were meaningless bits of nothing. "Some pain? Dalton, what happened to me when my marriage fell apart goes a little beyond the 'some' phase."

He looked at her, puzzled, but didn't dissuade her from continuing. "What do you mean?"

She sighed again, the sound ragged and uncertain. "Just as you did the other night, I'm going to start from the beginning."

He nodded. "All right."

She leaned forward to cross her arms over the chair in front of her, then placed her chin resolutely on the backs of her overlapped hands. Instead of looking at Dalton, she turned her attention to the blank screen before them, as if seeing there a return engagement of the film that had been her marriage.

"The man I married was my high school sweetheart," she began quietly. "Back then he was wonderful. His name was Dean."

"Is that the same Dean who fought with the projectionist after he made a pass at you?" Dalton asked.

"That's the one. I'm surprised you remember his name. I told you about him months ago."

His voice sounded sad as he said, "I always remember the names of my rivals."

She glanced at him from the corner of her eye. "Dean's no rival to you," she assured him before returning her gaze to the movie screen. "I don't even know where he is anymore."

"What happened, Ginnie?" Dalton asked her, his voice low and full of concern.

"At first, our marriage was perfect. Dean held this fabulous position as an executive vice president in one of Atlanta's most prominent banks, and I was teaching in a very prestigious private academy. We were extremely well-off and traveled in the most distinguished social circles. We had a great house and expensive cars... nothing but the best. Dean saw to that. For about seven years, we lived a picture-perfect life."

Dalton leaned forward in his chair, assuming a position identical to hers. "So what went wrong?"

She turned her head to face him then, settling her cheek on her hands. "The bank collapsed, and Dean lost his job. At first we didn't think it would be a problem. White-collar unemployment was almost unheard of then, and we were so sure he'd find something else in no time. For months, we kept living the way we had, spending freely, going out all the time. The bills started to pile up, and on my salary alone, we had no way to pay them.

"I don't think that was what bothered Dean the most, though. What ate at him was the fact that he couldn't find work. Here was a man with an advanced honors degree from Harvard Business School, and he couldn't find a job. It made him feel like a failure. It made him feel ineffectual and unwanted. Ultimately, ridiculously, I think it made him feel like less of a man. So, like a lot of people in his place, he started drinking. And drinking. And drinking. And drinking."

Her eyes met Dalton's then, and Virginia saw recognition in them. "You've seen it happen to people, too, haven't you?" she asked.

"It isn't all that uncommon in my profession," he told her. "The stress is very difficult."

She nodded her understanding. "At first, I honestly wasn't all that concerned about Dean's binges. I'd seen him drink heavily before when he suffered some terrible experience. After his father died, and once, when he lost several tens of thousands of dollars in the stock market. But on both of those occasions, he managed to pick himself up again. I thought he'd do the same thing this time. But he didn't. He just became more and more difficult to live with. He'd go out in the morning to look for work, and come home at night reeking of bourbon. We started fighting frequently. And then he became abusive."

She saw Dalton flinch. "He hit you?" he asked in a deadly quiet voice, the look in his eyes murderous.

"Not then," Virginia told him. "At that point he was just calling me names and blaming me for everything that was wrong in his life. As more weeks passed, though, the names became worse and he . . . he began to threaten me. I knew what he was turning into, knew what was coming next, and when the school year ended, I decided it might be better if I went home to Comfort for a while until he could cool off. But then . . . then I found out that I was . . . I was pregnant."

Dalton's expression changed to one of confusion. "I thought you said you couldn't get pregnant."

"I can't now. But back then I was fine."

"Ginnie, you . . . you have a child?"

She shook her head slowly, her eyebrows arrowing downward in worry. "No," she said softly. "No, I don't."

"But what happened?"

"When I learned I was pregnant, I thought it would be better to stay in Atlanta and try to work things out with Dean."

"But obviously they didn't work out."

Virginia shook her head. "No. They didn't. I was afraid to tell him about the baby, because I was afraid he'd be worried about the added financial burden. I just tried as best I could to get him to stop drinking, and encouraged him to get some help. But that only made him angrier. After about a month, when I realized how ineffectual I was being, and how much worse he was becoming, I decided I should leave him. I thought maybe the blow of losing me might make him come around."

"But it didn't," Dalton assumed, stating instead of asking the question.

"I packed my things while Dean was out one day," she said in lieu of a reply, "but I didn't want to leave him a note—that seemed so impersonal. I felt the least I could do was try to explain my actions to his face, so I waited for him to come home." Virginia leaned back in her chair, dropping her gaze to the fingers tangling nervously together in her lap. "When he came home that night, I could tell he'd been drinking all day. I'm amazed he was able to drive. When I told him...when I told him I was leaving him, he...he flew into a rage. I was a convenient target for his anger and he...he..."

"He attacked you," Dalton finished for her, feeling the rage swell inside himself at the realization.

When Virginia's eyes met his, they were filled with tears. She looked bewildered and frightened, as if reliving that day again in her mind. "Dean beat the hell out of me that night," she said quietly as one fat tear escaped to slide slowly down her cheek. Her voice was hollow as she continued, "I don't know how long it lasted, or what happened when he was through. When I woke up, I'd lost three days of my life, a kidney, an ovary, and..." Her chin crumpled and she began to cry in earnest as she added,

"And my baby, Dalton. Oh, God, in addition to everything else, he made me lose my baby."

A painful, searing heat surged through Dalton's insides like a fire raging out of control. He reached for Virginia, pulling her into his arms, but all he really wanted to do was get his hands on the sonofabitch who'd been her husband.

"The doctors did what they could, but apparently at some point, Dean just started kicking me in the abdomen and didn't stop until I was almost dead."

"Your surgical scar," Dalton said, recalling the thin pink line that had marred the white smoothness of her abdomen. He was amazed that his voice sounded so calm.

He felt her nod. "They thought they might have to give me a hysterectomy, too, but decided to try patching me up instead. I don't know why they bothered. The outcome was still the same."

"They bothered because the removal of any organ, even one that you might consider ineffective, is never a good idea unless there's a threat to the patient's life," Dalton replied in his best doctor's voice. "Removing an organ can be an enormous shock to the system sometimes."

"A shock to the system," Virginia repeated blandly. "I guess that's pretty much what the whole experience was."

Dalton didn't know what to say. He'd had no idea she had survived such an experience. She seemed like such a well-adjusted, happy woman. She'd offered no indication that there was a tragedy of this magnitude in her past. Had he not seen the photograph of her when she was a youth and been able to see for himself the changes in her features, he might never have guessed at what she'd gone through.

"So...so what happened to Dean?" he asked, wondering why he cared. Should the man ever show his face in Comfort again, it would be the last on which he saw the sun rise.

"I pressed charges. The police and my attorney wanted to see him go up for attempted murder, but after plea bargaining, he only wound up spending thirteen months in prison before they released him."

"Thirteen months?" Dalton asked incredulously. "Thirteen lousy months?"

Virginia sniffled and wiped away another tear. "It was the best I could hope for. Unfortunately the way the law reads regarding issues of domestic violence is pretty vague. There have been some changes made in the last few years, but not many. Not nearly enough." She rolled her shoulders in a halfhearted shrug. "Really, when you get right down to it, I was one of the lucky ones."

"L-lucky?" Dalton sputtered. "How the hell do you figure that?"

Virginia's gaze met his evenly. "I survived my attack. I lived. A lot of women don't, Dalton. A lot of women wind up dead."

He gazed back at her and nodded slowly, still not sure what he should say. Finally he simply mumbled, "I'm sorry." But his remark didn't seem to be nearly enough. Two crummy little words could never make up for what had happened to Virginia. He wished he could make it up to her somehow, wished there was some way to undo the terrible wrong she had been done. But he was helpless. Unable. Only she could deal with her tragedy. Only she knew how to help herself.

"I just thought what happened . . . I just thought it was something you should know about me, Dalton," she said as she rose from her seat.

When he realized she intended to leave him, Dalton wanted to tell her to stop, wanted to plead with her not to go. But why should she stay? he asked himself. He still had nothing to offer her, still couldn't alter the man he was. What she had told him changed nothing. In many ways, he wondered why she had even decided to describe her experience now, when things between the two of them were clearly over and done with. He was glad she had confided in him, glad she had thought enough of him to share her past, but nonetheless considered such sharing unnecessary. Unnecessary, because soon he would be gone from her life completely. Sooner, even, than he had originally planned.

"I'm leaving Comfort tomorrow," he told her suddenly.

Virginia collapsed back into her seat as if her legs had turned to rags. "Tomorrow? But why? I thought you would be staying until July."

He shook his head. "I can't. The hospital where I work in Indianapolis called me last week. They need me to come back early."

"Why?" she asked again.

He hesitated, wishing now more than ever that he could remain hidden in this little corner of the world with Virginia, free from worry, free from stress, free from pain. But he knew that was an unrealistic desire, knew there was no way he could stay. Although it was true he'd managed to keep his worry and stress at bay during his brief sojourn here, he knew his pain would be with him always. And now he would be going back to it, fairly begging to be hurt again.

"I have to perform surgery this week," he said quietly. "They have a patient, a boy, seven years old, scheduled for an operation."

"But can't someone else do it?" Virginia wanted to clap a hand over her mouth after uttering the question, appalled at how selfish and petulant she sounded. "I mean, they've done without you this long. Can't whoever's filling in for you do the operation?"

Dalton shook his head. "Not this time. The procedure the boy needs is a fairly new one. Only about a half dozen surgeons in the country know how to perform it correctly. I'm one of them. I'm close, and I'm available. I can scarcely tell his parents I refuse to do it, can I?"

"No, I don't suppose you can," she said. "But that's one operation, Dalton. And they have you covered until July. Couldn't you come back to Comfort afterward? Who'll take care of the theater when you're not here?"

"Randy Caswell. She's the woman I hired for the management position. She's been kind enough to start a few weeks early. I gave her a crash course last week in running the Palace. And I told her if she has any problems to get in touch with... to get in touch with you. I hope that's all right."

All right? Virginia wanted to scream. All right? Was it all right if he walked out of her life forever, all right if he went back to a life that held nothing for him? She wanted to shout that no, it wasn't all right, that he could come back himself and take care of the damned theater. Instead, she only nodded silently.

After a moment, she said, "Indianapolis is only an hour away. Maybe you could come back to Comfort now and then." She smiled weakly as she added, "For a movie or something."

He watched her closely for a moment, wanting more than anything to promise her that he would be back. Back every week if it meant glimpsing Virginia, if only from a distance, if only for a little while. But he knew he would never be able to keep such a promise. And when his rational side finally won out, he asked, "What would be the point of coming back?"

His words stung her. Virginia hadn't assumed he would come rushing back into her arms immediately after she'd told him about what happened to her during her marriage. But she had hoped he would at least give himself an opportunity to rethink the way he was living, that he might look upon her as an example of what he himself could achieve with time. She had survived a brutal experience and gone on to rebuild her life. She had even chanced falling in love again—with him. Why shouldn't he do likewise and take a chance with her? Why couldn't he give himself the same opportunity she had allowed herself to take?

But instead of allowing himself time or even stating a willingness to think about what she had told him, he had evidently decided to turn tail and run away. Back to Indianapolis and a life that held nothing but heartache, back to a future of certain unhappiness. That's what he was choosing over her, she thought. Instead of opening himself to let her inside, instead of accepting her love and making an effort to rebuild his life, Dalton Cameron was turning her away.

"Maybe I was wrong about you after all," she said softly as she rose again and began to make her way toward the aisle on her right. "Maybe you're not the man I thought you were."

"Ginnie, wait. What's that supposed to mean?"

But she simply shook her head silently and continued to walk away. She had done her best, she told herself. She had given him herself as an example that people did overcome tragedy and go on to live full, happy lives. What more could she say or do that might cause him to think he was capable of the same thing?

"I love you, Dalton," she called out as she turned to look at him one final time. "I love you."

Then she turned again and made her way up the aisle, through the lobby and out of the Palace Theater, feeling more than certain that she would never see Dalton Cameron again.

Chapter Thirteen

August dawned as it usually did in Comfort, hot and humid and thoroughly unbearable. The days were long, the nights were short, and everyone seemed to be in a bad mood, especially Virginia. Or perhaps she was the only one in a bad mood, she amended at times, and everyone else in town simply picked up on her ill humor and threw it right back at her. With school having been dismissed for the summer, she had felt oddly useless for weeks, something she hadn't ever felt before. Normally she would have volunteered to teach extracurricular art classes to the summer students, but this year she hadn't felt up to it and had opted out of the program. Now she wished she had agreed to teach. She needed something to occupy her mind. Anything would be better than her overactive thoughts and concerns about Dalton Cameron.

Nearly ten weeks had passed since he had left Comfort—and Virginia—behind. Ten weeks since she had last felt anything akin to a good feeling, ten weeks since she had harbored even the slightest amount of hope. At first she had been so certain he would come back, that he would feel some psychic pull, some cosmic attraction and return to the woman who loved him. Surely he would come to realize what he had abandoned, what he could have had, she had reasoned then. Surely he would come to his senses, and come back to Comfort and her. But with the passage of every week since his departure, Virginia had become less and less hopeful, and more and more morose. Finally she had forced herself to accept the fact that he wasn't coming back. And then she began to despair.

On more than one occasion, she had caught herself trying to contrive a reason to travel to Indianapolis. There must be something there that she needed but couldn't find here—besides Dalton Cameron, of course. But then she had envisioned herself approaching his front door, and having the door thrown open in welcome by his next-door neighbor, who had by this time become the new Mrs. Cameron. Quickly Virginia had banished the fantasy, reminding herself that Dalton had assured her there were no romantic ties between himself and Shari. But the melancholy feeling lingered long after, a piercing kind of sadness she hadn't quite been able to shake.

So she had remained in Comfort, muddling through her summer as best she could, wondering what she was going to do for the next forty or fifty years of her life. The prospects seemed bleak at best. Although she still preserved her dreams of teaching and growing old in peace, that peace seemed less stable now, less likely, thanks to what she was sure would become a lifelong preoccupation with the man who had come to town to renovate a theater and help her rebuild her trust, only to leave both behind.

Natalie had told Virginia that Dalton hadn't yet sold the Palace, despite a number of more than fair offers he had received for the old place, both from local members of the community and people from out of town. Virginia thought that news odd. Why would he hold on to a place he'd been trying to unload for five years? Why, after spending months of labor and countless dollars, would he refuse to sell the establishment? Natalie hadn't been able to provide any adequate reasons, either. She only said she had spoken to Dalton to tell him of the offers, and on each occasion he had told her he'd think about it and call her back. Yet those call-backs never came.

And when Virginia idly asked her friend if Dalton had ever inquired about her during those phone calls, Natalie could only shake her head sadly and tell Virginia no.

Obviously she wasn't a concern for him as he was for her, she forced herself to admit on those occasions. And clearly, he had no intention of coming back.

So Virginia stopped hoping he would, stopped believing the two of them had a chance for a future and tried to get on with her life as best she could. She cleaned her mother's house from top to bottom, sorted through closets and storage areas to discard old clothes and belongings that had become unnecessary, painted shutters and tended to the yard, then searched for more chores to do. Symbolically, at least, she felt as if she were cleaning up her act and getting her life in order, even if emotionally, she knew that might never happen again.

It was on such a day of hard labor that she went to retrieve the mail and found a puzzling piece of correspondence. As she sifted through the assortment of bills, catalogs and advertisements, she came across a perfectly square, white vellum envelope addressed to her in an unfamiliar hand, postmarked locally, but with no return address. Curious, she immediately ran her thumb beneath the flap and extracted another piece of square, white vellum, this one an invitation of some kind.

"You are cordially invited," the note began in the same unknown script, "to attend a private screening at the Palace Theater. Monday, August ninth, half past seven p.m. Champagne reception at seven o'clock. Dress: formal." And that was all it said. Virginia turned the envelope over to study the front again. It was addressed to her alone, with no mention made of her mother. Another quick search through the rest of the mail indicated her mother hadn't received a similar invitation.

How strange, she thought. She hadn't read anything in the paper about an upcoming special screening of any kind at the Palace. And Monday was the day the theater was normally closed. She hadn't even attended a movie there since the grand reopening, although Lana had visited the theater once or twice every week. Why would Virginia be invited to a private screening but not her mother? Then she realized that today was Saturday the seventh. Who sent out invitations to a formal function two days in advance of that function?

Shrugging off the odd request, she decided not to attend. She didn't much feel like going out, and really, what would be the point of participating in something festive and fun when that was the last way she'd been feeling lately?

Her mother exited the house then, on her way to her usual weekly meeting of her bridge club. When she saw Virginia holding the mail in one hand, a white card in the other, she asked, "What's that? A wedding invitation? Who's getting married now?"

Virginia started at the sound of her mother's voice. "No, it's not a wedding invitation, but I've been invited to some kind of private screening Monday night at the Palace."

"Oh, that sounds like fun," Lana said with a smile. "What are you going to wear?"

Virginia shook her head. "I'm not going."

Her mother's smile quickly reversed to a frown, and Virginia could tell she was about to receive what Lana used to call "a good talking to." "Why not?" she demanded.

Virginia sighed. "Because I don't want to, Mom."

Lana pulled the front door closed behind her, slamming it more than was necessary for the lock to catch. "And why don't you want to go?"

"You know very well why."

Although Lana knew that things between Virginia and Dalton had indeed progressed to the romantic stage, she didn't realize how seriously her daughter had begun to take the romance. At least, Virginia didn't think her mother realized that. She had explained away her overnight stay at Dalton's house as an all-night gabfest, an explanation she wasn't sure whether or not her mother believed. She was sure Lana knew Dalton's absence was primarily the reason for her daughter's lousy mood of late, but her mother didn't press the issue of his disappearance. Usually. For some reason, though, Virginia got the impression that her mother's silence on the subject was about to come to an end.

"You can't avoid the Palace forever, Ginnie."

Virginia lifted her chin defiantly. "Oh, no?"

Lana shook her head. "You love movies too much," she reminded her daughter unnecessarily. "You may be smarting now, but eventually you're going to have to face up to things. Eventually you'll go back to the theater."

This time Virginia was the one to shake her head. "I don't think so, Mom. I'll just go to the video store and rent movies the way I always have since the Palace first closed."

"It isn't the same and you know it."

No, it wasn't, Virginia ceded. Watching films meant for the big screen on a thirteen-inch TV was nothing at all like enjoying them in a dark theater. Just as movies themselves were nothing at all like real life. Just as real life was nothing at all like a fantasy one wished would come true.

"No, but it's good enough for me," Virginia replied quietly.

"Is it?" her mother asked.

She nodded, but said nothing more.

"You know, you never go out anymore, Ginnie," Lana complained.

"Mom, I never went out to begin with."

"You did when Dalton Cameron lived here."

"But he doesn't live here anymore, does he?" Virginia said softly, willing away the little ache that sprang up from nothing in her heart.

"No, he doesn't," Lana agreed. "But you do. And there's no reason why you should cloister yourself away and pine for some guy who isn't coming back."

Although Virginia had spoken those very words to herself on more than one occasion, to hear her mother's crisp, clear alto underscore them now made her want to brutally deny the assertion. Unfortunately she knew a denial would be untrue.

"I'm not cloistering myself," she insisted. "And why are you complaining anyway? The house looks great lately, thanks to me."

"And I thank you for making it look so nice. But, Ginnie," Lana told her daughter as she draped an arm across her shoulders, "you don't have to work so hard on the house. I'd rather have my house fall apart than my daughter."

Virginia stared at the white card in her hand, wondering again why she had been issued the invitation. "All right, Mom, I'll go," she heard herself say. Funny, though, how she had meant to assure her mother she would not.

When Virginia pulled her car to a halt in front of the Palace Theater at precisely 7:00 p.m. the second following evening, the place appeared to be deserted, despite the merrily dancing marquee lights and the illuminated sign that announced Private Screening—Return Engagement—One Night Only. She checked the invitation on the passenger seat beside her for perhaps the tenth time to make certain that she had the date right, then tossed the piece of paper back down, realizing it did indeed read Monday, the ninth. She lifted her watch to her ear to make sure it was running properly, only to hear the steady *tick-tick-tick* that assured her it was indeed keeping the proper time. Perhaps most of the people were foregoing the champagne reception, she thought, and would be arriving shortly, in time for the movie. Still, she had to wonder what kind of person would turn down free champagne.

She stepped out of her car and smoothed a hand over her short, figure-hugging, amethyst-colored cocktail dress, wondering again how she had let Natalie talk her into wearing the garment when she'd gone to her friend to borrow a dress appropriate for the occasion tonight. Virginia's wardrobe consisted primarily of dresses suitable for work and ultracasual clothes for play and a few bits and pieces in between. She had nothing that might be deemed "formal" save the black gown she had borrowed from her mother the night of the reopening, and she certainly wouldn't be putting that dress on again. It brought with it too many reminders of her solitary night of lovemaking with Dalton, something she had enough trouble trying to forget. So she had turned to her best friend for help, and Natalie had foisted off the most revealing dress in her arsenal.

"Evan loves it when I wear this," Natalie had said as she drew the small garment out of her closet. "It was what I was wearing the first night he... Well, you know."

Virginia had known only too well. Natalie and Evan had been going hot and heavy ever since the night of the Palace reopening. Her brother had forsaken all other women in his life to focus his attentions on his sister's best friend, no easy feat for him, Virginia was sure. She was more than pleased that the couple had gotten together and appeared to be ultimately headed for eternal bliss. But watching their love blossom when her own love life lay in tatters had been more than a little difficult for Virginia to bear. Still, it was nice to know someone had found happiness from this whole ordeal.

She fingered a long length of her hair, pushing it back behind one ear. Natalie had even forced Virginia into a chair long enough to whip through the strands with a curling iron, and now the pale red ends turned softly inward. She wondered again why she had even bothered to go to lengths to look nice for tonight's screening. Who cared what she looked like? She had no one to impress.

When she pushed through the lobby doors, it was to discover that the inside of the theater was as deserted as the outside. Although the lights were on, and popcorn popped with quiet irregularity and a wonderful aroma in the popper behind the concession stand, Virginia saw evidence of no one. No guests, no employees, no one. She frowned, feeling as if she'd stepped into one of Hitchcock's more bizarre thrillers. Then she saw a shadowed movement near the auditorium doors to the left of the concession stand, and she strode warily toward them.

Even before she arrived at the double doors, Virginia knew somehow that Dalton would be standing inside the auditorium to greet her, and her heart thumped wildly behind her rib cage as she drew nearer. He stood halfway down the aisle, dressed again in his white dinner jacket and black trousers, bow tie and all. But his hair was different, cut short and expensively styled, and his beard, his wonderful, luxurious beard, was gone. It was the first time she had seen his face bared since the day she had met him, the first time she had seen him completely clean-shaven at all. Without his beard, the hard lines of his face were quite distinguishable, the square jaw stubbornly set, two deep grooves in each cheek resembling something she supposed might be considered dimples.

But his eyes were what caught Virginia's attention most. Still every bit as vividly and clearly colored as before, something in them had changed. There was something there that hadn't been there before, but she couldn't quite decide what it was. A compassion, perhaps, or an understanding. She shook her head in bewilderment as she approached him to get a better look.

Dalton didn't think he'd ever seen a more welcome, more wonderful sight than that of Virginia walking toward him after having denied himself the pleasure of her company for so long. God, he'd missed her. He sighed deeply, feeling as if his lungs were taking in fresh air for the first time in months. He didn't know how he'd survived the past ten weeks without her.

The surgery he'd been called back to perform had been successful. The little boy was thriving with his family at their home in Minnesota, and would have no more need of the doctor in Indianapolis who had saved his life. Dalton had been tempted to return to Comfort once his patient was out of danger, feeling for some reason a need to share his relief and happiness at the operation's success with Virginia. But then he had assured himself such a journey would lead nowhere. A visit would only be temporary, he'd told himself then, and saying goodbye to her once had been difficult enough. He wasn't sure he'd be able to do it a second time.

Now, of course, he knew he wouldn't have to. Because now he had come back to Comfort for good.

"You look incredible," he said when she drew within a foot of him.

Virginia lifted a hand as if to touch his face, then pulled it back again and placed it against her own instead. "Your beard," she said softly.

He brushed his curled fingers over the rough skin of his cheek. "I had to shave it off when I went back to work. The hospital is privately owned and operated. They have a dress code of sorts. No beards, short hair. The administrators like to run what they think of as a nice, clean-cut operation."

"I like you better with it," she said, speaking her thoughts aloud before she realized how rude they would sound as a verbal comment.

But Dalton only smiled. "Do you find me so unattractive, Ginnie?"

Her eyes widened in panic, something that made him smile even more. "Oh, no," she assured him hastily. "Of course not, nothing could be further from the truth. I—" She stopped abruptly when she heard how anxious her words sounded. "I mean, no, you look . . . you look wonderful."

"Thanks."

She nodded her acknowledgment, but asked, "What are you doing here? Why are you back in Comfort?"

He took a single step forward, an action that brought his body close enough to hers that they were almost—but not quite—touching. "There's something I forgot to tell you when I was here before," he said quietly.

Virginia inhaled sharply and was assailed by the well-remembered fragrance of him, something dark and rich and exclusively Dalton. "What's that?"

He threaded the fingers of both hands slowly through her hair until he had it bunched in two fists at her nape. She could only stare at him helplessly, could only watch in wonder as his pupils grew large with wanting, could only sway toward him as he lowered his lips to hers in a whisper-soft kiss.

"I love you, Ginnie," he murmured against her mouth. "I forgot to tell you that I love you."

She felt herself go a little weak in the knees at his roughly uttered declaration, but pressed her mouth against his again. Hooking her arms around his neck, she pulled him closer, her fingers searching for the curls at his nape that were no longer there. Instead she encountered a short growth of hair that reminded her he wasn't back in Comfort to stay, but would soon return to a career and a life almost a hundred miles away, a life that didn't include her.

But before she could pull away from him, he began to speak again, telling her things she didn't want to hear, things she knew would only bring her more sorrow when he was gone.

"Every night in Indianapolis," he said, "I lie awake for hours wondering what you're doing, where you are, whether you're with someone else or by yourself. I remember the one night we spent together, the way you looked, the way you smelled, the way you felt . . . that tiny, helpless sound you made whenever I kissed you in places you thought were too intimate to kiss. And all I can do is wish you were in bed beside me, so I could kiss all those places again."

"Oh, Dalton," she groaned softly. "Please, don't do this to me. Don't come here for some one-night-only return engagement appearance, turn my emotions upside down and then leave me feeling empty inside again. It isn't fair."

"Don't let the words on the marquee outside fool you, Ginnie," he said softly. "I think we both know by now that appearances can be deceiving."

She gazed at him with eyes wider and bluer than he ever recalled them being, her lips parted in what might have been confusion or desire. "I don't understand," she said. "What do you mean?"

Instead of answering her right away, he kissed her once more before releasing her, then circled her waist with an insistent arm and encouraged her back up the aisle. When they emerged into the lobby, he led her to a small bench in an alcove made even more private by two potted palms adorning each side. There, he silently bade her to sit down. He himself remained standing, however, feeling restless and a bit edgy. He had so much he wanted to tell her, but no idea where to begin. Then he remembered that when the two of them had spoken of serious subjects before, starting at the beginning had seemed to work best. So that's where he began.

"The surgery I was called back to Indianapolis to perform went off without a hitch," he told her. "The boy came through it beautifully. Even before the procedure was completed, I knew he was going to be all right. And I was so happy, Ginnie, so incredibly pleased that I had been successful, that everything was going to be fine."

Virginia smiled, but the happiness never quite reached her eyes. "That's good news, Dalton," she said. "No doubt you're going to be more in demand than ever."

He shook his head. "No, Ginnie, you don't understand. I felt *happy* after the surgery was over. Happy and relieved and . . . and overjoyed."

She gazed at him curiously. "You're right, I don't understand. I'd think that's how you always feel after a successful surgery."

"But it's not," he told her, his excitement at odds with his statement. "At least, it wasn't before. I never felt *anything,* good or bad, before. I always forced myself to feel *nothing* when I had to perform surgery, regardless of the outcome. That way, if my patient didn't survive, I didn't have to feel grief. I didn't have to experience that pain of loss that had become so difficult to bear. And if my patient came through surgery with no complications, I simply found satisfaction in knowing I'd done my job correctly, but nothing more. I never felt *happy* about it before. But this time I did. And I wanted to share that happiness with someone. Ginnie, I wanted to share it with you."

She narrowed her eyes at him in puzzlement, still obviously not understanding what he was trying to say. So he tried a different tack.

"Remember, after we made love, I told you about a place inside myself that I retreated to a long time ago in order to avoid feeling the pain of loss?"

She ducked her head, focusing on the fingers that wove nervously together in her lap. "How could I forget?" she said softly. "You told me that was why you could never love me."

Dalton sat down beside her, pulling her hands apart, catching one in both of his. "Don't you see?" he exclaimed, a wide, happy smile splitting his features. "I tried to retreat there again before I performed surgery, tried to hide myself away there in case the procedure didn't go as well as I hoped. But that place is gone now, Ginnie, I can't find it. It isn't there anymore."

She scrutinized him more closely, but he could see that she still wasn't quite able to allow herself to believe what he wanted so desperately to tell her.

"You patched me up, Ginnie," he said with a small chuckle. "I don't know how you did it or when it happened, but somehow you filled in the emptiness inside me. And now, instead of feeling numb, instead of feeling distant and cool . . . all I can feel is love. For you.''

Virginia was afraid to believe what he said was true. It was too easy, too clean an explanation for his change of heart. There had been so much between them when they parted ways ten weeks before. How could she let herself believe he had put his past to rest so readily, so completely, simply because he had suddenly decided he loved her after all.

As if he knew she still experienced some doubts about what he was telling her, Dalton squeezed her hand more tightly. ''I've spent the past ten weeks thinking about my reaction after the surgery,'' he said softly. ''At first, I really wasn't sure what to do. When I realized how much I'd come to love you, I began to feel guilty, as if I were somehow betraying Penny and Dylan. Why should I be allowed to be so happy, when they had been denied so much? At one point I . . . I went to the cemetery, to visit their graves.''

His voice grew softer as he continued. ''I know this sounds crazy, Ginnie, but I talked to them that day...really talked to them for the first time, as I never had when they were alive. I told them all the things I wish I'd said but didn't—how much I loved them, how sorry I was that I wasn't there when they needed me. And as strange as it may seem, I got the feeling that both of them understood, and that neither one blamed me for what happened. Wherever they are, Ginnie, they're together—they have each other. They aren't alone, and I don't think they'd want me to be alone forever, either.''

He took another deep breath before concluding, ''I don't know why I didn't allow myself to think they might forgive me. I don't know why I didn't realize before that there was nothing I could have done.''

Virginia lifted their joined hands and pressed them to her cheek. She smiled as she said, ''Because you never allowed yourself to think or talk about it. I did the same thing when I first came back to Comfort four years ago. I felt responsible for everything that had happened to me, from the loss of Dean's job to the fact that he had beaten me up. Somehow I twisted around all the facts until I was the culprit, even though that wasn't true at all. I didn't want to talk to anyone about what had happened. But once I did, it was like a dam bursting apart. All my pent-up bad feelings spilled out, and only then did I have the chance to refill myself with something different, something better. Only then was I able to convince myself that I deserve to be happy as much as anyone else does."

She scooted a little closer, cupping his jaw with her hand, marveling at the warm skin where once there had been a silky beard. Quietly she told him, "But it wasn't until I met you, Dalton, that I allowed myself to fall in love again."

He covered her hand with his, his gaze searing into hers. "Then you still have feelings for me?" he asked. "You still . . . love me?"

She nodded. "How could I ever stop?"

"Say it then," he instructed her. "Tell me that you love me."

"I love you," she whispered immediately.

The relief in his eyes was an almost palpable thing. "That's good. Because I love you, too."

She lifted her face to his, and he bent to kiss her, a gentle, light caress of his lips against hers. The gesture was an unspoken promise of devotion, a reassurance that they would never again allow their pasts to interfere with their futures.

"There's only one problem," Dalton said when he pulled away again.

Virginia's eyes were as warm and clear as a hot spring when they met his. "Only one?" she asked with a smile. "That's not so bad."

"It's a big one," he cautioned her. "Could be a lifelong one if we don't work it out right."

"Then we better be sure we do the right thing," she said with a hearty nod.

He nodded back. "Now that I've relegated my past experience to the past for good, I think you and I should start looking to the future. A future that includes the two of us. Together. Forever."

Her heart pounded madly at his quietly uttered statement, the bonds of worry that had restrained it for so long finally bursting free. She wanted to shout her agreement with his suggestion to the highest rafters, wanted to throw her arms around him and drag him to the nearest chapel for the speediest wedding on record. But there was still one factor restricting their complete happiness, one fetter still not freed from Virginia's heart.

"What...what about children, Dalton?" she asked softly. "We've both lost one—we both feel the keen sorrow that comes with that loss. And I'll never be able to provide either one of us with another."

He draped an arm across her shoulders and pulled her close, settling his chin affectionately on the top of her head. His hands stroked over the vibrant strands of her hair from top to bottom, his fingers entwining themselves in the silky shafts. He hugged her close as he said, "All I want, all I need, in this life is you, Ginnie. Nothing else matters. Nothing. I can live without my career in Indy, without my big house there, the restaurants, museums, everything. I can even live without children. But I can never, in any way, live without you."

She still felt a little melancholy, but tilted her head back to meet his gaze. "Are you sure you want to surrender your career? You trained to be a doctor for a decade, and you're so good at it. How can you give that up?"

"I only said I'd live without my career in Indianapolis," Dalton reminded her. "There's a pediatrician here in town, a Dr. Warren Radcliffe?"

"Dr. Radcliffe?" Virginia asked with an affectionate, reminiscent smile. "He was my pediatrician when I was a child."

"Apparently he was just about everyone's pediatrician in this town."

"Dr. Radcliffe has always been very popular in Comfort," she stated unequivocally.

He swept her hair back from her forehead. "And now he's getting ready to retire."

"You're kidding. After all these years?"

He nodded. "And he's been looking for someone to take over his practice for quite some time. He needs someone he can trust to take care of his patients, someone who will take a vested interest in this community. In other words, someone he knows will make Comfort, Indiana, his home for life."

Virginia's lips stretched into a smile so broad, she felt her cheeks ache. "Gosh. Who could possibly be suitable for a job like that?"

Dalton shrugged humbly. "Well, Dr. Radcliffe *has* approached me about the possibility of taking over for him."

"And are you interested?"

"Very."

She straightened in her seat. "What about the Palace Theater?"

He spread his fingers wide in a gesture that clearly indicated a significant lack of concern. "I think the new manager's doing a terrific job. I wouldn't want to interfere with her running of the theater at all."

"I hear a 'but' coming somewhere."

"But," he qualified, "I'd like to keep doing the bookings myself."

"Your uncle Eddie would be proud of you," she told him.

"Well, I'm sure I'll be getting a little input from my wife, as well," he added for good measure. "She was once an employee here after all."

"No kidding?" Virginia said, feigning surprise. "What was her name? Maybe I know her."

"Oh, you know her intimately," Dalton assured her in a lascivious voice. "Almost as intimately as I plan to know her myself."

"I think you're presuming a lot here, Doctor," she said with a grin.

"Not as much as I intend to presume later," he told her.

"So are you asking me to marry you?" Virginia asked him bluntly. "Or are you just going to shamelessly use my body and my incredibly good taste where filmmaking is concerned?"

"Yes," he said with a smile.

"Yes to what?" she demanded playfully. "The marital proposal, the sexual exploitation or the cinematic savvy?"

He leaned forward to nibble her ear. "Yes to all of it," he murmured.

She giggled, then bent her head to nibble him back. "Oh. Okay. Then I accept."

"Great," he whispered.

"Mmm...it is great," she agreed.

As they embraced more insistently, a soft silence fell over the theater. Outside, the day grew late and the sun sank low in the sky. But inside, a new day was just beginning. And not for one night only, Virginia thought as she felt Dalton's arms come around her in a reassuring, protective embrace. But for all time. Forever. Wondrously, gloriously forever. Just as love should be.

Epilogue

"Okay, Freddie, I think you're all set here. Looks like I'm not going to have to saw that arm off after all."

Freddie giggled, running one stubby finger over his sling from shoulder to wrist. "How long do I gotta wear the cast, Doc Cameron?"

Dalton smiled at the boy before turning to the stainless steel sink in one of his three examining rooms, then washed the last bits of plaster from his hands. "Oh, about ten weeks ought to do it," he told his nine-year-old patient. "It's not a bad fracture, but it's pretty close to your elbow. We can't be too careful. I'm going to need you to pitch next season."

Freddie beamed. "You gonna coach soccer again this year, too?"

Dalton nodded. "But don't even think about trying out for the team with that arm in a cast, mister."

"Aw, Doc. I don't need my arm for soccer. Can't I play in just a few games?"

Dalton shook his head resolutely. "Absolutely not. I mean it, Freddie. Besides, your lungs are good and strong. We're going to need you on the sidelines egging us on."

The little boy frowned. "It ain't the same."

"It isn't the same," a cheery, feminine voice corrected him.

Both Freddie and Dalton glanced up to see Virginia poking her head through the examining room door.

"Hey, Mrs. Cameron," Freddie greeted her with a smile. He held up his plaster-encased arm. "Lookit. Doc fixed me up real good."

"Real well," she corrected him again.

But Freddie shook his head in refusal. "It's summer, Mrs. Cameron. I don't hafta bother with school rules."

She lifted her brows in mock censure. "Oh, no? Well just wait until I tell Mr. Graves—who's going to be your English teacher next year—about that. He might just want to tutor you in grammar over the summer."

Dalton could see that Freddie wasn't sure whether or not Virginia would make good on her threat, but apparently decided to play it safe. "Okay. I'll be good." Then he screwed up his face in confusion. "Or will I be well?" he asked no one in particular.

"Behave yourself and you'll be good *and* well in no time," Dalton told him.

That seemed to satisfy the little boy, and he scooted toward the edge of the examining table where Dalton carefully lifted him down. "Now I've already talked to your mother," he said as Freddie walked to the door, "and I've given her a prescription for some pills in case your arm starts to hurt again. If you have any problems, you have your mom call me, okay?"

"Okay."

Virginia smiled as the slight figure then disappeared through the door with cries of "Mom! Mom! Lookit the cast Doc Cameron put on my arm. Mom?"

"He's such a handful," she said as she closed the door behind her.

"That's the second tree he's fallen out of this summer. I'm just sure it will be only a matter of days before he's back in here again, and next time, I'll probably be plastering his leg."

"I'm sure he'll be good after this," Virginia said in the little boy's defense. "Surely a cast on his arm will slow him down a bit."

"Hah," Dalton muttered, clearly unconvinced. "Don't be too sure."

She smiled at him, wondering how he still managed to make her feel giddy and aroused just by looking at her, even after seven years of marriage. He appeared so professional in his white doctor coat, his beard neatly trimmed. His unfashionably long hair was the only physical characteristic that hinted at his laid-back personality. His green eyes glittered as they caught the late-afternoon sun and reflected it back more warmly than the summer day outside. Yes, every time he looked at her that way, a little piece of Virginia melted into him, stealing a bit of his heart to join it with her own.

"What brings you out here?" he asked finally.

"I missed you," she told him. "I wondered if you were free for an early dinner."

He tossed the file in his hand onto the examining table Freddie had just vacated, then approached her with slow, measured strides, pausing only when his body was in total and complete contact with her own. Virginia inhaled deeply, winding her arms around his neck, then pulled his face down to hers for a very heated kiss.

"You bet I'm free," he said in a ragged whisper when he pulled away. "What did you have in mind?"

A pounding on the door behind her prevented Virginia from describing in vivid, erotic detail the plans she had for her husband later. Instead her shoulders slumped in defeat, and she lowered a hand to the doorknob.

"I bet I know who that is," Dalton said softly with a huge smile.

Before she could turn the knob and open the door herself, Virginia felt herself thrown forward into his arms. Two identical, white-blond heads shot past her in a blur, racing to see who would be first to come to a halt behind Dalton, clinging to his coat with wild affection.

"Daddy!" the two little girls said in unison.

"Hi, kids," he greeted them with a smile. But his eyes held Virginia's. "Dinner for four, I'm assuming is what you were going to describe."

She shrugged. "Mom's got a date tonight. And Natalie and Evan are celebrating their anniversary. I'm afraid the four of us are on our own."

Dalton bent to scoop his four-year-old daughters into his arms. Lily burrowed her head against his chest while Rosie splattered a wet smack on his cheek.

"Mommy bought us Popsicles," she said. Her comment was unnecessary, really, as Dalton could already feel his beard puckering under the sticky mess.

Virginia wrinkled her nose comically. "Sorry. Guess I could have warned you."

He laughed as he lowered his daughters to the ground, making the two little girls giggle hysterically as he began a huge production about cleaning himself off, saying that now he would have to sterilize everything in the office. They jumped and squealed in delight when Virginia announced that Daddy would be joining the three of them for dinner—a picnic to be eaten at Baltimore Park in the center of town.

Dalton and Virginia had adopted Lily and Rosie four years ago, only a few weeks after the two little girls were left orphaned by an accident in Indianapolis that had ended their parents' lives. Addison Parker, Dalton's former boss at River Crest Hospital, had tended to the parents, and when confronted by the fact that the two children had no other relatives and would become wards of the state, had contacted the Camerons in Comfort. He'd told Dalton and Virginia that he knew what a burden two infants could be, but wondered if they might be interested in adopting the two little girls if he were able to pull a few strings. Naturally Dalton and Virginia had been delighted. And the Cameron family had grown from two to four virtually overnight.

And now as Virginia watched her daughters dance and cavort around their father, all she could do was smile. Her future had turned out better than she'd ever thought it could. Although she and Dalton would never be able to completely forget the things that had happened to them in their pasts, now they had so much more to look forward to in their future. She rejoiced daily at the certainty of a lifetime with the family she never thought she'd have.

As he watched the satisfied, peaceful smile that curled his wife's lips, Dalton could only smile, too. He knew exactly what she was thinking about, because her thoughts so often mirrored his own. He shook his head in wonder at the three most beautiful women in the world, then shed his white coat and hung his stethoscope up for the day.

"Okay, who wants to see *Bambi* this weekend?" he asked as the four of them exited the examining room and headed down the hall to the front office.

"Oh, no, not again," Virginia pleaded. "You've shown that every weekend for two months."

"But the girls love it," he protested. "And so do you, Ginnie. Admit it."

She grinned. "What I love most of all is you," she told him. "You and those two little monsters terrorizing your receptionist."

Dalton's heart swelled as it always did when he viewed the twin terrors that were his daughters, and he nearly burst with love when he turned his attention back to his wife. He looked forward to being the best husband, the best father he knew how to be. And he was thankful he had a lifetime ahead of him to do it.

"Come on," he said softly, tilting his head toward the door that would lead them all outside.

"Where are we going?" Virginia asked him.

He inhaled deeply, a sigh full of satisfaction. "Anywhere," he said. "Everywhere. We have a lot to keep us occupied for the next fifty years. I say we get started now."

She nodded. "As long as you're with me," she murmured quietly, "nothing will ever be wrong again."

And with that, the Camerons exited out into the sunny afternoon, happy, satisfied, and full of plans.

* * * * *

**It takes a very
special man to win**

That

SPECIAL

Woman!

She's friend, wife, mother—she's you! And beside each Special
Woman stands a wonderfully special man. It's a celebration of
our heroines—and the men who become part of their lives.

Look for these exciting titles from Silhouette Special Edition:

August   MORE THAN HE BARGAINED FOR by Carole Halston
Heroine: Avery Payton—a woman struggling for independence
falls for the man next door.

September   A HUSBAND TO REMEMBER by Lisa Jackson
Heroine: Nikki Carrothers—a woman without memories meets the
man she should never have forgotten...her husband.

October   ON HER OWN by Pat Warren
Heroine: Sara Shepard—a woman returns to her hometown and
confronts the hero of her childhood dreams.

November   GRAND PRIZE WINNER! by Tracy Sinclair
Heroine: Kelley McCormick—a woman takes the trip of a lifetime
and wins the greatest prize of all...love!

December   POINT OF DEPARTURE by Lindsay McKenna
(Women of Glory)
Heroine: Lt. Callie Donovan—a woman takes on the system and
must accept the help of a kind and sexy stranger.

Don't miss THAT SPECIAL WOMAN! each month—from some
of your special authors! Only from Silhouette Special Edition!

TSW3

Take 4 bestselling love stories FREE

Plus get a FREE surprise gift!

Special Limited-time Offer

Mail to Silhouette Reader Service™

**3010 Walden Avenue
P.O. Box 1867
Buffalo, N.Y. 14269-1867**

YES! Please send me 4 free Silhouette Special Edition® novels and my free surprise gift. Then send me 6 brand-new novels every month, which I will receive months before they appear in bookstores. Bill me at the low price of $2.71 each plus 25¢ delivery and applicable sales tax, if any.* That's the complete price and—compared to the cover prices of $3.50 each—quite a bargain! I understand that accepting the books and gift places me under no obligation ever to buy any books. I can always return a shipment and cancel at any time. Even if I never buy another book from Silhouette, the 4 free books and the surprise gift are mine to keep forever.

235 BPA AJH7

Name	(PLEASE PRINT)
Address	Apt. No.
City	State	Zip

Silhouette

SPECIAL EDITION ™

Coming in
October,
the third book in
Debbie
Macomber's

*From this
day
forward*

MARRIAGE WANTED

Dash Davenport didn't marry Savannah Charles for love, only convenience.
As a divorce attorney, he knew marriage was a mistake. But as a man, Dash
couldn't resist Savannah's charms. It seemed Savannah knew all the makings
of a happily-ever-after. And it wasn't long after saying "I do" that Dash
started thinking about forever....

FROM THIS DAY FORWARD—Three couples marry first and
find love later in this heartwarming trilogy.

Only from Silhouette Special Edition.

Silhouette Books has done it again!

Opening night in October has never been as exciting! Come watch as the curtain rises and romance flourishes when the stars of tomorrow make their debuts today!

Revel in Jodi O'Donnell's STILL SWEET ON HIM—
Silhouette Romance #969
...as Callie Farrell's renovation of the family homestead leads her straight into the arms of teenage crush Drew Barnett!

Tingle with Carol Devine's BEAUTY AND THE BEASTMASTER—
Silhouette Desire #816
...as legal eagle Amanda Tarkington is carried off by wrestler Bram Masterson!

Thrill to Elyn Day's A BED OF ROSES—
Silhouette Special Edition #846
...as Dana Whitaker's body and soul are healed by sexy physical therapist Michael Gordon!

Believe when Kylie Brant's McLAIN'S LAW —
Silhouette Intimate Moments #528
...takes you into detective Connor McLain's life as he falls for psychic—and suspect—Michele Easton!

Catch the classics of tomorrow—*premiering* today—
only from ▼ *Silhouette*

And now for something completely different from Silhouette....

SPELLBOUND
R O M A N C E

Every once in a while, Silhouette brings you a book that is truly unique and innovative, taking you into the world of paranormal happenings. And now these stories will carry our special "Spellbound" flash, letting you know that you're in for a truly exciting reading experience!

In October, look for *McLain's Law* (IM #528) by Kylie Brant

Lieutenant Detective Connor McLain believes only in what he can see—until Michele Easton's haunting visions help him solve a case...and her love opens his heart!

McLain's Law is also the Intimate Moments "Premiere" title, introducing you to a debut author, sure to be the star of tomorrow!

Available in October...only from Silhouette Intimate Moments

INTIMATE MOMENTS®
Silhouette®

SPELL1

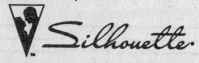

SILHOUETTE.... Where Passion Lives

Don't miss these Silhouette favorites by some of our most popular authors!
And now, you can receive a discount by ordering two or more titles!

Silhouette Desire®

#05751	THE MAN WITH THE MIDNIGHT EYES BJ James	$2.89	☐
#05763	THE COWBOY Cait London	$2.89	☐
#05774	TENNESSEE WALTZ Jackie Merritt	$2.89	☐
#05779	THE RANCHER AND THE RUNAWAY BRIDE Joan Johnston	$2.89	☐

Silhouette Intimate Moments®

#07417	WOLF AND THE ANGEL Kathleen Creighton	$3.29	☐
#07480	DIAMOND WILLOW Kathleen Eagle	$3.39	☐
#07486	MEMORIES OF LAURA Marilyn Pappano	$3.39	☐
#07493	QUINN EISLEY'S WAR Patricia Gardner Evans	$3.39	☐

Silhouette Shadows®

#27003	STRANGER IN THE MIST Lee Karr	$3.50	☐
#27007	FLASHBACK Terri Herrington	$3.50	☐
#27009	BREAK THE NIGHT Anne Stuart	$3.50	☐
#27012	DARK ENCHANTMENT Jane Toombs	$3.50	☐

Silhouette Special Edition®

#09754	THERE AND NOW Linda Lael Miller	$3.39	☐
#09770	FATHER: UNKNOWN Andrea Edwards	$3.39	☐
#09791	THE CAT THAT LIVED ON PARK AVENUE Tracy Sinclair	$3.39	☐
#09811	HE'S THE RICH BOY Lisa Jackson	$3.39	☐

Silhouette Romance®

#08893	LETTERS FROM HOME Toni Collins	$2.69	☐
#08915	NEW YEAR'S BABY Stella Bagwell	$2.69	☐
#08927	THE PURSUIT OF HAPPINESS Anne Peters	$2.69	☐
#08952	INSTANT FATHER Lucy Gordon	$2.75	☐

	AMOUNT	$ _____
DEDUCT:	10% DISCOUNT FOR 2+ BOOKS	$ _____
	POSTAGE & HANDLING	$ _____
	($1.00 for one book, 50¢ for each additional)	
	APPLICABLE TAXES*	$ _____
	TOTAL PAYABLE	$ _____
	(check or money order—please do not send cash)	

To order, complete this form and send it, along with a check or money order for the total above, payable to Silhouette Books, to: *In the U.S.*: 3010 Walden Avenue, P.O. Box 9077, Buffalo, NY 14269-9077; *In Canada*: P.O. Box 636, Fort Erie, Ontario, L2A 5X3.

Name: _____

Address: _____ City: _____

State/Prov.: _____ Zip/Postal Code: _____

*New York residents remit applicable sales taxes.
Canadian residents remit applicable GST and provincial taxes.

SBACK-OD

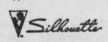